Anthony Ferguson is an author and editor living in Perth, Australia. He has published over seventy short stories and non-fiction articles in Australia, Britain and the United States. He wrote the novel *Protégé*, the non-fiction books, *The Sex Doll: A History*, and *Murder Down Under*, edited the short-story collection *Devil Dolls and Duplicates in Australian Horror* and coedited the award-nominated *Midnight Echo #12*. He is a committee member of the Australasian Horror Writers Association (AHWA), and a submissions editor for Andromeda Spaceways Magazine (ASM). A four-time nominee, he won the Australian Shadows Award for Short Fiction in 2020. Visit his website at https://anthonypferguson.wixsite.com/mysite.

T0118844

Rest in Pieces
Ghost Stories

by Anthony Ferguson

This is a work of fiction. The events and characters portrayed herein are imaginary and are not intended to refer to specific places, events or living persons. The opinions expressed in this manuscript are solely the opinions of the author and do not necessarily represent the opinions of the publisher.

Rest in Pieces: Ghost Stories

All Rights Reserved

ISBN-13: 978-1-922856-37-1

Copyright ©2023 Anthony Ferguson

V1.0

Stories first publishing history at the end of this book.

This book may not be reproduced, transmitted, or stored in whole or in part by any means, including graphic, electronic, or mechanical without the express written consent of the publisher except in the case of brief quotations embodied in critical articles and reviews.

Printed in Palatino Linotype and Penakut.

IFWG Publishing Australia
Gold Coast

www.ifwgaustralia.com

A dedication. There are so many people I could thank for helping me over the years.

Can I just say—For my dark muse.

TABLE OF CONTENTS

REST IN PIECES

"Kristi," she said as she reached across and shook his hand gently, climbing into the passenger seat. He made a mental note of the silver ring on her finger.

"Richard," he replied, easing the car away from the kerb. "You're brave, hitching at this time of night." He glanced at her, running an appreciative eye over the top of her blouse, two buttons undone to reveal a hint of pert creamy breast. "You running away from home?"

"Something like that," she said.

"Bad daddy?"

"Bad boyfriend," she said, with a grimace.

"Ah, good. He'll get the blame if you disappear," he said. Followed it with a laugh. *Not a wedding ring then. Different finger.*

She laughed too. Seemed relaxed. "Don't tell me, Richard. You're one of them serial killer types?"

"I was thinking the same about you."

She laughed again. A lovely lilting feminine laugh. Then a sudden movement caught his eye. A long-legged spider edged from behind the visor above his head and ran across the windscreen. Richard let out an involuntary shriek and jerked the wheel to one side.

"Jesus!" Without warning, Kristi forcefully grabbed the wheel and yanked it back again before they lurched off the road. Richard let his foot off the accelerator and the car shuddered to a halt.

In one swift movement Kristi snatched up the arachnid and flung it out the window.

"Jeez, are you okay?"

He caught his breath and his heart hammered.

"Yeah…sorry. I have a thing about spiders."

"No shit."

Once he had calmed down, he focussed his mind on the task to hand. He started the engine and eased back onto the road. Glanced sideways and saw her eyeballing him.

"So, what is your story, Richard?"

Fuck he was nervous. He'd never pulled anything like this before. Sure, he'd fantasised about it often enough. Written it down, tried to plan the exact process.

"Oh, me? I just like to help damsels in distress." He swallowed.

"Really? You've picked girls up off the street before?" She gave him a knowing smile. Her eyes twinkled.

"No." *Shit. Don't blow it.* "I mean I wanted to…help."

She laughed again. Not quite mocking. "You're a regular knight in shining armour, Richard."

Damn. It was all going wrong, and yet, was she flirting with him? He was going take a swing at her while they were driving. But he wasn't confident he could generate enough power behind the strike. She seemed feisty. She might fight back. He didn't want that.

"Where you headed, Kristi?" he asked.

"Anywhere away from here."

"I know a shortcut."

He nudged the car toward a nice quiet empty road. He knew these roads well. How you could cut through the farming communities to get from one town to the next. She didn't mind.

Kristi leaned toward the open window. Let the wind run through her long chestnut curls. He kept sneaking glances at her. She had her eyes closed. The wind lifted her hair from her smooth shoulders. Richard pulled the car over near some trees.

"What's wrong?" she asked.

"You hear that?"

"Hear what?"

"The tyre. Shit. I better check."

"Whatever."

Richard got out. Kicked the front passenger wheel. Swore. The tyre was fine. His heart was pounding now.

He went to the trunk and retrieved his tyre iron. Returned to the front wheel.

"Kristi."

"Yeah?"

"Can you come out here a sec? Give me a hand." He fought to keep his voice steady.

He expected her to come out her side and walk round, but she shuffled across the seat toward him and eased the door open.

"What do you expect me..." she started to say, turning and sweeping that long hair out of her face. Too late to see him pull the tyre iron out from behind his back and swing his arm violently toward her head in one swift movement.

She barely had time to scream.

Richard put the bloody weapon away and shut the boot. He leaned over where she was sprawled across the seat and lifted the hair out of her eyes. It was matted with blood. Her skull was cracked open right above her left eye, which was already starting to swell.

Checking the coast was clear, he moved the car off the road into the trees. He pulled her into the back seat, lay down beside her and cradled her in his arms. He tenderly wiped flecks of blood off her face. Told her he loved her as he undressed her. Tore his own jeans off. Then roughly pushed her legs apart.

Richard found that he adored Kristi so much it was hard to let her go. She was his first love after all. He took her home and carried her to his bed. By day he remained an anonymous office drone, by night an ardent lover.

However, like most loves, this one faded. His desire for her waned as the flesh drew back from her bones. He had to stab her several times to stop her bloating. Before long he knew it was time for them to part ways.

The dismemberment was the hard part. Richard had spent months studying anatomy and dissection online, but just like killing, the practical was a lot more intense than the theory. Finding no instructive guides for killers wishing to cut up human bodies. He relied instead on online medical texts. When he found these far too genteel—scalpels and surgical scissors—he turned instead to advice on the butchery of animal carcasses.

Thus, armed with a meat saw, bone saw and hardy apron, he set about dismembering Kristi in the bathtub, lacking a butcher's block. This brought on an unanticipated overpowering sense of loss, and at one point he found himself hugging her limbless torso to his bloody chest and sobbing, like a man cradling his beloved on the side of the road after a fatal car accident.

The work was long and arduous. Hacking through muscle and bone was much more difficult than anticipated. His limbs ached from the exertion of squatting over the tub, and he was covered head to toe in gore. Sweat dripped off his brow. Reams of decaying tissue clogged up the plughole, and he was forced to burn it in the embers of his backyard barbecue, only slightly tempted by the smell to try a piece of her roasted flesh.

In the ensuing weeks he scoured the media for news about Kristi's disappearance, always careful to maintain his anonymity. He was relieved and strangely aroused to find she was little missed. A child of a broken home, and a woman of a slew of toxic relationships. All of the boyfriends were questioned. None were charged. The investigation into her whereabouts tailed off, and she was written off as a runaway.

Still, as a novice, Richard lived in fear of detection. Hence his decision not to leave her intact in a shallow grave, but rather cast her asunder in a wide range of locations. Except for her head, which he kept in his fridge.

However, as time passed, he found himself noticing other women more. Live women.

He was ready to move on.

In the dead of night, he made one final trip to bury Kristi's head. As he held her by the hair, kissed her dried-out lips and lowered her toward the soil, the mouth dropped open and she spoke.

That's it, is it?

"What…what did you just say?"

In his mind's eye he saw her meet his gaze through her empty sockets.

I know what you're thinking. Ingrate!

Speechless, he lowered the rotting skull to the pile of dirt on the edge of the shallow grave. How did she know?

You've probably picked her out of the crowd already. Been following her, watching her. You're planning, waiting for your chance. Making sure there's nothing to connect you to her. You didn't do that for me, did you? I was just random.

Richard looked away, unable to answer. How could she possibly have seen him spot that girl at the station? Seen him linger close, eavesdropping until he got her name, Sophie. Seen him research her on social media. Seen him pinpoint where she worked, even where she lived.

How could you, Richard? I thought we had something special.

"Special?"

You felt it too. I know you did. From the moment you smashed my skull with that tyre iron, I knew I was the girl for you.

Richard gawped. His shock soon morphed into anger.

"No, Kristi. You mean nothing to me. I used you, and now, I'm done with you."

The head shook from side to side.

You can't mean it.

"I do. Sorry, Kristi."

I won't let you leave.

Richard sneered. "What are you gonna do? I'll kick your skull back into that grave. Not a damn thing you can do about it. I'll have one last bit of fun with you first if you don't shut it, bitch!"

Don't you dare!

"Too late."

Richard picked Kristi up by the hair, held her firm at his crotch while he unzipped.

I'm warning you, Rich...

Her words were choked off as he pushed his cock inside her mouth cavity. He grinned and felt a surge of power whip through him, and then he was screaming, pulling her head off his manhood and flinging it aside.

"You fucking bit me!" He hopped up and down. Folding his injured dick away, Richard stomped toward the discarded head and booted it into the grave.

Kristi looked up at him. *Right. I warned you.*

She opened her mouth wide, and a huge hairy spider crawled out of her maw, its fangs glistening in the moonlight.

"Jesus wept!" Richard watched it scurry toward the lip of the grave.

How's your arachnophobia, Richard?

"Please tell me that wasn't in there all the time we were…"

Not waiting for an answer, Richard grabbed his shovel and started flinging dirt back into the hole. When a pair of furry appendages reached over the edge for purchase, he let out a groan of dismay. As soon as the evil black-eyed head appeared, he bashed it in with the implement.

Hurriedly filling the grave, he turned and fled. As he ran back to the car, he heard Kristi's muffled voice calling after him.

I'm coming for you, Richard. Me and my little friends. We'll sink our fangs into you.

Richard heard it all, as he fired the engine up and fled into the night. He caught his panicked eyes in the mirror.

"Christ! I must be going crazy."

Something moved at the top of the back seat, and he almost drove off the highway. Then he saw it was the shadowy reflections of passing light posts. He blew a sigh of relief and forcibly slowed the car down, focussed on his breathing.

The dreams were bad. Half nightmare, half arousal. He found he still missed Kristi, even after all she had put him through. He had to get by this, had to wrest back control. In the following weeks, Richard turned his attention away from the dead and back toward the living. Back to Sophie. His itch grew stronger, overpowering his fear.

It needed scratching.

He already knew so much about her. Knew her intimately, even though they had yet to meet. It was hard work, but he enjoyed it. In some way the planning and anticipation was the best part. It brought him focus and calmness. Cleared his mind. Kristi was just a stroke of luck, right place, right time, but now he was more experienced. This time he would savour it.

He pulled the fridge open, half expecting to find… But no, Kristi's head was thankfully absent. Just the cold cuts and salad bowl. Richard made himself a delicious sandwich.

He flicked onto a football match on the flat-screen, sunk down on the couch. Took a bite and savoured the smoky ham, crunchy lettuce, tomato and onion, drizzled in mayo. He closed his eyes with relish, opened them and brought the serrated edge of the wholemeal up toward his mouth and then…something moved.

In between a fold of lettuce and the tomato, several legs unfurled and draped across the strips of ham. They oozed a green, pus-like substance as a pulpy body followed, parting the lettuce leaves as its leaking, bulbous form slid forward. Richard blinked and saw the empty space where two of the spider's legs and had been torn off.

He retched and gagged as he threw the sandwich against the wall.

"Jesus Christ!"

He spat up globs of half-chewed bread and ham as he watched the wounded arachnid limp across the white tiled floor. He raised a boot and squished it with an audible plop, spreading the rest of its guts beneath his boot.

That night he drove a hundred miles to another of the dump sites. It was well after midnight before he found the grave with its familiar markings. He remembered what he had interred here, the right arm and part of the chest cavity.

He brought his shovel, approached the grave, all the while thinking, *I must be crazy…*

Then he stopped and fought to choke down a scream.

The grave was open.

He rushed over and looked down.

Empty.

Someone had been here and dug her up. Either that, or Kristi had dug herself out.

A sound in the trees made him whirl around. Something dark flitted between the branches. His head said a bird, please let it be a bird.

A winged silhouette took off, and he expelled a deep breath.

Then around the nape of a thin bough he saw fingers curled, a ring glittered in the moonlight. A familiar ring.

Richard ran. Behind him came footsteps, something bounding through the bushes at a loping pace. He let out a wail as it seemed to edge closer until it was almost upon him, but he made the car, locked the doors, and fled.

Richard called in sick. Then he took some leave from work. At night he woke, seeing spiders crawl along his ceiling that were not there when he frantically turned on the bedside lamp. He dreamt of them. He dreamt of her. Kristi's head on a distended spider body, crawling up his paralysed body, opening her maw, showing him her fangs, edging toward his manhood. All the while telling him she loved him. That she was the only girl for him. That no one else could have him.

Richard stopped visiting the disposal sites. The dreams made him realise he needed a distraction.

Back at work, he asked one of the girls out for a drink. He knew Emma had a thing for him. It was easy to arrange. She was sweet, blonde and curvy. Not his type at all. Poor Emma. She was so excited, but at least she would live.

Richard arranged to meet her at Fenians, a local Irish tavern, on a Wednesday night. He knew that Sophie relaxed there with her girlfriends after netball at the local rec the same time every week. He knew what time her game ended. He would position himself, with Emma as his cover, close to Sophie's group and eavesdrop. Partly to add to his collated information on the minutiae of her life, but also so he could drink in her beauty and add to his mounting excitement. If it got him worked up enough, he might even fuck Emma just for kicks.

The night came. Rain drizzled on the bar window. Richard endured Emma's boring small talk, plied her with drink to shut her up. His heart popped when Sophie came in with her gang, right on time. He had positioned himself perfectly. Sophie was close enough for him to hear most of her conversation, without her even noticing he was there. Bloody perfect.

Then, just above the hubbub of the noisy bar, he heard it, a *tap tap tap* on the window to his side. Richard turned slowly as Emma jabbered on about herself, and outside on the footpath, a monstrosity glared back at him.

He recoiled, and Emma followed his gaze, but clearly did not see what Richard beheld through the greasy window.

A bloated mass squatted there, propped up by at least three spindly legs, one of which looked distinctly human. Another long appendage was tapping on the window, and at its end there sat a human hand with a silver ring on one finger. A ring it was using to rap on the window.

Sitting at a wrong angle lopsided atop the awful body was Kristi's head, with white staring eyes. Its bloody mouth formed a wide "o", and it was screaming something at him, something he didn't want to hear.

"Richard? Richard? Are you even listening to me?" He heard Emma yell above the hubbub and the tapping. He looked at her in horror, away from the thing, and when he turned his gaze back it was gone.

"What's wrong, Richard?"

The moment that defined his childhood happened when Richard was five years old. It was raining, and his mother ordered him to play inside out of the wet. Looking out the bedroom window, he spied his favourite truck out in the sandpit. It was bright yellow, and just about his favourite toy in the whole world.

It sat there, looking back at him. He looked up at the grey teeming sky. He listened to his mum pottering around in the kitchen. She was singing along with the radio. Mum said he was not to go out and get wet.

He chewed his lip.

Richard snuck quietly down the hallway and stuck his head around the door. Caught a glimpse of her auburn locks. Ducking back before she saw him. He edged toward the doorway, all the while fearing the sound of footsteps on the wooden floorboards heading in his direction. But the only pitter patter was the constant drum of rain hitting the drainpipes.

He cautiously prised the back door open and slipped out. Ran and grabbed the yellow truck and snuck it into his bedroom, closing the door.

For the next quarter of an hour he happily played with the truck. Working the mechanism to pick up small objects and drop them again. At one point his hand slid into a crevice and he felt something squishy.

He stopped. Even at his tender age he knew the soft, spongy thing wedged in between chassis and tyre was not part of the plastic and metal structure.

He held it up to his eye and seeing nothing untoward, he poked two fingers in the crevice again. There it was, soft and slimy. He thought it was maybe a piece of chewing gum.

And then it moved.

Recoiling in terror, Richard pulled his fingers out of the dark fissure, but the slimy thing came with them.

To his horror he saw a big black spider, clinging determinedly to his fingers by a pair of dextrous limbs.

Richard yelped and tried to fling the awful thing away, but instead, it redoubled its purchase on his flesh, and swung itself onto the ball of his palm.

Yelling now, Richard started to dance on the spot, his legs thrashing. Compulsively he wrapped his fingers around the hideous spider and squeezed.

That's when he felt the bite.

Richard's scream brought his mother running. She grabbed him in her arms in a mother's panic.

"Richard! What's wrong? What is it?"

Heaving and sobbing he pointed at the offending arachnid as it scurried across the floorboards. His mother screamed when she saw its horrid black carapace heading for the dark shelter under the bed. In two steps she had crossed the room and brought a heavy foot down on the monster, spreading its gooey innards across the floor and eliciting another scream from them both.

Sobbing, he raised his open hand to show her the already swelling wound where the two-pronged fangs had entered the tender meat of his palm, sending her into another flurry of panic.

By the time they reached the hospital, Richard had started

vomiting. The nurse had to sedate him to stop him clawing at the wound, screaming, "It burns!" Then they had to sedate his hyperventilating mother.

After almost a week in intensive care, they finally sent Richard home. He had a nice little necrotic scar to remind him of his probable encounter with a brown recluse spider, its venom only toxic to small children like himself. The doctor said he was very lucky, and praised his mother for getting him to the hospital so quickly.

Things could have been so much worse.

A week passed, nothing happened. Richard put the sighting at the pub down to his fevered imagination. He continued his surveillance of Sophie. Tailing her home on the subway had proved easy. He was buoyed by his growing skill. Now he knew her address he put the next stage of his plan into operation. It was risky, but the successful application would be worth it.

After phoning in sick at work, he carefully donned the overalls he had purchased a month earlier. Added the fake corporate logo and the make up to his face in accordance with the guidelines he found on the packet.

He checked his watch, making sure Sophie would be at her college in a nearby county. Then he calmly walked up and rang the doorbell. As anticipated, her flatmate answered the door.

"Yeah?"

Mandy, doughy, fleshy and pale. No threat to his plans.

"Morning, Miss, I'm from the electric company. The council asked me to run a routine check over the points, if that's okay?"

She looked over his shoulder at the street as if for confirmation. As expected, she was fooled by the van he had hired and tricked up with a fake logo.

"Well, alright, I guess that should be okay."

The girl stepped aside, eyeing him suspiciously.

"Thank you, miss. You just go about your business, and I'll be done in no time."

A look of mild concern crossed the girl's face, making him squirm. She grabbed her purse off a coffee table. "Actually, I just gotta run down to the corner store. I won't be long. If I'm not back, let yourself out and lock up."

Perfect. Even if the bitch was running to get help, or calling the cops, Richard only needed two minutes to install the miniature camera in Sophie's room. He bounded up the stairs and found it instantly on the trail of her perfume, so familiar was she becoming. Soon, she would be all his.

He was gone before the flatmate returned.

That night, overcome with anticipation, Richard tuned into channel Sophie and masturbated furiously. Especially as he watched her undress after netball. The sweat making the tunic cling to her lithe young body.

Unable to sleep and unwilling to resist, he took a drive, parked a distance away and walked by her house. He enjoyed the advantage of a row of trees running along one side of the property, their thick foliage beneficial to his needs.

He was congratulating himself on how well this was all going when a sharp voice hissed at him from the darkness.

Richard!

He looked up in shock, and there, around the bough of a tree, unfurled a long dark bristling appendage, ending in a pale hand with painted fingernails. It was followed by another. Then the hideous visage appeared. Kristi's head on a bulging carapace. Two twisted human legs jutted out of the black shiny body at a hideous angle.

Richard's own legs turned to jelly, and he felt an involuntary stream of piss soak through his jeans.

I'm coming for you, Richard, it said. *I told you to leave her alone. You belong to meeee!*

The horrid thing scrambled toward him, but it was slow. Some of its legs were dragging, as if they were not quite fully formed.

Richard stumbled backwards. "Get away from me. You're not real."

It lumbered forward again, falling and righting itself on clumsy legs, half-human, half-arachnid.

Richard turned on his heels and fled with a yelp, its voice

hissing through the air behind him.

I love youuuuu!

Holed up in the flat with every door and window barricaded, Richard sat on his bed clutching a can of insect repellent and tried to rationalise. He was losing his mind. He was seeing things nobody else was seeing. Hearing voices. Once the rational part of his brain resumed control, he determined there was only one course of action that would resolve the Kristi issue once and for all and banish her back to the grave. He was going to have to replace her.

To his delight, the camera showed him that Sophie went jogging before work three days a week in the early morning darkness. He watched her pull on the sweatshirt and pants, and later by discreet observation pinpointed the park just down the block from her apartment.

Making a mental map of the park quietly in daylight hours, keeping an eye out for giant deformed love-struck arachnids, Richard pinpointed the exact place to lie in wait for his prey. A point where the roughly hewn track dipped and circled a patch of thick foliage. He even lay there twice in early morning gloom, watching her run by and timing her. His lust for Sophie overpowering his fear of deformed spider-women. He noted she was a girl who kept to strict deadlines. She was disciplined and focussed. He admired that about her.

Finally, the momentous day arrived. Richard marked it off in his calendar, then set the calendar alight and destroyed it. He placed a large container of acid by the bathtub. No dissection this time. He would only keep the bit he wanted. He put on his best aftershave and tucked a ball-peen hammer into the loop of his jeans belt, secreted beneath a bulky jumper. The mornings were still crisp and cold. He parked a stolen car within reach in a small empty car park, close to the bushes, and walked the rest of the way in darkness. His nerves jangling with every step.

Reaching his hiding spot, Richard slid down on his stomach

and secreted himself in foliage.

He checked his Fitbit and waited. Felt his erection pushing at the cold earth beneath him.

He stole another glance. Three minutes and she would be along. Two minutes and she would be his.

One minute and he withdrew the hammer. Squeezed it tight.

Thirty seconds, any minute now, footsteps would signal her approach

Ten seconds.

Five…

Nothing?

Puzzled, Richard looked at his Fitbit, half expecting it to show he had misread. But no, it was correct.

Where was she? It was Friday, her third run of the week. *Don't tell me the lazy bitch slept in!*

Perhaps she was sick.

Annoyed, frustrated, Richard stood up and walked out onto the track, tucking the hammer and his ebbing erection away. He walked in the direction she should have come from.

Finding no sight of Sophie, he considered his options. Daylight was breaking, he would have to call it off and adjust his plans. He was so distracted he wandered off the path and found himself in the woods.

A sudden whooshing sound turned him on his heels. Something plummeted from the trees, bulky and wrapped in silk. It stopped with a jolt, suspended several feet above the ground before his face.

The impact made a slender arm drop from the silky bindings it was woven in. To his horror he saw a face protruding from the mummified wrappings—Sophie's face. Blood dripped steadily from her hair. Her eyes were wide with shock.

"What the fuck?"

I warned, you, Richard, a voice hissed from the trees.

Richard stepped back, away from the swinging corpse. His plans in ruins, he wanted to put as much distance between himself and this horror as quick as possible.

He blundered straight into the web.

"Shit!"

Richard tried to prise his arm loose. Tried his leg, but he was stuck fast in the thick silky strands. His heart sank as he realised which monstrosity had produced a web so strong.

The leaves rustled above him, and the awful misshapen carapace lowered itself down on a trail emanating from its swollen abdomen.

The thing that was Kristi waved a twisted limb and bared its fangs at him.

"Kristi, I'm sorry…"

Too late, she said. *I had to deal with her for you.*

He glanced at Sophie's swaying corpse and shuddered. "You're right, baby," he swallowed. "You are the only one for me. Now get me out of here." He felt the weight of the hammer dangling from his hip. If he could just reach it.

Nice try. She began to edge along the web toward him. *You know what they say about female spiders, Richard?*

"No."

Yes, I think you do. She reached out with a hairy limb and caressed his face.

"Please, Kristi."

After mating, many female arachnids devour the male. And as you know, we've already mated…and I'm awfully hungry.

Richard screamed.

BRUMATION

I always like to tell folks it was the weather that brought me across state lines to Texas, but that ain't really so. Nor was it the gators, even though catching and skinning 'em was my line of work for a piece.

Not a lot of people know that gators get as far west as Texas. But yessir, state lines don't mean a damn to them. Long as they got agreeable water, they'll get all the way from Florida through Louisiana and into oil country.

Truth is it was Willie Nixon that dragged me west. Even if I didn't have proof of his true nature at the time, I came trotting along on account of him, and them things he done. Real awful inhuman stuff. Like some kind of beast rather than a man.

I say this as one who knew folks got caught up in the Indian wars and seen some of the atrocities them savages committed. Cutting up folk and taking scalps and sometimes whole heads and putting 'em on display. Christ, even cutting off the lower regions as well. Then there was what they did to white women.

I heard sure as night follows day that some settlers got to leaving their last round of bullets to put into the heads of their women and children, rather than let the Injuns get at 'em. Then again, I also heard talk of some of the stuff the whites did to the Indians too, and that was just as bad. Raping and butchering their women and children, burning their villages and such like. Pure horrible stuff, and I was a mite grateful that the Indian wars were about done by the time I headed west back in '88.

It goes without saying them days were hard, and a lot of

people did a lot of suffering. I know that well enough on account of what Nixon did to my sweetheart, Annabelle, but I see I'm getting ahead of myself. So, I'll start at the beginning.

As a young man I set out working on whaling ships out of Nantucket. A fine sort of life for a lad, adventuring on the high seas with a bunch of rowdy coves. Made a man out of me. But comes a time when a man wants to settle and start a family, like I wanted with Annabelle.

While I don't wish to dwell too long on my love, on account of how she ended up and all, it's important for you to know that she came from out west. Put herself out a lot for me, good woman that she was, but we both came to agree that it aint no good for a marriage to have the feller away at sea for months on end, especially on journeys which he may not return from, as many didn't. God rest their souls.

So, it turned out there weren't that many jobs around for a feller skilled with a knife. Least, not the kind of work that paid enough to set up a home for a wife with a baby on the way.

That's how come I took to the gator skinning game. Plus the sallying forth by boat made it so I didn't miss the high seas and ships too much. Even better, none of the gator trapping trips lasted more than a day or two, week at the most, and only in the high season.

Gatoring is hard work, mind, and like whaling, you get paid by the amount of beasts you catch and skin. I sank most of my savings into my first boat, a real little beauty. Can't catch gators alone. Well, you can, but it's a mite easier with a buddy. Gotta have one feller to navigate, the other to haul up the traps. Both have to be good and quick with the knife once you drag the critter on board.

Had me a good partner in ol' Solly Marsh. Stayed with me a good two years afore that gator took off most the fingers on his right hand, the skinning hand.

I was a mite sorry to see Solly go, but I done him right with money and all. I made damn sure of that. Matter of fact it was down near Solly's old place the first bodies showed up. First ones we knew of anyway. Found 'em floating downstream in the river, caught up in the bulrushes. What was left of 'em.

Sure the gators had been at them, but it weren't that which made us swallow hard and cuss. It was the ropes tied around the wrists, and the obvious signs that someone had been at them with a knife. Solly had to usher his kids away, hollering at them not to look backwards.

They was women both, except that someone had taken to cutting out their private bits, their titties too. Punctured 'em fulla holes and even took out their eyes.

"God almighty," I recall saying to Solly at the time. "Damn gators didn't do all this."

It didn't make a lick of sense, Solly agreed, why anyone would do this to a body, no matter how much they felt they'd been wronged. I knew of men who had offed their wives for running around with other fellers, but this…this was beyond what any man would do. This was monstrous.

Well, we reported it of course, and the sheriff took up the case. Two women, unrelated. Though it musta been hard to tell from the state of them. They blamed the Indians of course. We let it go at that.

I had other stuff on my plate round the time, like finding me a new offsider. That's how I met Willie. He was just a few short years older than me. A real man's man. Had spent much of his youth out west serving in the US cavalry, as he told it. Matter of fact he sure reminded me of pictures I'd seen of Custer, with his flowing golden locks, bushy moustache and bright blue eyes. Willie sure turned the ladies' heads.

It surprised me that he weren't hitched himself, till he told me that he lost his sweetheart to the savages. Damn near made me lose my dinner when he described what they did to her, cutting her up something awful after they'd had their way with her.

The way he described it brought up images of them two bodies in the river, so I told him about that. Then I near choked again when he let on there had been others. More bodies turning up in rivers, in several towns along the state line.

When I called him out, he pulled from his rucksack some

clippings from the papers about the killings. Said he kept them on account of what happened to his girl. That he hoped to catch them at it one day. Then he pulled out his big Bowie knife and espoused on what he would do to them when he caught them.

"Rogue Indians for sure," he said. "No civilised man would behave in this manner."

I had him read some of the accounts out loud to me, seeing as I never did learn to read too good, having left home to go to sea at the age of twelve. But Willie seemed to have himself a decent education.

Seemed a mite odd to me he didn't have no steady woman either. Given every time we stopped off somewhere for a bite or a libation, the young ladies seemed to gravitate toward him. They ignored me of course, on account of my ornery looks and my wedding band, but Willie had him a way with words and a certain way about him the ladies seemed to find appealing. Like bees around a honey pot. I even felt a pang of jealousy. Was almost tempted not to take him home and introduce him to Annabelle. Did though. Damn my sorry hide. He was sweet as, though, and treated her like royalty. I swear she was even sweet on him too, though she insisted otherwise.

More important though was how good Willie was at his work. Wasn't long afore we was bringing in near twice what poor Solly and me used to do, and I was suckered in by all that money that would be so handy for my impending family. Willie was a breeze to work with. Always whistling and smiling, and I've never seen anybody handle a knife like that man. Had that gator out of its skin quicker than a whore out of her britches on payday.

I paint this picture so as to illustrate I never had no inkling as to Willie Nixon's true nature. That wouldn't come out till way later, and by that point, it was too late for me. No, it was like Willie was wearing a second skin of his own. One that somehow disguised his real face. That's what Deputy Briggs would say to me after, or words to that effect.

Suffice to say that them women's bodies kept popping up. Not in a flood, mind, but a steady flow. Always along the rivers and creeks. All of 'em desecrated in a similar manner too. With eyeballs, teeth, hands, and sometimes the whole heads removed. Sometimes the monsters even cut out their hearts.

Not that I ever saw any of it, thank the Lord. What I seen out back of Solly's was bad enough. But Willie seemed to take a keen interest in the matter and would regale me with lurid tales from the press cuttings he acquired.

The law was still running around in the dark on the killings, and it seemed it didn't matter how many stray Injuns, or negroes or gunslingers they strung up, them bodies kept on piling up. They even questioned poor old Sol and asked to look at his knives, but I knew damn well my old pal had nothing to do with it.

I should stress that policing as it was weren't too flash in them days, and if a killer managed to cross state lines, well, that sheriff there had to cede to the next one along, and so on. It was like the killer or killers knew this and was deliberately sewing confusion among the decent law-abiding folks to terrorise them. It worked.

That's how I come to that day… I don't want to dwell on the details none. God knows I talked enough about it in the weeks and months after. My Annabelle was only just startin' to show, and it pained me to think the savages knew it when they cut her.

I was screaming by the time they dragged me away from her. I just wanted to hold my Belle one more time, even if it woulda been hard to do on account of what state she was in, but the wedding ring on the hand still attached did me in.

Willie was good enough to keep the boat running for me till I got back on board 'bout a month later after the burial. Saw him too at the graveyard, but he kept a distance, just giving me a pat on the shoulder in passing.

Told me how sorry he was when we finally headed back out on the river. Vowed again to get his hands on the killers. I just nodded without speaking and he backed away. He knew it was still a mite raw for me.

Now this next bit is almost as hard to tell and near as awful as what happened to my kin. Thing is I knew the details of the savagery perpetrated on my bride, and I don't know if Willie knew that, or knew enough of it.

21

Anyways, we was drinking in a bar after another good day of kills on the river. I was drowning my sorrows as it were, and Willie was doing his best to help me.

At some point he took out a coin purse to pay for a round and I happened to notice the skin of it. Sort of a weird colour and texture. I asked him if it was gator, and when I reached out to touch it, he pulled it away.

Willie said it was from a boar he took down, but it was the way he said it that got at me. The look in his eyes was wrong, like it weren't him there at all, but someone else underneath. Best way I can say it. Twas then I really paid attention to the chain hanging around his neck. He hadn't had that piece when I first took him on, and I strained to recall when it first appeared on his person.

Now I did all this on account of two things. One being something the mortician let slip to me at the station. That the killer or killers were taking stuff from the victims. Sometimes body parts, other times accoutrements. Sometimes both.

Two. The sons of bitches had skinned my Annabelle's arm.

I didn't press him, but it occurred to me that Willie didn't want none of me touching his pouch. Whipped it away out sight real quick. I got to thinking why he would do that if it was just some old boar he'd taken the hide off. After all, he'd let me try on his gator skin boots not a month earlier.

I shoulda gone straight to the sheriff's office with my suspicions, but I didn't. Just sat there like a dunderhead, mulling it over in disbelief. Worse still, I let Willie see the look in my eye.

That night, I paced around in my now empty shack, a whiskey bottle on the table before me. I'd already downed one glass when it occurred to me how vulnerable I might be. Even me, a big strong feller in the prime of life.

Don't for the life of me know what made me hit the deck at that very moment. I turned toward the open window, strong breeze blowing the curtains Anabelle had picked out at the store before she…

Maybe I saw the muzzle flash, I don't know. But I hit the deck and the bullet crashed into the wall opposite.

I grabbed my rifle and ran out into the dark hollering. Damn fool thing to do, but maybe I hoped to scare him by it. As it was, there was no more shots. Whoever it was had hightailed it away into the woods.

Willie never showed up at the boat next day. In fact, he never showed up again. I reported it all to the sheriff, and they put out an account. But of Willie Nixon there was neither sight nor sound. Sheriff Polsen told me that Willie had no doubt crossed the state line and not to trouble myself. A telegraph had gone out for all bodies to keep an eye out for the suspect, set with a good photographical picture too. I say suspect because the law was still fixing to blame the whole mess on the Injuns. No white man could have committed these sins, was the general consensus of God-fearing folk.

But I knew what I knew, and I wasn't about to let it rest.

Another thing ol' Willie didn't know about me was that I'm an expert tracker of beast or man. Just got an affinity for it. Learned much of it at my daddy's side as a boy.

So, whether he knew it or not, I had old Willie's scent, and I was on his trail. I knew too that he would give me a sign, sooner or later. One way or another.

That sign came when I was drowning my sorrows one night in a tavern. I overheard a group of woodsmen talking excitedly. Another body had been found in the shallows of a river out west of Louisiana. This one at a place not far from Houston. This one feller was jabbing at the air, indicating the state of the body, and how and where she had been cut, dissected as it were. Sure the body was gator bit, but there was no denying the other handiwork had been done by human hand.

I swear this cove's eyes was fit to bust out of his head as he described how the poor girl had been carved. Straight away I knew it was Nixon's handiwork. It was as if he were calling to me. I quietly drained my tankard, walked home to my dead empty house, and started fixing to sell up and put all my worldly goods in store.

That's when I headed west, on the trail of new hunting grounds, following the water looking for gators, and another type of monster too.

On my travels I reflected back on some of the tales Nixon had regaled me with around the campfire, his eyes all shining with what I now figured to be excitement. He would ponder as to just how the killer had subdued and cut up them poor gals, carefully selecting which pieces of flesh to carve out. How he stuck his hands inside their guts and pulled out their innards. How he musta got some kind of sick pleasure out tampering with them like that.

Now I damn near choked thinking on all that stuff, on account of what the sheriff told me about my dear departed wife, how they had found the killer's seed on her. Then I thought deep about Nixon and gripped the handle of my gator knife real tight, giving myself an account of what I was fixing to do when I caught up with him.

Well, I made sure my appearance on the gator hunting scene was well publicised round that part of Texas. Advertised for an offsider, even though I had no intention of taking one, unless it was the one I was after. I set out my traps in more ways than one, now I just needed him to take the bait.

The next sign he gave of his presence came floating on the tide past my boat one morning in late summer. More than three months since we parted ways. The decomposing torso of another young woman, minus the eyes, all of its limbs, and a hole where her heart shoulda been.

I figured he cut out the eyes because he didn't want them looking at him while he worked at them, carrying out his vile acts of cruelty.

It did occur to me that I had a moral obligation to bring the law into it, and how it might save the lives of more unfortunate women, but to my shame I was now Hell bent on revenge. Too filled with bitter hatred to let anyone get their hands on the murderer but me.

Late summer marked the end of gator season. As the leaves turned to brown and the waters grew colder, an idea started to fix itself in my brain.

I knew Nixon wasn't a true gator man. Soon as the weather turned, he always lit out for warmer climes. Taking himself anywhere he could practice his true calling with the knife. This time I knew he would stick around because of me, but I would be ready.

I set up home in an old shack not far from the river's edge and sat and waited for the snows to come. I knew he would come for me soon enough.

Took to sitting myself out on the porch in full view, braving the cold, wrapped up tight in blankets. Shotgun on my lap. It was a risk, but one I had to take.

Late one afternoon, as I was starting to doze despite the cold, a voice hailed me from the edge of the woods.

"Mite cold to be sittin' out, aint it?"

My eyes eased open to try and pinpoint the voice, while my fingers slid around the barrel of my shooter. Then I fixed on the figure skulking under the trees, dressed in furs. The golden curls were gone, his head shaved bare. The moustache too, but the piercing blue eyes still glittered with hidden knowledge.

"That you out there, Willie Nixon?" I asked, showing him my hand.

He stepped forward into the light, the wind whipping around his collar. He held his own rifle out before him.

"Been a long time, Zeke. Too long. I know you got me figured. Thought we could sort this, man to man."

He edged closer. I sat upright. Both of us pointing our weapons.

"Why d'ya do it, Willie? Why d'ya take my woman?"

He shook his head. "I'm damn sorry, Zeke. I just can't control it. The fever comes over me, and I just gotta cut 'em. See what's inside them beautiful critters." He looked down at his rifle. "Even these things don't do it for me. Makes it too impersonal, if you understand."

"How comes you tried to shoot me through my window back east then? I figure that was you."

"I fired over your head, Zeke. That's why you're still sittin' there."

When I thought back to it, I recalled how high the bullet went into the wall. Nixon weren't lying to me.

"Well, if you aint fixing to shoot me then, what do you want, Willie?"

He lowered his gun. "Well, sir, it occurs to me you tailed me out here for a reason. It's you that wants dealin' with me, not the other way round."

"True." I lowered my own gun slightly.

"So, how's about we do it man to man? My blade against your blade. Like true gator men."

As I watched him, Nixon lay his gun down in the snow, and slowly drew his knife out of his boot.

"Whadya say, Zeke?"

I laid my gun at my feet and rose slowly.

"If that's the way you want it, Willie, find me fair."

I drew my own blade and stepped down off the porch. Took a couple of steps toward him and stopped. I tried my damndest to keep my eyes on his, and not down on the ground between us. He frowned.

"You fixin' to trick me somehow, Zeke?"

"No, I'm fixing to cut you, Willie. She was with child, you know."

"I know, Zeke... But I weren't sure who's it were...yours or mine." A sly grin lit his face, and I screamed and charged at him.

"You son of a bitch!"

Willie forgot his hesitation and came at me, the blade held out afore him. I stopped in the nick of time, praying that I hadn't miscounted my steps under that day's fall of snow.

Nixon got within a couple of feet when I heard the sharp snap of the bear trap clamping around his foot. He let out a piercing scream and lurched forward. I swept my blade across his fingers, severing the front three at the knuckle and sending the knife spinning out of his grip. Blood sprang out of the bloody stumps and soiled the white earth.

Recoiling in shock, Nixon sat down hard on the seat of his pants. His good hand flew to the steel jaws of the trap, and he let out a series of involuntary moans.

I stood and watched him a good few minutes till he calmed down, then I went for him. Nixon raised his good hand up to protect his face and I hacked that son-of-a-bitch clean off. He screamed again and fell back into a dead faint.

I picked up the unconscious body and carried it indoors.

Nixon woke the next morning as I was hauling him fireman style through the woods. The sun was in the sky and the snows were waning.

"Where the Hell are we?" He said in a raspy voice.

"Hush now, Willie. I'll give you a sip of water when we get there."

"Where you taking me, you bastard?"

"Now now, Willie. That ain't no way to thank a man who tended to your wounds."

Nixon held one hand then the other stump up to his face to see where I had cleaned and bandaged his amputated parts. Least I assumed he did since his face was hanging down toward my rear end.

"Put me down and let me die."

"All in good time, Willie. Do you know what time of year it is?"

"Huh?"

"It's closing in on spring."

"So? Ain't going gatoring with these hands now."

I paused, a wonderful sight spread out before us. The mighty frozen river. I swung around to give him a look at it.

"You see that, Willie? Ain't that a sight to behold?"

He didn't answer, so I stepped gingerly out onto the ice, testing to see it would take our weight. Thank the Lord it did, and I motioned out like Jesus, carrying my burden.

When I reached the spot I had carefully picked out, I laid him gently on the ice. Then I dropped the ropes down off my shoulder.

"What…what are you doing?"

"You never stuck around the river during the winter, Willie. Not once."

"So damn cold."

"Look around you. What do you see?

Nixon craned his neck, did his best to scan the frozen waters.

"Ice, just ice, and a few dead trees stickin' up."

I smiled. "They ain't trees, Willie. Look closer."

He did, and it was as if he cottoned on to what I was about all at once.

"No! They… That can't be."

"It is. You ever heard the term, brumation, Willie?"

He shook his head.

I picked him up under the shoulders and held my canteen up to his lips. Then I lifted him upright and started tying him to the tree. He was too weak to fight me, as I planned.

"In the wintertime, gators don't hibernate like some other critters. They got a unique system shuts their body down, but they still need to breathe. So, when the river starts icing up, they prop themselves up like you see right there, with their snouts sticking out of the ice. That my friend, is what they call brumation. I learned that from an old gator man."

Nixon looked around desperately at all the gator snouts propped up in the ice.

"You can't leave me here."

I ignored him and tightened the ropes. Then I took a few steps back and looked up at the bright sun.

"Zeke, I know I done wrong. I repent." Drool ran down his chin and his eyes looked fit to burst.

"I ain't no preacher, Willie, no holy man, 'cept I can walk on water." I started to walk away across the ice. Nixon called after me.

"Kill me, Zeke. Cut me with your knife. I deserve it… please Zeke."

I turned and gave him one last sermon.

"I offer you the same quality of mercy you showed them girls and my unborn, Willie. Them gators look frozen to death, but they aint. Soon as the snows thaw, those big critters will spring right back to life. I figure they'll be a mite hungry, and them teeth look sharper than any knife."

That's my story about what happened 'tween me and Willie Nixon. Never did figure out what was wrong in that man's head made him do those awful things. I know what I did in return weren't nice neither, but I figure I was justified. An eye for an eye, the Good Book says. Never told no one my tale till now. In time my heart healed some and I found myself a new woman. She bore me two children who grew up fine and strong. I went back to gatoring till I couldn't cut no more. Never heard a thing 'bout Willie Nixon again, and no part of him ever did come floating on the tide past my boat.

DEMONTIA

The aural narrative of asphalt disappearing under the wheels of the car almost lulled Matt to sleep. The route between his house and his mother's, the old family home, had become so familiar he could have driven there with his eyes closed.

It was a mixture of anger and guilt which propelled him on the all too familiar journey. He chided himself for resenting her refusal to pull up stumps and move into a home after his father's death. Yet he loathed having to drive so far, so often, to complete the mundane tasks she could no longer perform for herself.

Having never learned to drive, she couldn't get to the shops, and the fact that she lived on an incline meant she couldn't even wheel her rubbish bin down the drive. Matt had to come over and do it for her. Yet she was stubborn and set in her ways, so she stayed put, a willing captive to her physical incapacity.

Matt shook himself out of the stupor as the old neighbourhood came into sight. He eased into the drive, got out, and stretched, nodding to old Bill Jeffries who loitered over his hedge with a pair of shears. He was almost of his mother's vintage but enjoyed greater mobility.

Matt picked the local newspaper off the driveway and walked up the rise to the front door. He saw through the flyscreen that it was open and watched his mother shuffle toward him from the dining room adjoining the lounge room. The faded aroma of pipe tobacco lingered like a memory. *Old Rogue* had been his father's brand. Rather appropriate, Matt had thought.

"It's okay, Ma, I can let myself in." Matt used his own key to unlock the screen door. He walked inside and waited for his eyes to adjust to the dim closed-curtained interior.

His father's passing had hit his mother hard. The whole house was a shrine to the old man. The cluttered paraphernalia that constituted his life still dominated. Pictures of Dad in his best suit, belting out a tune at the local club, Dad with his golf buddies on the first tee, Dad's coffee mug, Dad's pipe and ashtray, even the book he was reading when he passed still sat on the small table next to his favourite old armchair.

Edna Rogers held out her withered arms. It was all she could do to remain upright. Matt hugged her gently.

"Matthew. What brings you out this way?"

Matt edged past her into the dining room. She followed.

"You asked me to come over." Matt sat at the dining table and pushed a small mountain of papers, bills, prescriptions and old magazines aside. It looked like a scene from an apocalyptic film, where the inhabitants had vanished and left everything to rot.

His mother hovered at his side. "Did I?"

Matt held in a sigh. "You called me, remember?"

A light bulb switched on in her head and she reached for a piece of paper held down by a stained cup half-filled with tepid liquid.

"I need you to get a few things for me at the shops if that's okay. Then change the filters in the pond and water the roses. Oh, and feed Mr Binks. Cup of tea, dear?"

Matt looked at the empty pet dish by the stove. "The cat died, Ma. About ten years ago."

She looked puzzled. "Oh, did he?"

"Yeah. We buried him out the back." He rose and moved to the small kitchenette. "Don't worry, I'll make the tea." He filled the stained jug and switched it on, then busied himself piling up a stack of newspapers and faded periodicals.

When they had drained their cups, Matt readied himself to drive to the local mall. He picked up the list of items to collect. It was the length of his arm, written in her familiar cursive scrawl.

"Jesus, Ma. All this?"

She fiddled with her purse and muttered, "S'alright, I'll pay for it." She pulled a great wad of notes out and held them in her pale fist. Most were fifties with a few twenties thrown in.

"Jeez! What did you do, rob a bank?"

"You know I only go to the bank when I can. I don't like to be caught short." She limped toward the bench with the empty cups. "Would you like a cup of tea?"

"We *just* had one. You wanna be careful someone doesn't knock you on the head. All this cash lying around. I showed you how to use your card to pay for stuff. Don't you remember?" As he spoke, Matt's attention was drawn to his mother's shopping cart, which sat against a cabinet with produce overflowing from the lid. Matt started pulling it out. "What's all this stuff? Groceries, cat food, medical supplies..." He held a container of pills up toward her. "Mum, have you been to the shops?"

Edna gave him a blank look. "Ooh...that's right. The home help came last week."

Matt smiled. "Hopeless. I'll take this rubbish out to the bin." He picked up the pile of magazines and newspapers and made his way out front, where the bin had yet to be returned from the verge. Bill Jeffries looked up from his rose bushes.

"How's your mother, young Matthew? I worry about her a lot."

Matt dumped the periodicals and wiped his hands down his shirt. "She's hanging in there, Bill. She appreciates your company."

"I was gonna wheel that bin back up the drive for her later."

"That's okay." Matt smiled. Was it possible Bill was keen on his mother? He was a widower too after all. He thought about it, about them, *together*, and shuddered. He was a nice old guy though. "Still wearing that hat I see."

Bill looked up. "Eh?"

Matt pointed. "Your old fishing hat. You've had it since I was a kid. Don't tell me you've still got the boat."

Bill took the hat off and held it in his hands. "No, I had to get rid of it when Ruby passed on. To help pay for things..."

Matt's face dropped. "Oh, I'm sorry, Bill." He hated making the old guy sad. He hadn't meant to dredge up those memories. "Come over later for a chat?"

Bill lodged the hat back in place. "Sounds good, son." Matt

hoped he had already forgotten the previous line of thought. Old folk often did.

He pulled the bin up the drive and went back inside. He found his mother in the lounge room. She eased herself down into a frayed armchair. Matt rescued the remote before it had a chance to jab into her scrawny backside and set it on the coffee table. He contemplated sitting in his father's chair, thought better of it, and chose the couch. He pushed a bunch of cushions aside and found himself staring into his father's face in an old photo propped up on the busy coffee table. Dad in the seventies, his dark hair slicked back, terrible moustache, big toothy grin, decked out in a powder blue safari suit. It looked like he was about to wink at the camera, his eyes twinkled with life.

"He up to his old tricks again, eh?"

"Huh?" said Matt with a start.

"Bloody Jeffries," she said. "He's not getting the house."

"I don't think it's the house he's after, Ma. He's got his own. I think it's your body he wants."

"Don't be daft," she snorted. Matt looked up to see her reach for the television remote. As she leaned forward in the light of the window he noticed a trickle of blood running down the side of her head toward her neckline.

"Ma! What the hell happened to your head?"

"Oh, that dear? It's nothing to worry about. I think I recorded *Frost* last night. Let's put that on, eh?" She started fiddling with the remote, pushing a range of buttons.

"Nothing to worry about?" Matt snatched the remote from her hands. "There's a big gash on your head. What happened?"

He held the remote away from her, demanding an explanation.

"I had a fall. That's all. I fell and hit my head."

"Had a fall where?"

She thought for a long time; her gaze darted around the room. "Outside. Just out by the front door. I was trying to pick up a flyer that blew onto the lawn. I hit my head on a rock in the garden... Remote. Let's watch *Frost*."

"Christ, Ma, gimme a look." He handed her the remote and stood behind her to examine the wound. Blood had dribbled down her wrinkled neck and stained the shoulder of her flowered nightdress. He cursed himself for not noticing it before and pulled the curtains open. His fingers lingered above the wound, aching to pick at it, but not wanting to add to the damage. She leaned forward as the screen flickered to life.

"Leave it, Matt. I'm not hurt."

"Jesus, it doesn't look like it. What if you've fractured your skull? Why didn't you call an ambulance, or call me?"

"I did call you."

"You didn't tell me you'd cracked your scone!" Matt probed around the wound with an inquisitive finger. It came back red and sticky.

"Ow! Leave it, Matthew. I'm fine."

"Why didn't you use that personal alarm system I rigged up for you? All you gotta do is push the button and they send help straight away."

"What alarm, dear?"

Matt looked across toward the telephone where the alarm system sat, disconnected, a jumble of plastic cords. "Are you even wearing the device?" He checked her neck where the strap should have hung. The flesh was unencumbered by technology.

"I don't like that thing hanging around my neck. It stops me sleeping."

"It's there to keep you alive, you stubborn old goat!" Matt reached for the phone. She hobbled after him, pleading.

"Honest, love, I'm right as rain. Besides, I don't trust those doctors. They messed my pills up last time, almost killed me."

He stopped dialling. "You took the wrong dose, Mother, it wasn't the doctor's fault."

Her lip began to quiver. "Take their side. You were in on it, can't wait to get rid of your old mother, get your hands on the house."

Matt sighed. "Don't cry, Mum. You know that's not true."

She reached out and gripped his jumper. "Please don't make me go back to hospital again, son. Don't let them do me in. I just want to stay here in my own home. Where your father and I…"

Matt shook his head. "Why are you so stubborn? I'm going

to fix you some food, but I'm keeping an eye on you." He went through to the kitchen and spoke to her through the doorway as he fiddled with pots and pans.

"These dishes are all dirty, Ma. You need a bloody maid. Listen, I should take you to the doctor to get that thing checked out. It could get infected…"

Matt walked through the doorway with a plate of food for his mother to find her lying prostrate on the floor in front of the flickering screen, where DI Frost leaned over the body of an old woman. He dropped the plate and rushed to his mother's side.

"Ma!" He fell to his knees and grabbed her flimsy wrist, checking for a pulse. He leaned his ear over her open mouth and felt her shallow breath.

"I'm alright, love."

"Christ!" He jolted backwards. "You gave me a scare."

"I'm just having a rest dear."

"On the floor?"

"I'll be alright in a minute."

It was then that Matt saw it, growing out of the side of her head from the wound; a great glutinous mass, bloody and throbbing, trying to take shape. Matt pictured a snake trying to force its way out a sac made of veiny membrane.

His mother let out a series of low moans, sending him into a fresh bout of panic.

"Ma! What the fuck is happening?" Matt grabbed a wad of tea towels and wiped the blood from around the edges of the thing that pulsed from the side of his mother's head. It looked like something was trying to tunnel its way out of her skull.

Matt grabbed his mobile off the table. "That's it, Mum. I'm calling a damn ambulance."

Her eyes flared and a hand shot out and grabbed his ankle in a vice like grip. He yelped and dropped the phone.

"No ambulance, no bloody doctors. A…another trip to the hospital would just about do me in." She placed her hand over her heart in a dramatic gesture. "I'm okay, Matthew. Just let me rest here for a bit, please." The calm finality of her tone somehow terrified him.

"Are…are you sure?"

Tears formed in her eyes as she looked up at him.

"I'm 83, son. If it's my time, so be it. Besides, I miss your father. Can you just…get me a pillow?"

Numb with shock, Matt stood and looked down on the scene before him: his mother flat out on the old, faded carpet, the foetus growing out of her head, the growing pool of blood and the useless crumpled crimson tea towels with stained images of familiar landmarks visited long ago. He swallowed and went to fetch her a pillow.

Hours later, Matt watched over his sleeping mother. Her shallow chest rising and falling, head propped on a stained red pillow. The growth still attached to her, throbbing and pulsing. Perhaps it was feeding off her like some vampiric parasite. A wave of panic flooded his mind and he contemplated grabbing the old man's axe from the shed and cutting the bastard off, but to do so might kill her.

Matt switched on the table lamp as the evening grew dark, bathing the scene in sallow light, then reached down and pulled up his trouser leg to examine where she had grabbed his ankle. He was shocked to see a red welt forming. Where did she get the strength? He looked across at her serene sleeping features and mopped the perspiration from her forehead with a damp cloth, eliciting a soft moan. Matt pushed back the snow-white hair now stained a pink hue. Her lips moved and the occasional word slipped out from her dreams. He heard his father's name.

Dad's last days had been hard on them both. Many a night he had sat by the old man's hospital bed, listening to stories of his boyhood during the war. That was before he got worse, and Matt only had the hiss and beep of the life support machines for company. Matt missed his father too, but the old boy had a good run. It had been over a year; his mother needed to start letting go.

When the hour grew late Matt took a blanket from his parents' bedroom and lay it over his mother. She murmured in her sleep. He grabbed one for himself and hunkered down on the couch beside her. The thought of sleeping in his old room didn't appeal, too many ghosts. In the morning he would call the boss and ask for a week or two of carer's leave. Tony would understand. He lay with his phone in his hands, fingers paused over the buttons, and fell asleep. His father visited him in his dreams too. This was his bad Dad, shouting Dad, brandishing his belt. "You've always been weak, son. Letting people walk all over you. No wonder Susan left you."

Matt woke with a start from an awful nightmare to find his mother leaning on her elbow staring at him. The morning sun streamed through a crack in the curtains, shedding light on the scene. The growth that had been attached to his mother's head was gone. For a few, beautiful seconds he thought the whole thing had just been a terrible dream.

Then he saw the blood.

"Christ, Ma! Stop staring at me like that. You look a bit better. Where's it gone?"

His mother cast her eyes to one side, and Matt followed her gaze. Like a newborn burst from its foetal sac, bloody and raw, the growth lay on the floor. It opened a mouth-like aperture and let out a tiny wail, and Matt found himself both fascinated and repulsed.

"Matthew, I think it's hungry."

Matt restrained his mother as she moved toward it.

"Ma, don't go near it."

She tutted at him. "Don't be silly. You can see it's helpless. It's a newborn and it needs me."

Stunned, Matt relinquished his hold on her shoulder. "At least let me check your head."

With some impatience she let him probe her skull, never taking her eyes off the formless shape on the carpet as it struggled and kicked with ill-formed appendages. "I feel a lot better now."

"Weird, that wound seems to be healing itself."

Matt sat back on his haunches with a puzzled expression and watched his mother push herself to her feet with the aid of the armrest of the closest chair. "I think I've got some hamburger in the fridge."

"Hamburger… You're not seriously going to feed that thing?"

She returned with a packet of raw meat in her hands, moved to the wailing progeny's side and squatted down with ease. "Oh, hush now, Matthew. I'm a mother. Mums never forget how to do this, just like I raised you."

Matt edged closer as the monstrosity caught the scent and stretched itself toward the dripping mass in his mother's wrinkled hand. A serpentine tongue snaked out and licked at the offering. His mother cooed and dropped the morsel into the opening. Matt's mouth opened just as wide.

"Fuck me, it's got teeth!"

"Matthew!" she scolded.

Matt took some time off to nurse his mother following her ordeal. After a week she began to carry her strange offspring around, strapped to her side. He acquiesced to her request to fetch a supply of mincemeat from the butchers, but a few nights of watching her feed the thing and, even more disconcerting, seeing it grow and take a vague anthropomorphic shape, was enough for Matt. He went back to work.

When he returned a few days later he was relieved to see it was no longer strapped to his mother's hip.

"Oh no, dear, he's getting way too big for me to carry him around now," she said as she buzzed around, dusting the lounge room.

"*He*? It's a *he* now?" Matt couldn't help but notice the lack of clutter and general cleanliness of the place. "Who tidied up? Has the home care been?"

She stopped mid-wipe and grinned at him. "No dear, I... dispensed with their services. I cleaned the place myself. I've got a new lease on life. I think I enjoy being a mother again."

Matt rubbed his temples. "But you're *not* a mum again, Ma. That thing isn't human. Where is it, anyway?"

She folded her arms. "*He* is in the cellar. He seems to like it down there, living among your father's old stuff."

Matt scanned the room. His eyes came to rest on the door leading down to the cellar, where his dad used to love hanging out. To one side sat a folded pile of clothing, topped by a familiar looking hat. A pair of brogues sat next to the pile. Matt walked over and examined it. He held the hat in his hands, looking at the silhouette of an angler casting a line out to sea.

"What's this stuff doing here, Ma?" Matt twirled the hat between his fingers.

She gave him a sheepish look. "Oh…just some old clothes of your fathers. I've been meaning to take them to the op-shop."

"Is that right? You haven't thrown away a single thing of Dad's since he died. I know who this hat belongs to. What is going on?" As if on cue, a sound rose up from beyond the cellar door; a noise like something large being dragged along the floor.

Matt motioned toward the door. "It's okay, Ma. I'm a grown man. I understand if you and Bill have got a thing going on. Now what's he doing down there?"

Edna darted between Matt and the door. "Don't go down there, Matthew."

"Now you're being silly. What, is he walking around naked? I'll shout down to him to put his pants on." Matt glanced at the hat again and noticed blood around its rim. He picked it up and held it toward the light.

As he did so the cellar door was flung open, his nasal passages were assailed by the stench of rancid meat, and a bloody, broken face thrust itself into the light. Matt found himself staring into Bill Jeffries" ruined visage.

"Help me!" Bill gasped.

Matt looked from his mother to the neighbour, just as a large sinuous tentacle stretched up from below and curled around Bill's waist.

"Fuck!" said Matt, and as Jeffries grabbed at his arm, he lifted his foot and stuck it into Bill's midriff and shoved him back into the dark, slamming the door shut. There followed a muffled scream and then silence.

His mother looked placid. "He was hungry dear. You know how it is. When children get hungry, nothing else matters."

Matt dropped the hat back on the tidy pile. "Jesus, Mother! What the Hell?"

She strode toward the kitchen. "Oh, come on, Matthew, it's not as if anyone is going to miss Bill. Let's have some tea."

Matt regarded the discarded clothing and shuddered. He followed his mother into the kitchen, where she fussed around filling the kettle and spooning sugar into two mugs. Another subterranean thump echoed up through the floorboards, making Matt jump.

"Mum, just how big is this thing…?"

Edna Rogers proved as recalcitrant over her new companion as she had been over hanging onto her husband's memory. Matt was numbed by the peculiar turn of events and paled at his part in the demise of poor old Bill. The next time he dropped by, he found the homecare nurse's white Ford stored in the garage. Her glasses sitting on top of her discarded uniform in a neat pile by the cellar door. The following month he found a girl-guide uniform, two boxes of cookies and a half-full collection tin.

Fresh flowers littered the disinfected lounge room and kitchen. Their cloying scent fought for attention with the overpowering aroma of rotting meat. Edna started taking long walks in the fresh air, testament to her growing vitality, and Matt quailed at the rumours that began to circulate around the old neighbourhood. Rumours that she did not always return home alone.

Matt sat at the kitchen table with his head in his hands. Edna stood at the bench slicing through some thick red slabs of meat with a large knife.

"Matthew?"

He spoke without looking at her. "Ma…you just can't go around killing people… it's…not right. You have to stop."

The sound of blade on chopping board ceased. "You wouldn't turn us in, would you, son? Your own flesh and blood."

Matt jerked his head up. His mother stood over him with the bloody knife in her hand.

He jumped to his feet, the chair scraping along the floor. "Jesus!"

Edna looked at the knife as if she had forgotten she was carrying it. "Oh…no…Matthew… I wouldn't."

Matt ran for the door, her pleading voice rang in his ears as he slammed it behind him. "I love you, son…"

For several weeks Matt avoided his mother's house and its basement, afraid of what he might see down there. Terrified of what her demonic progeny had become, and just as afraid of what his mother was becoming. He fought a constant mental battle between his desire to call the authorities and his fear of what they would do to his mum. She was way too old to do time. He was also ashamed to admit his own fear of what her bloodthirsty companion might do to him if his mother let it.

It was the recurring nightmare that sent him back. His father, younger and returned to vigour, leaning over him. "I know why she left you, boy. You couldn't give her what she wanted, could you? The sound of tiny pattering feet…" The voice nagged him until he turned the car off the road away from his office and accelerated toward his boyhood home. He burst into the old house and stood before the cellar door, blood pounding in his throat.

"Matt?" His mother's voice came from her bedroom doorway. He didn't turn to look at her. He heard her bare feet pad down the hallway toward him.

"What?"

"If you're looking for him, he doesn't live down there anymore."

Filled with sudden inconceivable hope, Matt turned. His mother wore a skimpy nightie. Her body somehow full and ripe, like it had been when he was younger. Her hair dyed a blazing red. For a brief moment, he almost forgot she was his mother.

"Where is it then? Gone I hope."

A sly grin spread across his mother's face. She did not reply, but glanced over her shoulder toward the bedroom. Matt saw her nipples were erect and straining at the thin material. He raised a hand to his mouth and backed toward the lounge. "Oh God!"

An odd smell permeated the room. Through a wave of nausea Matt strained to place it.

"Won't you join us for breakfast, Matt?" his mother implored as she followed him, pulling a dressing gown around her near naked form.

"Won't you join us for breakfast, Matt?" another voice echoed.

It too was familiar, a deep throaty baritone. A voice hued from years of inhaling tobacco.

Then Matt recognised the stench in the air. *Old Rogue.*

He turned to see a figure sitting in his father's favourite armchair, garbed in Dad's old tartan dressing gown, and obscured by the morning paper, held in misshapen hands. A languid plume of tobacco smoke curled toward the ceiling. In the doorway his mother began to croon an old tune he remembered from his schooldays. A rich masculine voice joined in on the harmony. The paper lowered and a melted parody of his father's face curled its wet lips around the stem of Dad's old pipe, winked at him and said, "Morning, son."

ROAD TRIP

Richie shot Frankie a glance as his companion punched the keys on his mobile. He gripped the steering wheel hard. He could tell by the way Frankie was bouncing around in his seat that he was agitated. Richie didn't like it when Frankie got upset.

Nobody liked it when Frankie got upset.

"Christ's sake!" Frankie shouted and smacked the phone against the dashboard. "How d'ya get a fucken signal in this godforsaken shithole?"

He held the phone out of the Commodore's passenger side window and shook it vigorously.

"Where the hell are we anyway?" he said over his shoulder.

"We're just outside of Manjimup, on the way to Bridgetown," Richie said.

"How long till we get back to Freo?"

Richie chewed his lower lip. Frankie knew how long it would take. He had driven the reverse journey three days earlier. "About three hours."

Frankie flung the mobile over his shoulder onto the back seat via the roof of the sedan. Richie braced himself for the onslaught.

"I've had it with these inbred hicks and their redneck shitholes. Ya can't get a phone signal, ya can't get the Internet, everything's overpriced and ya can't get good service. That's when the shops are even open. Christ, ya can't even get friggin' Italian food out here. Only bloody restaurants are Chinko, and who runs those? Not the bloody Chinese."

Richie smiled. "Christ, here we go." He watched Frankie's

Adam's apple jiggle up and down with agitation before the tirade resumed.

"How 'bout that joint the other night eh? '*What's in the Chinese Hotpot*,' I asked that ranga waitress, and what did she say? '*Aw oi dunno, Choinese shtuff*.' What the fuck is Chinese stuff? What's wrong with a bit o' spag bol? And I'm jack of payin' fifteen bucks fer a sandwich too. Nup, ya can stick ya friggin' country as far as I'm concerned."

"Well at least we got the job done with no hassles, took out Jimmy the Bull, like Enzo wanted." Richie looked across for acknowledgement as he slowed to accommodate the vehicle ahead of them.

Frankie plucked a mint out of the packet sitting in the central console and stuck it in his mouth. Richie pictured the dissolving peppermint soothing his rage.

"Yeah, ya did okay on that one, Rich. Ya coming on good. I schooled ya well."

"How many hits is that for you now, Frank?" Richie asked, trying to shift the conversation onto safer ground.

Frankie's brow furrowed. "Let's see, that makes… thirteen now."

Richie whistled.

"Yeah, what can I say? It's a living," Frankie mused.

Richie gripped the wheel and stared at the chassis of the old pick-up truck in front of them. A tentative sun peered through a crack in the gunmetal clouds and shed its light on the road ahead. Even Frankie conceded the south-west was gorgeous this time of year. The rains had created a fertile paradise among the fields and forests, and they had lapped up what little sight-seeing their journey afforded them.

Richie hadn't known if he would be able to hack it when Enzo first brought him into the fold, but they threw him in the deep end and he had done whatever the Family asked. It was like Frankie said, "When you're a wop and you're stuff-all good at anything else, whaddya do? Ya join the Mob." Having family connections helped, and when you're Italian, everybody's family. Even third generation bums like him and Frankie.

"What's this prick doing?" Frankie motioned toward the truck ahead as they rode its bumper. "Bloody speed limit's a hundred and ten and he's sittin' on eighty."

"Yeah, I know."

"Can't ya overtake the dickhead?"

Richie waved a hand over the bitumen vista filling the windscreen. "Well, I can't go over the double white lines—too many sharp bends on the road."

Frankie lost it. "Shit! You can shoot a bloke in the head but ya can't pass on a double line?"

"Take it easy. There's a passing lane coming up. We'll take him then."

Frankie pulled the sunshade down and checked his reflection in the mirror. He adjusted the crotch of his jeans. "Geez I'm lookin' forward to gettin' home eh? Gonna give the missus a bloody good seeing to."

"Yeah?" Richie feigned interest. He cranked his window down a little to let the wind run through his hair.

"You still seeing that Saskia chick?"

"Nup. We broke up yonks ago."

"Oh, that's right. She was two-timing ya, hey?" Frankie shook his head. "Any bitch did that to me I'd rub her out."

"Angelica wouldn't do that to you, Frank. She's not that type of girl."

"Oh yeah? Know her *that* well, do ya mate?"

Richie felt Frankie's eyes on him.

"No, of course not. It's just… You been married three years, you got a kid… Hey we're coming up to Palgarup. We can lose this prick."

The car descended into the town. As they rolled down the main street Frankie spat the mint out the window. "Hey, pull up here, mate. I'm starving."

Two beef and mushroom pies and a ham and salad roll later they were back on the road.

Frankie had his mobile again and was fighting to get a signal. Richie kept his eye on the road while his tongue probed a crack in one of his upper cuspids for a stubborn sliver of onion. At the same time he replayed their earlier conversation for clues. Was Frankie prodding him for information back there? Nah, he's not that smart. Besides, everybody knows you don't cut someone's grass in the Family. Not if you want to keep your balls.

"Shit!" said Richie.

Frankie looked up from his phone. "Fucken country hick!" He reached across Richie's lap and leaned on the horn, then sprang back and stuck his head out the window. "Hey dickhead! Get outta the bloody way."

"Unbelievable," said Richie.

"Wait a minute. Isn't that the same prick who was holding us up before we got into Palgarup? Faded red pick-up? He should be bloody miles away by now."

As if in response, the pick-up slowed down. An intermittent stream of traffic sped in the opposite direction.

"I don't believe this arsehole. Is this some sort of joke?" Frankie squeezed the mobile in his fist as if he wanted to crush it.

"Thank Christ." Richie heaved a sigh as he hit the accelerator and pulled into the overtaking lane and passed the slower vehicle.

Frankie leaned out the window to give the guy a mouthful as they drew level, and the truck accelerated ahead of them.

"What the…?"

The passing lane narrowed into nothing and the pick-up was waiting for them, as impassable as ever.

Frankie said, "This guy is taking the piss. That's it."

Richie swallowed. "What's it?"

Frankie glanced over his shoulder toward the boot of the car. "I'm taking this guy out."

"Frankie, we ain't got time for this. Besides, we're on the open road, too many witnesses."

The truck ahead of them indicated a left turn, even though there was no road to divert onto.

"Now what?" said Frankie.

Several minutes later, a side road came into view. The truck slowed to a complete stop at the junction, its indicator still flashing.

Richie said, "What is he doing?"

Frankie broke into a smile. "The dumb prick wants us to follow. We'll give him what he wants."

Richie hesitated. "What if it's a trap?"

"Nobody would go to that much trouble. Look at the guy. He's on his own. Enzo doesn't have any enemies out here, none that are still breathing anyway. He woulda warned us."

The red pick-up eased around the corner and the white Commodore followed. A green road sign indicated the destination and the distance.

"Donnelly River. You know that place, Rich?"

"Nup. Never heard of it."

"I know it, been there before. Keep going. We'll teach this wanker to mess with us."

The road narrowed into a single lane with orange gravel framing each side. Dense forest hemmed them in. Richie wandered over the middle of the tarmac and glanced up at the sun as it began its descent toward the horizon. "Hope this don't take too long. It gets dark quick this time of year."

"Yeah, don't worry. This guy ain't got long to live. Anything coming the other way will take him out before it gets to us. Just watch out for roos. They like to hit the paddocks around dusk."

Half an hour later the pick-up slowed and rounded a sharp bend. They followed until it rolled down a slope and came to a stop by a crumbling wooden structure.

"Woah! What the hell is that?" said Richie.

"It's the old wood pulping mill. Don't follow him, go up this way. He ain't going nowhere. It's the end of the road."

Frankie guided them into a clearing by an abandoned cluster of stone buildings. They got out of the car and looked down the hill at the foreboding looking relic where the truck had parked. The decrepit mill was dank and dark and had collapsed in places.

"That place looks haunted," said Richie, wrapping his arms around himself to ward off the afternoon chill. He swore the cold was emanating from the rotting hulk itself, rather than the river beyond it.

"I bet it is. Lotta accidents happened there, from what I remember. Lotta accidents happened after it closed too." Frank smiled.

"Whaddya mean?"

"Funny that guy leading us here. I did my first hit here, five years ago, right over there where he's parked, as a matter of fact. Small world, eh?"

Frankie popped the trunk, rummaged in a leather carry-all, and retrieved a snub-nosed Glock.

"Should I bring my gun too, Frank?" Richie asked.

"Nah mate. Leave this one to me." Frankie slammed the boot of the car.

They walked past the crumbing main building and Richie's attention was drawn to a large notice board, hammered into the ground.

Frankie checked the gun's chamber. "This used to be a bit of a tourist spot back in the day, but all that died out yonks ago. People stopped coming here. The ones living here left."

Richie read from the notice board. "'Do not dwell in this sad place, where the dark ones watch from the shadows.' What do ya suppose that means, Frankie?"

Frankie fitted a silencer onto the pistol. "Stuffed if I know. Never saw it before."

"Says it's a quote from an Abo elder. Not a very touristy message, is it?"

Frankie ignored him, staring dead ahead. "I brought Angelica out here once."

Richie flinched.

"Screwed her right over there, up against the wall. She likes it out in the open, but you'd know that, wouldn't ya, Richie?"

"Frank…?"

Frankie turned toward him. "Nah, don't say anything mate, just start walking." He motioned toward the red pick-up.

"Aw shit! Come on Frank."

Frankie spoke with quiet authority. "Shut up, Richie. Turn around. Don't even look at me." Richie felt the barrel of the pistol pressing into his back.

Richie staggered ahead of his mentor. Down by the old mill, the occupant of the truck had alighted and stood with his back to them, staring out toward the river.

"I'm fucken disappointed in you, Richie. I taught you the ropes, and this is how you repay me, by banging me missus."

Richie wheeled around and dropped to his knees.

"I'm fucken sorry Frank, alright? I'm sorry. Please don't do this. Don't let a woman come between us. It was her fault mate. She forced herself on me."

"Don't make a spectacle of yourself, Richie. Try and act like a professional. We're hitmen, fer Chrissakes. We got a job to do here, remember? There's no use arguing. I'm gonna do him, and then I'll do you. Two birds with one stone. So, get up and keep walking."

Richie rose with the enthusiasm of a condemned man. He turned and placed one foot in front of the other. "Please Frankie…"

"The only question left, Richie, is whether you get it in the head or in the balls. Now move!"

A chill wind swirled up from the river as they approached their target and Richie noticed the silence which enveloped the area. There were no bird or insect noises, not even the sound of ebbing water. The man stood with his back to them, his hands in his jacket pockets. He was tall and angular, and dressed head to toe in black garb.

Frankie let out a bitter laugh. "Turned out quite convenient this, eh, Rich? Enzo insisted I bring you back home to face the music, but now I figure, stuff that. Had a bit of trouble with a guy, he took Richie out before I could get him. Sorry Enzo, but it's the nature of the business."

Richie shivered and his teeth chattered. "I don't like this place, Frank. We shouldn't have come here."

"What are you scared of Rich, the mill? It's just an old building, you dumb shit." Frankie shrugged his shoulders. "If there are any ghosts, you'll be joining them soon. You can all haunt me together."

Richie cast a sideward glance at the crumbling pulp mill. It felt even colder up close, like it was sucking the life out of the air itself. He didn't like the way it made him feel like he was being watched.

As they neared the truck, Frankie stopped several metres from the motionless figure and shoved Richie aside. "Hey! Hey arsehole! Turn around, so I can shoot you in the face."

The man turned to face them. Richie dropped to his knees for the second time. Frankie's jaw hung slack.

"Shit!"

The visage staring back at Frank was that of the man he had executed five years before. At least it was at first. Though it was difficult to tell for sure in the dull afternoon light the face seemed to exist in a state of flux. First angular with a wispy moustache, then pear shaped and clean shaven, then fat and double chinned. Calabrian, Sicilian, it mimicked the variation of human facial structures, but always in perpetual motion.

"Nooo!" Frank screamed. He backed away as the shadowy figure closed the gap between them with uncanny speed. Frank fired point-blank once, twice, a third time. The bullets smacked into the man's face which seemed to open up and swallow them within its fleshy folds. Strong, wiry fingers closed around Frankie's neck, and he stared into the dead eyes of his victims, one after another. The Glock fell into the dirt.

"Richie…" he gasped.

Kneeling in the mud, Richie saw Frank's eyes bulging.

"Richie…help meee!"

Richie saw the gun lying at the feet of the two figures, but thought better of it. Frankie let out a keening whine as one of the hands moved from his throat and crept up his face. Richie stood transfixed as two of the fingers dug into Frankie's eye sockets and squeezed. Richie heard a sound like a boot crushing a blowfish and saw a stream of viscera ooze between those skeletal fingers. Frankie bellowed in pain.

Then Richie was running, pounding the dirt. He ran toward the river. He looked back to see the thing drop Frankie and point a long bony finger straight at him. Its eyes seemed to glow. Richie saw the car sitting on the hill beyond the outstretched arm. Then he turned and fled into the bush.

He tore through thick foliage which grabbed at him like gnarled fingers and splashed along the shallows, not daring to look back.

After a while he slowed and stood, hands on his knees, panting. He listened for any sound, but the world was dead and silent. He hurried on, moving as far away from that awful scene as possible.

As he ran, he played scenarios out in his head. Frankie knew about him and Angelica. Enzo did as well. That meant that the Mob would have already whacked her. Christ, what was he thinking, crossing the Family? He couldn't go back, ever. He needed transportation. He should double back to the car. Then he would have wheels and a gun. He'd rather face the Mob than that thing back there. Maybe it only wanted Frankie. Maybe it had gone now. But it pointed right at him. Christ!

Richie slowed to a walk. He looked around, trying to get his bearings. He could hear the river somewhere in front of him. It was pitch black. No moonlight filtered through the clouds. There was no sound of movement from the forest. He was sure that thing was not chasing him. He allowed a flicker of hope to penetrate his despair. If he could find the river and follow it, maybe he could retrace his steps and get to the car, even if it meant going past that mill again. It seemed the best option.

If only there was light to guide him. Then, as if in answer to his prayers, he saw a shimmer through the branches. It flickered in the night sky, like a million tiny lights being switched on.

"Stars," he said.

Richie felt a surge of relief. He could use the stars to navigate his path out of the bush.

He moved toward the sound of the flowing water and focussed on the stars. They shone like spun gold through the canopy, seeming to form patterns. Then Richie stopped in his tracks, his heart hammering. He saw the dark edifice of the mill loom before him. He spun in a circle as the glittering orbs encroached upon him from all sides and realised too late that they were not stars at all.

WITH A WHIMPER

Dave missed the old world more each day. Going fishing with Ben and Nev. Hunting ducks with his best four-legged buddy, Nipper. Going for a sly massage and happy ending down the secret knocking shop populated by Thai immigrants with Greasy and Spud from the factory. Christ, he even missed getting up before the sun and going to work and punching on.

"Beats the hell out of this crap," he mouthed to the empty hotel room overlooking the Hell hole the world had become outside. Kind of ironic, he supposed. Some band Kara listened to as a teenager once asked, *When did reality become TV?* Now the question was reversed, *When did horror movies become reality?*

He slid the glass door open and stepped onto the balcony, letting in the incoherent swell of noise and the stench of rotting flesh. "Fucking zombies!" he yelled over the edge, incredulous, at the mindless, impassive hordes wandering around on the streets, moaning and bumping into each other on a desperate and endless search for meat.

Dave wasn't big on films but even he had seen a few zombie flicks in the old days. Thought they were pretty funny.

Weren't funny now.

How the fuck did this happen?

A few people, among the few who were left, had tried to explain it to him. Some proxy virus the bloody government created in a lab to use against the ragheads or something had got loose and infected every bastard on the planet. It brought the dead out of their graves, and it got into everyone who died, whether they were bitten or not.

The world was fucked.

All his friends were dead: Robbo, Thommo, Benno, Nev, Greasy, Spud, all the hot women, all the Thai hookers, even his dog, Nipper, his best mate. That brought a tear to Dave's eye and he wiped it away angrily.

The ex-wife, dead, probably, he hadn't actually checked. His beloved only child, Kara, gone, and he was left to deal with his layabout son-in-law, Kev the dickhead. Far out, he thought, if there was a God, the bastard had lifted the lid off Dave's world and taken a big dump in it.

Okay, fair enough Kev had saved Dave from becoming a zombie buffet that afternoon he rocked up in his ute and sprayed the reanimated dead littering his front lawn with an AK47. This was just after the virus took full control and nobody knew what the Hell was going on.

Dave certainly didn't. One minute he was watching Chelsea's French international striker curl an absolute pearler into the top corner, and the next the poor sod was being dismembered under a pile of extras from *The Walking Dead*.

Dave had laughed at first. Thought it was some sort of political protest. Then the front window caved in and he forgot the carnage unfolding on his giant flat screen. Kev yanked him toward the idling truck while one of Kev's mates stood on the apron giving the masses of dead bastards that had suddenly appeared a good spray. Even Dave knew from the movies you had to take them out from the neck up, but Kev's mate didn't seem to care. The weapon was so powerful there was guts and body parts flying from arsehole to breakfast. Judging by the look on his dial he was enjoying himself too.

"Kev, what the fuck's goin' on?" Dave asked as he was shoved into the passenger seat.

"End of the fucking world," Kev said, gunning the engine.

As the car shot off up the road, the rapid-fire shooting trailed off, and glancing out the window, Dave saw to his horror that the brisk propulsion of the vehicle had taken the shooter by surprise and sent him hurtling off the back of the ute. The gun went clattering away up the tarmac, and Kev's mate was swamped by the ravenous dead.

He made a futile attempt to get up and run, waving toward the car, but he was already covered in bite wounds and pissing blood.

Dave turned to Kev. "Should we at least help your mate?"

"No point," said Kev, glancing in the rear-view mirror. "He's meat." He planted his foot.

Dave thought he heard a final scream over the roar of the motor. That was Kev all over though. Selfish bastard.

Kev filled in a few of the details as they headed toward the Manningham Hotel. Situated just off the highway south of the city, it was high enough to allow them to reconnoitre the situation, being close to the centre, and easy enough to booby trap the entrance downstairs.

Dave knew he should be grateful that Kev had pulled him out of the shit just as it was hitting the fan, but subsequent knowledge had dampened his empathy for his former welfare dependent layabout son-in-law. There was Kev's missing missus and Dave's daughter, Kara, for starters. He still remembered the discussion that ensued once Kev had got them to safer ground, and he noticed Kara wasn't among the small group of survivors.

"You left her there in a shopping mall, during a swarm?"

Kev looked more belligerent than downcast, which made Dave's hackles rise sharper.

"I tried me best. She wouldn't take her bloody heels off."

"Whaddya mean?"

"Her bloody shoes," Kev pointed helpfully at his feet. "She said they were expensive. I tried to drag her along out of harm's way, but it all happened so quick. We were caught unawares, just like you."

"Christ!"

"She didn't realise what the things were, until it was too late."

"She was your wife!"

Kev spat on the ground. "Ya think I didn't try and save her? I tried to yank the bloody shoes off her feet. The zombies were on her, they almost got me too."

Dave couldn't stop the tears. Tears of grief, and of rage. "You left her there to die."

A silence ensued. The type of silence only possible between grown men unable to convey their emotions in words.

"I came back for you, didn't I?" Kev said, sotto voice.

"Only because you felt guilty." Dave walked away.

While Dave now spent most of his time brooding, over a world and way of life he had pretty much taken for granted, he also took it upon himself to start garnering knowledge about how to survive in the new one.

House design, for example, was very important in terms of avoiding being eaten. It was important to recognise the structure of buildings to avoid getting yourself backed into a corner.

It amused Dave to discover that the homes of the very wealthy, who he had always envied, were the most susceptible to zombie assault. With their expansive bay windows to allow for more light, and their multiple entrances due to their sheer size, they were now just invitations to a corpse buffet.

The homes of the poor, in contrast, tiny, reinforced and secure due the vagaries of living in shit neighbourhoods, were much better equipped for use as boltholes against the dead.

Dave picked up this and other useful knowledge during his regular foraging for food and supplies. Such as which areas to avoid because they were full of paranoid nutters with guns. It also pleased him no end to witness his flabby middle-aged body retract back into the slender rock-hard figure he enjoyed in his youth. Constant exercise and forced sensible eating had its benefits. He even managed to give away the smokes. He got fed up scavenging for them, and with the ceasing of production, most of the supplies soon grew stale anyway. His one remaining vice was thankfully still available: the hotel had a great supply of booze. As long as you only indulged when you were locked up and secure, you were fine to get off your tits and have a cry about everything you had lost.

Which was what Dave was doing this evening. Shirtless and admiring his abs in front of the mirror in his spacious room.

He raised a glass to his four-legged mate, Nipper, and brooded about the poor little bugger's untimely demise.

Dave still remembered that dark day like it was yesterday. Scrambling home with three dead ones on his tail, ragged and starving. All his foraging bringing no result. Almost being gunned down by some idiot with a shottie in the ruins of a supermarket. Dave still had a lot to learn at that point.

Once he had secured the compound, he was drawn to the rooftop balcony by the scent of something wonderful, something he hadn't experienced in months, the aroma of succulent barbecuing meat. His mouth watering, Dave found Kev, turning a spit over a roaring fire. Decked out in thongs and shorts, his ridiculous tribal tattoos on display, Kev turned and saluted him with an open stubbie.

Dave moved toward the roasting carcass in a Pavlovian trance. "You found something, what is it, rabbit?"

"Somethin' like that, yeah." Kev took a swig of his beer and continued to turn the spit slowly.

Dave followed the slow twirl of the crisp, golden brown flesh, its juices dripping, mesmerised.

When they sat down to eat, Dave experienced the gamut of emotions. The high of the sheer joy of partaking in what had once been the simple pleasure of enjoying a roast meal. He likened his contentment to the rare delight he had experienced as a child opening presents on Christmas morning.

Then came the transitional moment, when the mood turned swiftly from being his best experience since the world collapsed upon itself, to the worst.

It occurred to Dave that he wanted to share this bounty with his best mate. He plucked a sliver of meat from his plate, held it below the table and whistled. He was not met with the usual sound of happy yipping and the patter of little feet. "Where's Nipper got to?" he asked Kev.

Kev's look in response told him everything he needed to know.

Dave gagged and spat out the mouthful he was chewing.

"You killed me fucken dog!"

Kev got that defensive, recalcitrant look on his face, the one that always gave Dave the shits. "Yeah, well, we were hungry."

Dave's face reddened. "My best fucking mate!" He swept his plate across the table at Kev. The latter stood up and stepped back.

"Don't be a dickhead! We needed to eat."

Dave picked up the big carving knife Kev had used to cut up his beloved Nipper, and advanced on his hated son-in-law. "I will gut you, you bastard!"

Kev edged toward the ledge. Hands raised in self-defence. He glanced over the edge, where a small group of curious zombies had already gathered, drawn by the shouting.

Dave's eyes glazed over as he advanced on Kev. "First me daughter, and now this. You fucking murdering scum!"

Kev fired back. "I just did what was necessary. I saved your fucken life!"

Dave raised the carving knife. It was then that a moment of clarity sunk in. He looked from the blade, to the half-stripped carcass on the spit, and he fell to his knees and started weeping.

"Nipper, my little buddy. You made me eat my best friend…"

Stunned by the turn of events, but still unapologetic, Kev moved away from the edge of the building, stepped around his sobbing father-in-law, picked up his plate, and took it back inside to finish. He left Kev with some parting wisdom. "You need to get a bloody grip, mate. The old world is gone, finished. This is what we are now."

Dave glanced at Kev through his fingers from his position on the ground. It was at this point that he determined that the bastard had to go.

The unsteady truce between Dave and Kev had settled since the incident, but all the while, Dave was plotting and formulating ideas. Getting a good grasp of the lay of the land. He knew Kev was a self-absorbed, narrow-minded idiot, who didn't think much beyond his immediate needs and gratification. Dave sucked on a tinnie and ruminated, running scenarios through his head.

The mad gunman option was no good. Dave had already shared much knowledge about the no-go areas with Kev before the Nipper incident. With time on his hands, he thought about the type of things that might tempt Kev into letting his guard down. Guns. The idiot was triggered by them, the bigger the better. Food was a necessity. Beer, but the hotel already gave them an adequate supply even Kev would take a while to get through.

Women! Dave had always sensed that Kev was one of those blokes who couldn't keep it in his pants. Had heard all the rumours back in the day about how many short-term relationships he had got through. He had always assumed it was natural, that most women soon saw through his act and realised he was a user and gave him the elbow accordingly.

Yet Kara had seen something in him that had to be more than what was hanging between his legs. Dave had always given his little girl credit for having an inkling of taste. The thought that he might be wrong left a bitter taste in his mouth.

Dave got full confirmation of Kev's womanising tendencies one day a couple of years back when, dropping in on Kev and Kara unexpected when called away from work, he had caught the bastard in flagrante delicto with some little tart. Kara was at work—the wanker was unemployed as usual. At least most of him was unemployed, but his dick was clearly active.

Dave thought long and hard about the situation. He enjoyed the sight of Kev on his knees begging for mercy. Despite his strong urge to spill the beans and make life very uncomfortable for the bludging love-rat, he thought about how much it would tear his daughter apart. So, Dave held back, and blackmailed the bastard instead. Kev spent the next few months fixing Dave's car for free and mowing his lawn on request. Everyone thought Kev was acting out of the goodness of his heart. Little did they know!

Dave stroked his now-chiselled jaw and thought back on the situation. Kev liked loose women. After the zombie plague hit, the boundaries of moral decency had loosened. Dave knew from his knowledge of history that in times of great social upheaval, the masses would fall back on their vices for comfort and security.

Vices like tobacco, drugs, alcohol, and sex.

From his hunting trips, Dave also knew there were certain houses, places where women, abandoned by their men or widowed, would gladly exchange sexual comfort for food and drink. Not many, but there were a few around. Kev also knew some of these places. You had to be careful though, because men were now unbound by the former laws of society. As a result, women and children lived in constant danger of sexual assault, battery, and murder. Women who were known to be generous with their sexual favours were a particular target. The more the world changed, the more it stayed the same.

Nonetheless, Dave knew that Kev had a preference for a certain type of woman, and thus, he set out his stall and laid his trap.

"A curvy blonde, you reckon?" Kev asked, as they pulled up outside the house.

"Yep, real voluptuous, with huge tits," Dave added. "Tatts as well, don't forget."

Kev was triggered. They got out of the car, it was all going to plan. They approached the door, appropriately red in colour.

"Just knock three times," Dave said.

Kev knocked. A muffled sound came from the other side, and something slapped against the door from inside the house.

Kev took a step back, looking puzzled.

Dave handed Kev a six pack and a couple of tins of beans. "That's her signal," Dave smiled. "In you go, son, fill your boots."

Kev looked at Dave.

"I'll stay out here, keep watch for the undead. Then maybe you can do the same for me, eh? Let me have another crack at her."

That was all it took. Kev turned the handle. Dave followed him over the threshold.

The girl was voluptuous alright, but half of her guts were hanging out of a hole in her middle, and the once full breasts had turned an awful blueish colour with decay. She lunged at Kev from across the room.

"What the fu—" was all he got out before Dave pulled the dagger from his waistband and stuck it into his kidneys from behind.

"Cop that, you bastard!" he said as he shoved Kev into the ravenous embrace of the walking corpse. Distracted and shocked, still reaching for the fatal wound in his gut, Kev failed to stop the zombie sinking its teeth into his neck.

Dave grimaced and wiped the knife on his pants. Kev fell to the floor and lay on the mouldy carpet.

The rotting blonde leaned over Kev and got ready to feed, but Dave had other ideas. He stepped across and slammed the blade into the side of her head.

"Sorry sweetheart, nothing personal," he said, pushing the now truly dead corpse away.

Kev looked up at him and spoke through the pain of his wounds. "Why, Dave? Why?"

Dave looked incredulous. "Why? Why do you think, you lazy, selfish, murdering piece of shit? For Kara, for ruining my daughter's life, and most of all, most of fucking all" — he pointed the knife at Kev, then raised it high in both hands over the prostrate bleeding figure—"for making me eat my best little mate."

Dave paused, still holding the blade in the air. Kev gasped, spitting out blood.

"Do it, Dave, just do it. Don't let me suffer."

A look came into Dave's eyes and he lowered the blade.

"No. Fuck that. I got a better idea, son. I'm gonna let you become one of them," he pointed at the dead blonde, "so you can suffer an eternity with the living dead."

"No!" Kev shook his head, sending blood spatters flying. "Please!"

"Walking the earth, looking for meat. Until the flesh rots and falls off your stinking bones. That's what you deserve. That's poetic justice."

Dave left the door open. "Better hope none of your new mates find you before you turn," he said to the soon to be corpse. Kev mouthed something but Dave had moved out of earshot.

Time passed. Dave acclimatised to the new world and found it not so bad after all. He knew where the safe places were. He knew where to look for food and other comforts. Sometimes he let one of the women come and stay with him for a while. Until they bored him. He stayed in the hotel, enjoying the free booze. All of the other stragglers had departed, still hopeful of finding some semblance of community. Sometimes weeks went by without him even seeing another living face. Even when they invited him to join their ragtag communities, he turned them away.

Dave had given up on that as a bad idea. He knew the world was stuffed. The hordes of wandering dead grew ever larger, and it amused him to see his former son-in-law among their number.

Dave got his kicks out of tormenting dead Kev for fun. Separating him from the herd, teasing him with pieces of meat, leading him into traps he had set up, and poking him with sharp objects. He took to cutting bits off Kev for his own amusement. His nose, ears and genitals. Sometimes Kev looked at Dave like he knew what was going on, like he was hurt, but Dave knew that wasn't possible. He would have his fun and then set his dead son-in-law loose, until he found him wandering and started over again. Dave found himself enjoying doing all the malicious stuff he dreamed about doing to Kev in the old days. Things he never would have got away with back then.

He was comfortable now. He had everything he needed right here. Even the sad memories of Kara and Nipper dissipated over time. Dave grew wiry and strong, sported a long beard. He did whatever he wanted, whenever he wanted, within reason. He was heavily armed, and people learned not to fuck with him.

Dave was confident in his surroundings. He knew the booby-trapped entrance to the hotel and how to bypass it. He had seen its effect on would-be intruders to his sanctuary, both living and dead. This was why his hackles had risen when he heard the hotel lift ping as it came to a stop early one afternoon.

Half-cut on whisky, lying in a steaming hot bath (thank God for the generator), Dave cursed as he hurriedly towelled himself dry and pulled on his pants. He cursed again when he realised he had left his gun on the bedside table.

Getting slack, Dave.

How the fuck did someone get through his defences? Maybe, he thought, as he hurried down the hallway, past the now empty lifts, a walker had triggered the trap, got caught up, and somehow another one had managed to clamber over it and…work the lift?

Didn't make sense. These things couldn't think. They had no rational thought.

Dave rounded the corner and headed toward the open door of his room, visualising the gun. He recoiled when he got there to find it gone.

Fuck!

A noise from the balcony jolted him to attention. The bay window was open, the curtain billowing. Had he left it open? He couldn't remember through the fog of alcohol.

Dave stepped out into the open air gingerly, shading his eyes. The sun blazed in the sky. The sight he beheld made his eyes bulge out of his head.

The stench hit him first. The stink of rotting flesh.

He peered down the barrel of his own gun. A gun held by his zombie son-in-law.

"How the fuck?" asked Dave.

Kev grunted and shuffled around Dave in a wide arc, turning him around in the process.

"How did you remember how to work the booby traps…and use the lift?" Dave asked.

Dead Kev grunted and motioned for Dave to back-peddle as he moved toward him.

Dave raised his hands.

"How do you know about guns? You're not supposed to think!" he yelled at the corpse. "You never thought when you were alive, you stupid fuck! Why are you thinking now?"

Dave stared down the gun pointing at his face. Kev shuffled closer, forcing him back toward the edge of the building. Too late he realised the zombie's intention in turning him around. Dave looked over his shoulder, down three flights to where the hungry dead beckoned with open arms.

He turned back to Kev. "Can we talk this over?" he asked.

Kev opened his rotten mouth and grinned, shaking his head.

BURN FOR YOU

Like most of Western Australia, the sleepy little town of Prospect had emerged unscathed from the great conflagration of the Second World War. As with all the fellow tiny settlements pocketed down the great south-western coast of the giant island nation, Prospect had puttered on, unimpacted by the rock and roll social revolution of the fifties, and eased gently into the counter culture era of the sixties in the shadow of the rise of communism and the Vietnam War.

The only visible impact of the latter was the plaque the town councillors stuck up in the local park, the only piece of man-made greenery in the shire. Joe Warren, the local police chief, just as his father had been before him, reckoned they put the bloody thing up too soon, given the damn war was still dragging on, but Joe knew when to hold his tongue, his own tour of duty had taught him as much.

It was another baking hot summer afternoon, the sort only WA could throw up. Dry as a dead dog's donger, as the old man used to say. The proposed tourist bureau across the street might as well have stayed the pile of rubble it began as—such was the dearth of visitors. Nobody in their right mind would want to visit a dead gold town anyway, as the settlement of Prospect was woefully misnamed before the small pocket of gold unearthed in the 1850s quickly dried up. The place emptied even quicker than it filled and was lumbered with the ironic misnomer ever since.

Joe leaned back in his chair, slapped the page of the glossy magazine in his hands and shook his head. He addressed Carole

Farr, the rookie *cum* typist and the only other occupant of the station.

"Would you look at this, Caz? Yanks reckon they're gonna put a man on the moon. On the moon, I ask you. Never thought I'd see the day."

Carole stopped typing and looked across the station through a plume of smoke. "Whadda they wanna go up there for? What's up there? Little green men?" She took a thoughtful drag of her cigarette and recommenced bashing the keys on the Remington.

Joe grinned and wiped his brow. "It's just progress. Hard to imagine all that's going on out there while we're tucked away here, in this tiny corner of the British Empire." He got up and strolled across the room. "Sometimes it feels like the world is passing us by, Caz. Still, this place is home. Wouldn't wanna be anywhere else." Joe parted the shades and looked out the window of the station at the mob gathered on the sparse brown lawn outside. Their cat calls reverberated through the partly open window.

"Come on, Joe, send him out here so we can give him a dose of country justice," yelled a disembodied voice.

Carole looked up from her typewriter. "Sounds like we got half the town out there, Chief."

"Just a minor lynch mob," Joe sniffed, turning away from the window.

"You want me to call in reinforcements?" she asked, stubbing out her butt in the burgeoning ashtray on her desk.

There was a pause and they looked at one another and laughed.

"Yeah, right. Nothing Reg and I can't handle," said Joe. "Besides, when was the last time we had any contact from those clowns up or down the coast? By the time anyone got here, that mob would have already lynched poor old Greg, or whatever it is they're doing to that effigy out there. You keep an eye on the cells, make sure Greg's alright. I'll go out and try and calm them down."

Carole nodded as she shook a fresh ciggie out of the pack.

"You know I read in a journal that those things give you cancer?"

Carole laughed as she struck a match and lit up. "Yeah right. Next you'll be tellin' me sugar is bad for us too. You have three spoons in your coffee."

"Touché, Caz. We all have our vices I guess." Joe sucked in his midriff as he headed out the door. "Put the kettle on, eh? And make it two sugars, I'm cutting down."

Outside on the verge by the gravel pit that passed for a car park, the mob stood in front of their motley collection of cars and trucks, surrounding a poorly constructed effigy on the baked lawn. Someone had crudely scrawled Greg Gilchrist's name across its chest in black marker.

Joe shook his head as he approached. It looked like Brodie Ross was the ringleader. He was giving orders to the others. Sharon Baker, proprietor of *Gutbuster's Café*—makers of the self-professed best burgers south of Mandurah—was pouring petrol from a tin onto a makeshift torch. Daryl McGuigan, the local publican, chucked on a pile of twigs and small branches he had picked up from the surrounding scrub. The rest of them were shouting and egging them on. Joe spotted Sheila Davies from the chemists, Ron Nooks the butcher, and Hugh Ramsay, proprietor of the town's only garage, where Brodie worked as a grease monkey.

Reg Hamilton, Joe's deputy and the only other copper in town, was there, trying to calm them down. His uniform was already dishevelled, the shirt half hanging out of his pants.

"Come on, fellahs," said Joe. "Give it a rest. This isn't helping anyone."

"Just drag him out here, Joe," said Brodie Ross. "We'll do the rest." Reg put a restraining arm across Brodie's chest. Brodie shook it off, and Joe saw him give Reg a death stare.

"You know I can't do that, Brodie," said Joe. He felt Brodie's eyes bore into him and shivered internally. Joe thought he had seen eyes like that before, on men he served with on his tour of Vietnam. He thought it was a pity Brodie's number hadn't come up.

"He's a monster," Sharon joined the chorus. "What sort of a sicko burns down a bloody school, Joe?" Her voice caught in her throat. "Thank gawd they got the kids out in time."

"Yeah, too bad about Benno," said Daryl, scratching his gut. "His old legs couldn't carry him outta there before the blaze got him."

"They say he climbed into his tool shed and curled up to die," said Ron Nooks taking up the story.

Joe chewed his lip. He knew they weren't bullshitting. The bush telegraph never missed a beat. Joe had prised the janitor's charred remains out of that shed, and the stench of burned flesh had taken his mind right back to 'nam.

Sheila Davies took the bit between her teeth. "What about them two firies we lost, fightin' the blaze? God rest their souls." She crossed herself and snuck a look toward the town's one and only church in the near distance.

"Yeah alright, Shaz, Ron, all of you. I know. People lost their lives. It could have been much worse. But the law is the law. Greg Gilchrist is innocent until proven guilty."

"He bloody confessed!" said Daryl, his buttoned shirt straining to hold in the beer belly. "You caught him hiding in the bush beside the school, watching it go up."

"Means nuthin', Dazza." Joe shook his head. "We all know Greg's a bit soft up top. Remember when he confessed to touching up old Mrs Swann, God rest her soul? Turned out it weren't him at all. Greg just likes to be the centre of attention."

A beat-up old sedan screeched to a halt in a spray of gravel, and Magda Kowalski, a waitress in Sharon's *Gutbuster* café, slammed the door and stormed across the car park.

"Ah shit," Brodie grunted. "Here comes the fun police."

Magda flung her braided hair back over her shoulders. Her bell-bottoms swished through the dry air. "Have you yokels lost your minds? Isn't it bad enough that people died in this town? This isn't gonna help matters."

"Ah give it a rest, Magda," said Sharon.

"You should know better, Shaz, at your age." Magda glared at her employer through her John Lennon frames. Sharon's lower lip briefly quivered before she fixed the young upstart with a steely glare.

"Magda," Brodie stared a hole through the wiry waitress, "One of them firies that died was Joanne Inkster's bloke. They got three bloody kids. Fatherless 'cos of that mongrel in there."

Magda shook her head. "Have you all taken leave of your senses? Greg Gilchrist is mentally ill. He needs psychiatric help, not a lynch mob."

"Shut up, Magda, ya bloody do-gooder," said Daryl.

Brodie stepped forward and growled low into the interloper's face. "How come whenever anyone in this town steps up to the plate and tries to do something about no good ratbags, you always take their side?"

"Probably because I'm not a fascist redneck bully like you, Brodie Ross." She squared up to Brodie, who stood head and shoulders above her, as if daring him to hit her.

"Ya stupid hippie bitch," said Daryl, working himself into a lather. "Why don't ya piss off back to the city and smoke some more dope? Let us deal with this."

"Yeah, nick off, ya bloody stuck-up mole," Ron threw his piece in.

There was a commotion as Father Roy Battersly, the town priest, strode into view, his robes flowing behind him in the breeze. Brodie turned toward him. "What do you say, Father, innocent or guilty?"

Battersly looked from face to face, coming to rest on Sheila's intense pious gaze. "Bugger him," he said. "Let's torch the bastard."

There was a roar and fist pumping among the throng. Joe shook his head. "Christ's sake, Father. I expected better from you."

Daryl pulled out his lighter, it flickered into life with a small orange glow. Even as Reg jumped forward to stop him, he chucked it at the effigy. The crowd stepped back as it went up in flames and cheered as the fire crackled and hissed.

Joe looked toward the station, where Carole stood watching from the door, cigarette burning between her fingertips.

"You're next, Greggy," Brodie Ross shouted at the building.

They jeered as Joe marched back to the sanctuary.

"We're comin' for him, Joe," Daryl yelled. "You can't hold him in there forever."

Reg tugged a hose pipe across and unleashed a big jet of water over the burning effigy. The crowd howled but it had the desired effect. They dispersed quickly, muttering among themselves.

Inside, Joe sat down for a chat with Greg through the bars. Reg shadowed him, sipping on a coffee and eavesdropping. Greg sat on the bunk looking down at his own feet, which were still encased in the worn pair of thongs he was arrested in.

"You sure you don't want me to get you some socks, Greg? Keep your feet warm."

"Nah. I'm alright, Joe."

Joe sighed. "You know I only stuck you in the cell for your own protection. I know you didn't do it."

Greg shook his head. "I did do it, Joe. I set the school on fire."

"I got a witness coming in tomorrow. A friend of yours. Reece Graham. He's out rounding up stock at the minute, but he's coming back in. He reckons you were out at his place on the day the school was set alight."

"Reece… Nah, he's me mate. He's just tryin' ta cover for me."

Reg slurped at his coffee. They both turned to look at him.

"Sorry, Joe," said Reg.

"Okay Greg. Why don't you tell me why you set the school on fire?"

"Huh?"

"Well, you must have a reason. What were you trying to achieve?"

"Well…" Greg swallowed. "It's sort of personal." He looked at Reg.

"Ah, don't mind Reg. He doesn't tell tales. You can tell us, mate."

"Ah, jeez…" Greg pulled at a loose thread on the crotch of his corduroys, and looked from Joe to Reg. He leaned forward conspiratorially. "Can Carole hear us?"

Joe and Reg leaned in closer.

"Not from here," said Joe.

Greg swallowed, and his eyes glazed over. "When I was a kid,

I was always gittin' in trouble off mum after dad shot through. One day I found a big pack of matches in the laundry cupboard, so I nicked 'em. I sort of lit a few little fires here and there. Ya know, chucked a few things in garbage bins and set 'em alight. But the weird thing is…it gave me a kind of thrill, ya know, down there."

Joe shook his head. "Are you saying that starting fires made you…sexually aroused?"

Greg flushed red. "Yeah, yeah it did."

Joe looked at Reg, who wore a look of fascinated awe. Then Carole's disembodied voice interrupted them.

"Joe? We got a call coming in. Domestic disturbance out on Russell Road. Sound of gunshots."

Joe and Reg jumped into action. "We'll pick this up later, Greg." Joe grabbed his hat and jacket. "Who called it in, Caz?"

"Didn't give a name, Joe. A neighbour. Number 38."

"Righto, we're on our way."

As the town's only police car sped away into the night, Brodie Ross and Hugh Ramsey stepped out of the shadows under the eaves of the station. They waved into the near distance and Daryl McGuigan, Ron Nooks, and Sharon Baker came out from the dark corner of the pub. They congregated on the grass verge outside the building now only occupied by Carole and the suspect.

In the car, Reg spun the bullet chamber on his service pistol and turned to Joe. "What did you make of that stuff Greg was saying? About the fire giving him a hard on."

Joe glanced up at the heavens and mused. "It's a strange world we live in, Reg. I been reading a lot, about psychology and criminal behaviour. You wouldn't believe some of the shit that goes on."

"Try me."

"Well, it seems the more I read into it, the more there appears to be a pattern to these sort of events, like with the fire."

"You don't think anyone bore a grudge?"

"Nah! We covered that angle. Who the hell would try and murder a bunch of kids? It just makes no sense. Nobody in this town had a reason. So, maybe whoever did this, did it for their own pleasure."

"I don't know what you're getting at, Joe."

"That's the thing. This idea of killing strangers just for the hell of it. Just for some sort of sexual kink. You ever hear of the Moors murders?"

"No. Who are the Moors? They from round these parts?"

"The Moors is a place over in England. The Yorkshire Moors. It's like a huge wide open plain. Like the Stirling Ranges over here. Only colder and wetter. Anyway, the murders were done by a killer couple, names were Ian Brady and Myra Hindley. These two lured little kids out onto the Moors and sexually abused them. Then they tortured them, murdered and buried them."

"Christ, Joe. What the hell for?"

"That's just it. No reason at all, other than for their own sadistic pleasure. The act of murder made them sexually charged. They even recorded the kids' voices, pleading for mercy."

Reg squeezed the handle of his pistol. "That's fucken disgusting! There's things in this world I just don't understand, Joe. When I think of Jess at home with little Kelly… If anyone ever laid a hand on them, so help me I'd kill them. I hope they strung those bastards up."

"Nup. They canned the death penalty just before they caught 'em. They're still in prison over there. My point being, like Greg was saying, there is something in this fire lighting business that isn't a million miles removed from the Moors thing. There's plenty of other cases like it too, going back to before the War even. A growing link between sex and random murder."

Reg shook his head. "What happened to the age of Aquarius, Joe?"

Joe pulled the car to a halt in front of the homestead Carole had directed them to. It was quiet. The porch light out front was on.

"You sure this the place?" Reg asked.

"Yup." They pulled their guns for security. As they stepped out of the car, the front door swung open and a male figure stepped out, his large, rotund form squeezed into a blue singlet and tight footy shorts. As soon as he saw the guns, he raised his arms.

"Wooh! Steady on there, youse blokes. I'm unarmed. Me shotee is inside. What's the go? Is that you, Joe?"

Joe recognised the voice and lowered his weapon. Motioned for Reg to do the same.

"Hey, Clance. Didn't realise this was your joint. We got a call for this address. Domestic disturbance. Is Ruth alright?"

"Yeah, she's inside snoring her box off. That's the only disturbance around here. Probably woke the neighbours all around. Come in and have a look if youse like. I'll put the kettle on."

Joe hesitated, then he and Reg followed the local inside. They holstered their guns, but Joe kept his hand within easy reach just in case. He knew Clancy had an issue with booze, and the big bloke's breath let loose enough ethanol that you wouldn't want to strike a match.

"Ruthy? You awake, luv?" Clancy pushed the bedroom door open gingerly with a toe. "We got company."

Joe tensed, his hand hovering over the holster.

A spluttering sound issued from within the dark room. Followed by a series of rasping coughs. A minute later, a bleary-eyed, wild haired woman came out wrapped in a pink dressing gown and matching slippers. "Joe? Reg? Shit, I'll put the kettle on. What's going on?"

"Never mind the coffee, Ruth. I think someone's thrown us a red herring."

"A what, Chief?" asked Reg.

"Someone's playing funny buggers, Reg. We've been tricked. Someone wanted us away from the station... Shit!"

Joe was off and running. "Cheers, Clance. We'll have ta take a rain check on the cuppa. Ooroo, Ruth. Come on, Reg."

"What's the go?" Reg puffed as he pulled on his seatbelt.

"Ah, Christ! Someone pulled a swifty to get us away from the station, and I've got a fair idea who." He glanced at Reg's blank face as they powered back down the road. "They're after Greg."

"Aw shit!"

Daryl held Carole back while Brodie disabled the station's two-way radio.

Carole tried to tear herself free from Daryl's grip. "What the hell are you playing at, Brodie Ross?"

"Shut up, Carole. Keep out of it."

"What's goin' on out there?" Greg's voice came from the cells. Daryl looked at Brodie. Brodie went into the lock up and walked up to the only occupied cell. Greg eyeballed him through the bars. Brodie absent-mindedly fiddled with the crotch of his pants.

"So, ya like settin' fires, do ya Greggy?"

The accused looked at Brodie open-mouthed. His mind ticking over. "Yeah, that's right... I do." Greg's Adam's apple bobbed up and down in his taught throat.

"Why'd ya fucken do it, mate? You tried to murder them kids. Ya killed three people." Brodie bit down on his rage.

Greg swallowed. His face dropped. "Jeez, I'm sorry. I...I didn't think."

"You didn't think? Fuck's sake!" Brodie lunged at the bars. Greg jerked back. "I should fucken come in there and kill ya. I should go get the fucken keys."

Greg slumped onto the bunk and curled his legs up to his chest. He spoke in a small voice. "I didn't do it."

Brodie squeezed the bars. "What?"

"I...I didn't do it... I just wanted people to notice me."

"Bullshit! Now ya fucken lying to me. Ya got this comin' to ya mate."

Greg stood up as Brodie stomped away. "Got what coming? Brodie? I didn't do it, Brodie!"

Brodie strode back into the main office, where Daryl still held onto Carole. "Get her out of here." He turned to Ron, Hugh, and Sharon. "Go get the gear."

"Brodie!" Carole yelled. "What are you doing?"

As Daryl dragged her out the door, she saw the trio coming back in with cans that stunk of petrol.

"Aw, hell, no! You can't do this!" Carole yelled. She watched, helpless, as the group poured a trail of fuel across the floor toward Greg's cell.

"What the fuck's goin' on?" Greg's voice rang out and the bars shook.

Carole hung on to the frame of the door as Daryl tried to pull her out. "You can't torch the station."

"Hey! I didn't fucken do it... Brodie?" Greg's panicked voice rang out, growing more strained and ragged. "What's that fucken smell?"

Carole screamed as they threw her out onto the grass verge. She heard Greg's muffled yells through the walls. Daryl pinned her under his bulk. Sharon handed Ron a torch made of rags, soaked in fuel. Ron raised his lighter to it and set it aflame.

"No!" Carole screamed. Greg followed suit.

Brodie nodded at Ron. He threw the torch through the open door. The petrol trail ignited into flames and swept like an orange tide down the corridor toward the cells.

They stood on the front verge, watching the orange and red glow through the windows, listening to Greg scream and plead his innocence. Daryl sat on Carole's back, holding her down. Eventually her screams dissolved into broken sobbing.

Greg's shrieks of agony were punctuated by the sound of the bars of his cell rattling, until they died away to a low whimper, like a wounded beast. Sharon leaned into Brodie and whispered, "Burn, ya murdering bastard." Brodie hugged her into his chest.

Through the smoke they watched Magda's car screech to a halt and saw her run across the verge. She tried to get inside but the flames burned too high. Then Brodie jumped on her and dragged her away from the inferno. She fell to her knees in front of the building and threw her arms in the air and wailed.

Within minutes, the familiar sirens and flashing lights of the town fire truck approached, quickly followed by a police car which screeched to a halt. Joe and Reg sprinted across the car park. Joe barrelled into Daryl, knocking him off Carole. Reg manhandled

Ron and cuffed him. Hugh waited meekly to be restrained.

A small crowd of townsfolk had gathered, drawn like moths to the flames. Father Battersly appeared and made the sign of the cross before scurrying back to the sanctuary of the Lord's house.

Sharon looked around, wondering how Brodie had somehow slipped away into the night. When Joe came for her, she put her hands out willingly for the cuffs.

Carole looked up to see Joe stride purposely into the station. He turned his nose up at the lingering aftermath of petrol and burning embers from the ruined cell down the hall.

"Carole, pull out that file on Brodie Ross again."

"What's up, Joe?" she said, pulling the cabinet open and fishing through the small pile of alphabetised cards.

"I been doing some snooping. Got some reports of fires in other towns. Running down the coast from here all the way to Albany. All a few months apart. Damn the lack of communication around these parts."

They both studied the report on Brodie Ross.

"A few minor priors, break and enter, fencing stolen goods. Any news on him?" Carole asked.

"Nah. He's gone to ground. It's like he never existed."

A sudden thought occurred to Joe. "Hey, Reg."

Reg stuck his head in from the next room. Joe slid the file back in the cabinet. "Did anybody else happen to leave town round about the same time as Brodie Ross disappeared?"

Reg gave a blank look. "Not that I know of, chief. I can look into it."

"Magda Kowalski."

They both looked at Carole.

"Say again," said Joe.

Carole took the cigarette out of her mouth and repeated. "Magda, the hippie waitress. Her and Sharon had an almighty blue just before the fire that killed poor Greg. Told Sharon to stick the job up her arse. Can't say I blame her. She was a sensitive girl. Not like she was a local. She probably didn't wanna stick around after that."

Joe's mouth hung open. "Reg, grab your hat and your gun."

"Where we going, chief?" He followed Joe toward the door.

"Up the coast to Danning. Strike me fucken pink!"

Carole motioned after them. "Wait, Joe. Who's gunna look after the station."

Joe smiled at her. "You are, Caz."

"Me! But I'm…"

"You're what, Caz, a woman? It's your time, Caz. Women can do anything blokes can. You're in charge. Don't take any shit from anyone. Ring Nev and get him to bring your service revolver in. We might be a couple of days. Just cut down on the bloody ciggies!"

Joe turned and dragged Reg toward the car. "Come on, Reg, I'll explain on the way."

Reg jumped into the car, holding his hat down with one hand. "Damn, Joe! There's things in this world I just don't understand."

Joe cocked his service pistol and refilled the bullet chambers. "You don't know the half of it mate. Wait till you hear this one…"

At a junction in the middle of nowhere on the one road running through the great south-west, an old sedan sat in the scrub just off the gravel, under the shade of a big old gum tree. Magda sat on the bonnet, toking on a freshly rolled joint.

Eventually, another car appeared on the horizon. It drew up, slowed, and pulled off the road to a halt right next to Magda's sedan. The door opened and Brodie Ross got out.

"Took you long enough," Magda said, proffering the spliff.

Brodie knocked it flying from her hands and pounced on her, forcing his tongue down her throat. A small brushfire sprang up from the discarded joint. Magda wrapped her legs around his waist as he tore at her clothes. She saw the flames reflected in his irises as they rocked and bucked and screamed like banshees on the bonnet of the car. The flames licked around his ankles, and Brodie roared as his seed spurted inside her. Magda dug her nails into his back as her own release washed over her.

Later they sat side by side in Magda's car. Still half undressed, sharing a smoke. The smell of scorched earth from the recently extinguished fire permeated the car.

"Show me the book again," said Brodie.

Magda opened the glove box and retrieved her A4 journal. It was ragged around the edges. Her pupils dilated as she flicked over the worn pages. "Details of every fire, from the age of twelve," she said.

"Read me the next line," Brodie whispered. He leaned back and closed his eyes, his hand sliding down between his thighs.

"I used to set a fire, then go home and touch myself as the world burned," she said.

Brodie pulled out his lighter and fired it up. Magda looked at the flame, mesmerised, and let out a sharp breath. "Show me the scars," she said, her voice trembling.

Brodie pulled his shirt over his shoulders. Magda gently stroked the rough, pock marked craters on his chest. "Your mum did this to you." It was a statement rather than a question.

"Every time I was bad. With her cigarette. Your touch burns me like fire too."

THE ARDENT DEAD

was six hours into a twelve-hour shift at the helm of the cab when it happened. BANG! The left rear tyre blew out and the vehicle lurched over the tarmac as invisible hands tried to wrench the steering wheel from my grasp. I bit down hard on my lip as I wrestled the car over to the kerb.

Under normal circumstances a flat tyre should have been a minor inconvenience to a cabbie, representing a pain in the ass and perhaps the loss of a couple of fares. In this new world it threatened something much more dangerous.

Swearing to myself, I killed the engine and jumped out of the cab, sprung the trunk and retrieved the jack and spare wheel, all the while watching out for any sign of them. I was in a built-up area but it was a wide road so I had a pretty good view all around. The last thing I wanted was to encounter a herd; they were pretty slow moving and you could handle one or two, but a large number would overpower you in no time. Seen it happen myself.

I thanked Christ I had plenty of experience in the field of changing tyres on account of my profession. I had the hub off and the four nuts loosened in no time. I reckon I could've got a job with a racetrack pit crew, I was so good at this. Had it jacked up and the wheel off in two minutes flat. I was just balancing the new tyre making sure it was on straight before I tightened her up again when I heard it, the shuffling of worn-out feet, accompanied by the ripe stench of decaying meat.

I turned and backed up against the door as he approached—

male necro, not too far gone, most of the flesh still intact. He grunted something unintelligible at me through his ruined mouth. I didn't need further clarification of his intent. I could see it sticking out the front of his pants—rigid member covered in a film of tiny vermin.

I swallowed my bile and managed to get to my feet as he made a lunge for me. I manoeuvred around him, but that just meant he was now between me and the car, my one means of escape. Nice going jackass. I did a quick scan of the area to make sure we were alone, then addressed my new friend.

"Now look, buddy. I know you want to get it on but you're barking up the wrong tree here. I'm not that way inclined, and I'm just not that into necrophilia."

He wasn't taking no for an answer of course and he continued to pursue. I scrambled back and forth, trying to dodge around him, but there was no way I'd have time to tighten those nuts before he emptied his and then it would be over for me too. I'd be one of them. What the papers call the "ardent dead". This must be some deity's idea of a cosmic joke, infesting the world with a plague of horny zombies. They didn't want to feast on your brains, they just wanted to hump them out.

I tried to remember my training. I knew you weren't supposed to kill them. They are pretty harmless as long as you keep out of their way. Let them screw the bejesus out of each other until the government rounds them all up. But whatever you do don't let them touch you. They'll be all over you like a rash, kissing and licking and sticking God knows what into God knows where and within a couple of hours you'll be joining their orgy of the undead.

So, keeping this in mind I did what I'd been taught, I lined the putrefying pervert up and kicked him fair in the balls. He may have been dead but the effect was pretty much the same as on the living. He went down in a heap, gasping in pain.

"Sorry, chum, but I'm on call," I explained as I finished fitting the tyre and banged the hubcap back into place. "It's not that I don't like you, but I've got a fare to collect."

Crap! The fare!

By now he'd be wondering if I had been waylaid by necros enroute. I threw the jack and punctured tyre back in the trunk, jumped in the cab and gunned the engine. To hell with the speed limit. Weren't so many cops on traffic duty these days anyways. They were otherwise occupied keeping the dead at bay. Last thing I wanted was for the fare to give me up for undead and ring the company for another cab.

I heaved a sigh of relief as I rounded the corner on Valentine Avenue and saw him poke his head out of a doorway. I screeched to a halt right out front and hit the meter. I heard my rear door open and shut amid a volley of imprecations followed by the sound of quick stepping feet, and then another door open and shut. That's when I looked in the mirror and screamed.

The thing in the back seat grinned at me through rotting gums and, as it opened its mouth, I saw the obscene blackened gristle of its tongue. A large chunk of flesh was missing from its left upper arm and there were maggots hanging off torn strips of flesh. They stood out from the navy blue ruin of its burial suit. I noticed with some relief that its hands were cuffed and that its still breathing minder seemed to have it under some kind of restraint. There was a steel collar attached to its neck by a chain.

I met his gaze in the mirror.

"Get out," I said.

"I can explain."

"Don't wanna hear it. Get that abomination out of my cab. Jesus Christ! You know how much it costs to keep that upholstery clean? He's dripping maggots on it, man."

"Please, I need you to take me—us—to 39 Jefferson Street over in Bakersfield. I can make it worth your while. I'll pay you double the meter."

My ears pricked up at the magic words.

"Show me the green, pal," I said.

He did. There was lots of it. More than I'd seen in all my time on the company payroll.

"You sure that thing is under control?"

"One hundred percent. Trust me. I've done this before. You just get us there," he said.

He pulled a generous wad out of the bundle, wrapped a band around it and threw it over the front seat. It landed on the passenger seat with a satisfying thud. I shoved the cab into gear.

"Strap yourself in, son, and don't let go of that chain."

I kept one eye on the road and the other on my strange fare and his even stranger companion. He was a weedy little guy, didn't pick him for a necro lover. He didn't look strong enough. Middle aged, a little paunchy, maybe the kind of guy who liked to hang around in gay bars soliciting younger men back in the old days.

"Christ! Crack a window back there pops, your buddy stinks. No offence, gorgeous," I said to the corpse. It looked at me like it almost understood for a moment.

"Sorry," the fare said.

"So, what's the deal, Jack? You get off on bumping uglies with dead guys? Ain't ya afraid you might turn into one yourself?"

He let out a deep sigh like a deflating tyre and seemed to shrink back into the leather upholstery.

"No, nothing like that. It's not for me. He's not for me."

"Well, come on, chuckles, spill the beans."

He perked up a little. "Might be easier if I showed you when we get there. I could use your help, big strong fellow like you."

"Hey, don't get any funny ideas there, pal. I'm not some kind of pervert."

"No, you don't understand. I just need you to help me with him." He nodded at the crumbling Casanova by his side and another bundle of cash thumped on the front seat next to its neighbour. "Consider that a down payment, half now, half later."

The necro itself seemed to have lost interest in our conversation. It was half dozing—if the things ever did sleep. It looked out the window, waving to some of its festering friends. I had to slow the cab to a crawl at times to weave around the ones copulating in the middle of the road. Not supposed to run the idiots down you see, even though I found the thought of it tempting on occasion. I felt a bit sorry for them to be truthful. They didn't ask to come back with an insatiable libido after they'd popped their clogs. Thank God it was just the adults. I don't think we could have coped if the kids came back as well.

Soon enough we arrived at the joint, nice two storey townhouse in one of the more salubrious parts of town. I felt a little more at ease and less like someone was going to jump me as soon as my back was turned. There were no other necros loitering around so I stuffed my down payment in the glove box and helped the guy manoeuvre the frisky corpse through the door while trying not to get too much putrefaction on my shirt and pants.

"Up these stairs, if you don't mind. Bring him up here."

"Stairs? Horseshit man, this is gonna cost you extra."

"Yes, yes. I'll pay you whatever it takes. This way please."

He led the way up, jerking the corpse's chain in a similar way to which I felt he was jerking mine. On the landing we pulled the dead thing up to a closed door. The fare turned the handle, pushed it open and we lumbered in. My jaw hit the floor for the second time that day.

There on the bed, buck naked and trussed up by a decaying limb to each post was a prime example of the female of the necro species. She was probably beautiful once, but now her hourglass figure was an abomination of rot and her sexual parts looked like roadkill left out in the sun a little too long. Once again I fought to suppress my gag reflex.

"What's your name, cabbie?" the fare asked me.

"William. But my friends call me Bill."

"Bill, I'd like you to meet my wife, Patricia."

At this point the hunk of mouldy man meat at our side was champing at the bit to get unleashed, and Patricia looked like she wanted the same thing. She was moaning and thrashing and pulling at her restraints like a well drilled porn actress.

"Well hump my ass and call me a choirboy, if this doesn't beat all," I said. "So, where's the camera?"

His eyebrows curled up into his furrowed brow. "Camera?"

"Yeah. I assume you're filming this. Big market for necro porn and all that."

He tutted. "I loved my wife, Bill… I still do. I'd do anything for her, can't bear to let her go. But I just can't touch her anymore. Lord knows I've tried, with all kinds of protection, but she's just so damn wild now, biting and scratching and clawing. I couldn't take it anymore."

He looked over at our virile guest. "This is the best I can do for her now."

I put my arm around his shoulder. "You don't have to say any more. I understand." Godammit if I didn't have a tear in my eye as well.

"So, how do we do this?" I asked.

"Go and stand over by the door. As soon as I let this thing off the leash, we high tail it out and lock the door. They'll wear themselves out after a few hours. Patricia, she's a feisty one. She'll take all this one can give her. Later on, we'll truss him up and release him back into the wild. You'll get the rest of your money then."

That was how it went down. How it went down in the bedroom of the natty two storey townhouse, or who went down on whom I didn't care to speculate too much about. I left the fare in the doorway where I first collected him. Made sure he had my name and number in case he needed my help in these matters again. Then I went and parked the cab in the lockup and headed straight for the first high security bar I could find.

I liked how that enormous stash felt in my pocket as I snuggled up to the barstool and had a good few drinks to wash away the images burnt into my retinas from the day's events. It wasn't such a bad world after all. There was us still going about our breathing lives as best we could, and then there were the necros, doing the one thing left they were wired to do. Then there were those who flitted between the two worlds trying to maintain a balance and their sanity, like my fare today. Funny what love can move a soul do I thought, before cogent contemplation deserted me for the evening and sweet oblivion swept me into its loving embrace.

OVERBOARD

When the boat went down I headed straight for Connor. I saw him going under and knew he couldn't swim. I was a former school champion. Made it over in a few easy strokes Got my hand up under his chin and tilted his head back.

He panicked. I expected that, but managed to calm him, let him know I wouldn't let him sink like the boat. A small craft I purchased last summer. Room enough for two.

"Just paddle with your feet, buddy, let me keep your head above water."

Not easy to do. The ocean was choppy, no land in sight, but I knew which direction to head, and moved us against the current.

"I'm choking, Dunc," he said. Eyes wide with fear.

"No, you're just taking in water. I am too. Can't be helped. I'm just glad it was you out here with me, and not Sasha."

I looked right at him when I brought up my fiancé's name, saw him flinch. Saw that calculating look, the same one she had. The look they shared these past few months. Like they were thinking, *How much do you know?*

"I'm sure she doesn't want either of us to drown, eh mate?" I added.

"No…she'd want you home safe, Duncan."

There it was again, that pause before he spoke. I let his head slip a little bit.

"You too, Connor. I know she's pretty fond of you," I said through gritted teeth.

"No, mate…" he began, as a huge wave swept over us. I lost

my grip. I resurfaced, looked around desperately. Saw his arm above the waves, a few metres away. I grabbed it, and hauled him above the surface again, coughing and spluttering.

"I got you, mate. It's okay."

Connor spat another mouthful.

"I can't do this," he said. Panic setting in again.

"Yes, you can. We both can."

He shook his head. "You can swim, I can't. There's…no land in sight."

I followed his despairing gaze. "It's not far. Trust me. Can I trust you, Connor?"

The pause again. "With what?"

"Trust you to trust me with your survival?" A look of relief crossed his face. Then I added. "Trust you with my fiancée?"

"Duncan…there's nothing to…"

"It's just this weird vibe I've been getting the past few months," I cut in, "every time I see you two in the same room."

"You're imagining it." I felt him kicking violently beneath the waves, the pair of us corks bobbing in the vast ocean. "Are there any sharks, Dunc?"

Trying to change the subject, even now.

"Yes, but we'd be unlucky to encounter one this time of year. Too cold."

Christ, we better not. That wasn't part of my plan. We were still way offshore. Had some swimming to do. I wanted to be home before dark.

"I'm scared, Duncan." He started to cry now. This was all too much.

"Me too, mate. The world can be a scary place. That's why trust is so important." I squeezed the back of his neck with my free hand.

"Funny that you never learned to swim. I remember you at school, screaming when they threw you in the pool. Who fished you out back then?"

"You did," he sobbed.

"Now look at this predicament we're in. Lucky for you I'm here to save your skin again."

Lucky, yes. Lucky for me that Connor would never believe I'd do something as heinous as scupper my own boat or remove the life-saving gear.

"I'm sorry," he said at last.

"For what?" I wanted to hear it.

"For Sasha. I didn't mean for it to happen. I fought against it."

"How long…?"

"About three months, oh Christ! I'm so sorry."

I sighed. "I sort of knew anyway, mate. I remember the exact moment the atmosphere changed. I knew that a part of her was gone, lost to me. The rest would follow soon enough. Most of all, it was the deceit I couldn't take. My two best friends in the world, running around behind my back."

I said all this to Connor, but he didn't hear a word.

I turned in silence and started swimming toward the coast.

A RIP IN TIME

You hold the music box up for closer inspection. It is the one from the catalogue, you are certain. Found in a slum on the London docklands in 1986. Sold by Sotheby's in 1989 for one hundred thousand pounds. You place it next to the brooch and several other items of interest. Another one crossed off your list.

These worthless baubles will one day sell to collectors for a fortune. What's more, they will be sold on that far distant day by yourself. You smile, aware of your anomalous status in late nineteenth century London. Just another stopover on your voyage of discovery.

Gaslight flickers on the filth encrusted window. A crack in the glass emits the smell of rotting fish and the river. This tiny doss hole reeks of stale sweat and something else. A cloth cap and a dark stained apron hang over a rickety chair.

You lift the device from your pocket and place it on the decrepit table. It is the key to your success, this shiny little mechanism, for it allows you to travel through time.

You handle the vessel with the same blood-stained hands you used to obtain it. How was the old inventor to know he would stumble across such a treasure after years of fruitless experiment? It was his misfortune to share his secret with you. All that matters now is that it belongs to you.

You were wise to apply its capacity to your trade as a dealer in artefacts, and what riches your secret travels bestow upon you. You read enough about Victorian London to note the East Enders had a habit of leaving doors unlocked for easy access. The poor have nothing of worth to protect.

As the waning moon descends past the grimy window, you check your watch against the faithful chiming of Big Ben. It is almost dawn. Time to move on.

You pick up the music box, turn its key and hold it to your ear. Distracted, trying to place the wistful tune in your memory. A quiet footfall causes you to turn around and you are face to face with him.

The two of you stand motionless, eyeing one another as the lilting melody winds down. Caught off guard, you take in the image of this vagabond in all his shabby gentility.

His dark eyes scan your strange clothing. He suspects your unnatural presence in this place, just as you begin to perceive his. It is then that you see it, the bloody knife protruding from the sleeve, held in a purposeful grip. With sudden realization you are aware that you cannot know the face, but you do comprehend the name.

Until this point, he had been nothing more than a bloody phantom, a demon stalking the pages of history, a symbol of the misery of life for the poor of East London on nights like this, in November of 1888. No time for that now. You cast a furtive glance at the table behind you where the device awaits. One click and you are no longer here.

His eyes follow your every move and you are unnerved by his uncanny stealth. In desperation you chance your arm, lunging for the timepiece, but he is too quick. In an instant a gnarled hand covers your mouth. The cruel blade shimmers in the gaslight and your throat is slit from ear to ear.

You fall before him, undone by the whims of time. The age of gaslight will draw to a close in the next few years. Herschel's science of fingerprinting will remain unappreciated by a capricious government until the turn of the twentieth century. These things once worked in your favour. Now they work in his.

You lie looking up at him as the light flickers out. Linger long enough to see him pick the object up and examine it, turning it over. He has no idea what it does, but he will learn.

HOUSE OF CARDS

I woke to find another brick gone this morning. That made six in the past month. Janet didn't notice of course. The light was shining right in my eyes through the hole where the brick should have been. She looked at me like I was mad, as she usually does.

But as I had told her insistently, this had been happening for some time. I put it down to the wayward youths who always seemed to be hanging around our street. I was sure they were doing it. I would watch them through the curtains in the evening, while Janet tut-tutted at me, flicking through the television stations with the remote.

Why do they have to loiter out there all night? Don't parents discipline their kids anymore? Don't they care where they go, what they do? It was frustrating to me. When I was their age, my old man wanted to know everything I was up to. He'd always find out too, and wallop! I'd get it, a back-hander right across the face. But at least I knew who I was.

I made my way down the hallway, treading carefully to avoid the mounds of old newspaper and sundry other obstacles. That woman was getting very lax in her housework, I thought. I must speak to her about it. There were more bricks gone from here too, and in the lounge. You could see right out into the road through some of the cracks now, and the wind moving through them made an eerie whistling noise. Like the house was making its own protest at the neglect. A family needs its privacy, this wasn't right.

I thought I heard the boy pottering in his room. I made to knock lightly on the door, but thought better of it. He wouldn't back me up either, he never does. I still remember when he was a kid. I built this big sandpit out front of the house for him to play with his Matchbox toys in. Every day when I came in from work, he'd be there in that sandpit, racing the cars around the little tracks he'd made. But never once did he acknowledge me. Not once. It was supposed to be like the movies, where the boy sees his dad coming up the street and he runs up squealing with joy to give him a hug, "Daddy, Daddy! You're home." But not him, he was always a strange one that kid. So quiet and morose. It really hurt me, made me angry.

I used to buy him these little chocolate cars wrapped in bright crinkled paper. They only cost a few cents and it was worth it just to see the expression on his face. The chocolate had raisins in it. It was always a dilemma whether you'd keep the car in its wrapper and play with it, or unwrap it and eat it. You had to peel the gaily-coloured paper really carefully or else you'd rip it. You could see his mind working over as he studied them. Those were the only times we were truly together, me, Janet, the boy, walking around the shops and laughing, every Friday evening, on payday.

I got into the car and stared out through the drizzle from the carport. Winter was coming on again. Got to get those holes fixed. I pulled out of the driveway warily and scanned the road for any sign of those damn kids, but they probably wouldn't be out yet. Too early for them, they mostly come out at night.

I parked it out back and climbed the short stairwell to the lift and my office, which stood on the third floor of a dilapidated brownstone on the old side of town. Out the window, the few remaining employees of the once mighty merchant companies scuttled around the decaying edifices as the pounding and clanging of heavy equipment sounded a death knell for somebody. The whole thing seemed to be held together by grime. I swear it often felt like a good puff of wind would bring it all tumbling down.

On certain days you could almost see the ghosts of old buildings that were no longer there. Sometimes, stone and mortar can be as fragile as memory. Once something has gone, we forget all too easily.

Old Bill Johnson shuddered involuntarily at the sight of a nearby tenement imploding noiselessly before him through the rain-spattered window. For as long as I could remember now the company appeared to consist of him and me. The others had just faded away over the years. It didn't faze me. I was always better suited to working alone I reckoned.

He stood before me briefly and I looked up into his watery pale blue eyes. Those eyes spoke to me of loss. I figured Johnson suffered the kind of loneliness prevalent among the elderly, having watched the life slowly drain out of those they loved.

"Should have sold up and taken their money when I had the chance." He gesticulated toward the clouded pane, his frail presence almost tactile as he brushed beside me, footsteps leaving an insignificant trail in the dust on the floor.

Dusk was starting to fall as I pulled into the driveway and, to my consternation, I noticed some of them gathering in the lengthening shadows. I had begun to regret the time the previous week when I had reproached them, asked them what they were doing on the streets after dark. Now they seemed to be following me, watching every move I made. Maybe I was overreacting. Perhaps it was just a generational thing. All the same I found it hard to ease my suspicions.

I counted the number of missing bricks as I put the key in the door. Was it six or seven now? I had lost track again. Janet looked at me strangely as I peered through a crack in the curtains. "They're out there again," I warned. She didn't seem to care. Just carried on with what she was doing.

Janet never wanted to have a second child. *Not after what I went through the first time* she said. I wouldn't have minded, but never pushed the issue. Best let her have it her way. But I often wondered if the patter of a child's voice around the house might have brought her back from wherever it was the woman I married had gone.

She was getting worse lately. I figured she was going through the change that all women experience, and sadly, the encounter seemed to have drained her of all vitality. Now every minor task seemed to vex her, and nothing could alleviate the pall of gloom that had descended on the house.

I had a terrible fright on the way home the following evening. A group of them surrounded the car as I slowed to pull into the driveway. They gripped the chassis and began rocking it up and down. They were all around me, glaring malevolently through the windows. Yet they never said a word. It's the darkness that makes them bolder. Thankfully, they appeared to tire of it after a while and went away, but I was shaken nonetheless.

Janet seemed particularly miserable, even more than usual. It must be very boring, stuck in this house all day. I had often asked her why she didn't get out and find herself a job. Something appropriate, a position in a typing pool perhaps.

A sudden rustling sound made me jump, and I took a precursory glance through the blinds. I'm sure I saw them moving in the twilight out there. Then the sound came again, and I was relieved to discover it was just the wind echoing through the cracks in the wall. There were more of them now.

Had trouble starting the car this morning. No doubt those kids had been tampering with it. I made a mental note to give it a thorough check when I got home, but it eventually fired up okay so I made it into work. As soon as I reached the stairs however, I had another shock.

The builders had finally encroached upon our doorstep, and now they'd roped our entire building off with yellow tape. There was a sign attached to the wall which read: *Demolition site. Keep clear*. This didn't make sense. I tried the lift but it wasn't working. Any further ingress halted by a locked door.

I stepped back onto the street and yelled up at the darkened window for Bill. He didn't respond. He was getting a little deaf, I recalled. A sense of impending panic overtook me and I hammered on the door, dislodging a pall of dust from the faded lettering of the company sign. Someone had put a rock through one of the lower panes. More vandals, I'll bet.

I went back to the car in a trance.

When I got home, the front door was wide open. There was

a van pulled up to the kerb outside. I walked in slowly. There were people inside, but Janet wasn't there. They were moving things, putting them in the truck. Someone was asking me if I was alright, a young woman.

A man put his arm around my shoulder and guided me toward the door. I was asking them what they had done with my wife. I had this memory of an argument, Janet rushing at me and pummelling me on the chest. She was screaming at me, her eyes teary and wild. "You drove him away! You never loved him!" She said it over and over. She clawed at my face.

They had to cut him free from the wreckage, the boy. They had to prise the mangled steel open delicately, like they were unwrapping something precious. I remembered it now. It was on the six o'clock news. Then I broke free from their grip and ran back across the threshold, into the house. They followed me into the boy's room, coaxing me gently. On the shelf by the bed, I picked them up and held them, the little chocolate cars wrapped in tinfoil, one for every year he'd been away.

BLIND DATE

Blair parked and checked the GPS again. The address was correct. He glanced at the directions the girl, Amber, had given him. Saw that it must be up the stairs in the faded red brick building.

He crossed the almost empty street. The only activity came from the meatworks adjacent. Blair saw the red swinging carcasses on hooks through an open roll-a-door. A truck idled out front. An odd location for a residential zone.

"Okay," he said. "I'll play."

The online fetish site hadn't let him down so far. This Amber was his latest hook up, and she sounded very eager. A hint of submission about her. Just his type.

His blood rushed as he pressed the buzzer. Images of previous conquests, pulling at their restraints, flooded his mind.

The face that greeted him as the door swung inward confused him. She was ancient, decrepit, a shock of white hair. Surely he had the wrong address? Worst of all were the eyes, white and filmy like a television zombie. Only a sturdy stick held her upright.

Before he could excuse himself, she spoke in a harsh whisper.

"You must be Blair." Her dry lips parted into a smile he mistook for a grimace, revealing the rotted black stumps of teeth. "Don't worry, dear. This is the right place. It's my granddaughter you want."

"Amber?" He let out a sigh of relief.

"That's right. I may be blind, but I know what she gets up to. She's a spirited girl. She just popped out, but said she won't be long."

Blind. That explains the milky eyes and the stick.

She stepped aside to let him in.

"Come in. It's alright. I was young once. I know what it's like to have those *urges*."

Blair didn't like the emphasis she put on the last word. The door closed behind him, shutting out the evening light. Neither did he like the way her sightless gaze seemed to follow him. For a moment, he thought he saw erect nipples straining at the sheer negligee that hugged her emaciated frame, but quickly dismissed it as a trick of the light. She ushered him into a seat.

"I'll make you some tea," she said, and he could hear her pottering about in the kitchen. He perused the mementoes dotted around the room. There were several framed photographs which caused him to expel a breath of air. They were all of Amber as he recognised her from her Internet profile, but the things she was doing in the photographs would have made her grandmother blush, had she eyes to see.

"Christ!"

The rattle of cutlery alerted his attention to the old woman's return, carrying a tray with a teapot and single cup. He stood and eased the platter from her unsteady grasp.

"Here, let me take that for you."

"You're very kind, dear."

The air in the apartment was suffused by a cloying sickly-sweet smell. The old woman's perfume? Amber's? He noticed there was another smell lingering beneath as well, like something dragged in on the bottom of a shoe. He sniffed the teapot as he poured.

"Nice photographs," he couldn't resist saying.

The woman cast her sightless eyes around the room. "I assume they are, dear. Amber gave them to me."

A noise from somewhere in the house drew their attention.

"I must have missed her coming back in. She's in her bedroom." He looked to where she pointed. "Third door along. She'll be waiting. I usually pop out to the shops around this time."

Blair gulped the tea and rose, uncertain. He made his way down the dingy hallway where soft music ebbed from beneath the third door. The underlying smell grew stronger here. His mind flickered back to the meatworks. He glanced back toward the exit, his thoughts swaying between flight and desire. He heard the front door open and close, and that decided for him. He knocked and, receiving no answer, gripped the handle and turned it.

The stench hit him full in the face as the door swung inward. A volley of flies rose from a shape trussed to the large bed which dominated the room. The red painted walls were covered with a range of implements swinging from hooks; cutting tools, whips, and massive rubber dildos.

On the bed lay a naked body, tethered by its arms and legs.

Blair clamped a hand to his mouth and stumbled forward. The young man's blue eyes, as sightless as the old lady's, stared at the ceiling. His greying skin was covered in welts, and flayed open to the bone.

Then, incredibly, the lips moved, and for one awful moment he feared the youth might still be alive. Then a maggot, fat and white, popped out between the swollen blue gums.

As Blair retched, the door clicked behind him. He swung around just as the old woman dropped the flimsy negligee at her feet.

Her body was grotesque. Not only sagging and rotting with age, the once full breasts hanging over her shrivelled stomach, but the whole torso displayed the scarring of decades of flagellation and other vile abuses. Only her sexual organ appeared to retain a sense of vitality, plump and swollen—a horror in itself. Despite himself, Blair felt a twitch downstairs.

He began to move toward her, thinking he would shove her aside, but a sudden savage pain rocked his gut, and his head begin to swim.

The tea!

Those translucent eyes now fixed him with a look he recognised, too late, as lascivious. She reached up with gnarled fingers to retrieve something long and shiny from one of the hooks embedded in the wall and whispered.

"Let's play."

CHRISTMAS PAST

"Where did you say you saw this thing?" Marius took his helmet off to wipe his brow. He was breaking protocol, but the lab had cleared the atmosphere. Whatever had happened to this civilisation—something cataclysmic judging from the remnants—it had occurred a long time ago, taking everyone with it.

"Through there." I pointed as I led the way through the large break in the wall into a massive amphitheatre. Part of the ceiling had gone, but the scale of the walls suggested it had been built high.

I stepped over some rubble, and Marius followed on my shoulder. "This better not be another of your hallucinations, Andreus, after last time."

Marius stopped short.

"There, by the throne. I told you."

The figure had appeared out of the shadows. A large being, much taller than us, and round. Dressed in thick red garb. Clothing that suggested the temperature here must have been much cooler at one time.

"How does it live," I asked, "when all others are dead?"

Marius scanned it from a distance, shaking his head. "It doesn't appear to be carbon based."

"How is that possible? If it doesn't breathe, is it a spirit?" As if in response, the being flickered out of sight and back again. "Hey!" I tried to draw its attention, but it ignored me, waving its hands in the air in front of its big red face. A face totally covered in the same flowing white mane that grew from its head.

"It doesn't acknowledge our presence," Marius said. "Notice its repetitive behaviour."

He was right. The being repeated the same actions in a loop, throwing its arms wide in gesture, its hairy mouth opening and closing, all with no sound. Behind it sat a strange metal construction; a seat at its rear, some kind of transportation device. Next to that, a huge elevated throne of burnished gold and red.

Marius approached the figure. "Be careful," I whispered.

"It's okay. I think I know what this is." With that, Marius swept his arm straight through the red being. It reappeared again on the other side. The alien ignored the attack and continued with its strange ministrations.

Marius turned to me and grinned. "It's an avatar, some sort of hologram. You must have triggered it when you first approached."

"Why is it here?"

"To provide a message? The raised throne intrigues me," said Marius. "We have much to learn about this species and what became of them, but this is a breakthrough." He climbed up the plinth and patted the empty throne. "Andreus, I think this is their God."

We both stood in awe and beheld the name of the God, carved above the throne. Like the avatar it too had survived the ravages of time.

I swept the translator across the strange wording and the machine spoke the name to us.

"Santa's Grotto."

ONE FROM THE HEART

Michelle flinched when she heard the familiar rattle of the postie's engine. Should she check the box or wait for Trish to get here? It was a dilemma having to rely on snail mail for the stuff she ordered on eBay. Yet it was the only way to get the kind of materials she needed. Not the sort of things you could purchase down the shops. She unbolted the door and peered out, feeling the light drizzle on her face. Then on checking the street both ways, she wrapped her gown around her and ran out to the mailbox.

No parcels at all. Just a letter… No, a card. She swallowed and flipped it over. She knew what day it was. Sure enough, there was his handwriting in the familiar scrawl, an ugly deformed heart inked in the top corner.

Michelle hurried back inside and slammed the door, slitting the envelope open with a steak knife. Her knees almost buckled as she read the poorly scripted words.

Dear Shell, my heart will always belong to you.

"Hi, Shell."

She turned at the exact moment she realised she had forgotten to lock the door behind her and dropped the knife to the floor.

Brian stood in the closed doorway. She should have smelled him. Could have kicked herself. He stank, and rags hung from his shrivelled, mottled flesh.

"Jesus! How did you get in here?"

She motioned to go around him but he lurched toward her, sending her scuttling back across the room.

"You got my card I see."

Michelle threw the item on the table in disgust, as if even touching it somehow soiled her.

"Ten years in a row. Surely you've forgiven me, after all this time?" His voice was a dry rasp, words struggling to fight their way out of his desiccated throat.

"What do you want, Brian?"

He gestured as to move forward, but stayed hovering in front of the doorway.

"You know what I want, Shell. I can't function, I can't move on without it."

Michelle felt a surge of anger diffusing her terror. "You should have thought of that before you did what you did. It was unforgivable, on Valentine's Day too."

Brian exhaled, a grating scrape through ruined lungs.

"But the price I paid, Shell." He reached out a gnarled hand toward her. "Surely I've suffered enough."

Michelle made a rush for the door, but he moved across to block her.

"You're weak, Brian. Getting weaker by the year. You can't hurt me."

"Just try me," he said, "and don't bother running out the back. I locked it." He held the key up in front of her.

"Bastard!"

He grinned, his mouth a black, cavernous ruin, and at that moment, Michelle saw the front door open behind him. Trish stepped forward and smashed Brian on the back of the head with a ceramic pot. He fell forward in a heap of soil and broken clay.

"I thought we told you never to cross this threshold again, you bastard!" said Trish, stepping around the fallen figure.

Michelle hugged her sister.

"Where the Hell have you been?"

"Sorry, sis. Traffic was a nightmare. Speaking of nightmares, what is this piece of shit doing here?"

Brian picked himself up off the floor, rubbing his head.

"Now, ladies, let's not fight. Just give me what I came for, and I'll be on my way."

The sisters exchanged a glance, emboldened by their strength in numbers. Michelle reached into a drawer and withdrew a huge silver knife. She waved it at her ex-husband.

"Fat chance," said Trish. "Now you better get packing, or Michelle might cut off the piece of you she should have taken ten years ago."

Brian looked down at his crotch. They stared at the faded dark stains on his shirt, and the ragged hole in his chest.

"But how will I ever love again?"

"Shoulda thought of that before you broke my heart," said Michelle, prodding him toward the doorway with the knife. "Go on, get."

He backed toward the open door. "I'm going, but I'll be back."

Michelle bolted the door behind him. Turned and leaned against it.

"That was close. He's never got back inside before." She tossed the knife on the table where it landed with a clatter.

Trish filled the kettle with enough water for two and flipped the switch. She fished the Valentine's card off the floor, sat and read it.

"Insincere bastard!"

"Exes, hey? Can't live with them."

"Can live without them," Trish finished her thought, and they cackled.

Trish twirled the knife in her fingers.

"You know, that's the very knife I used." Michelle smiled.

"Christ!" Trish dropped it on the table. The carved ivory guard of the blade glittered in the light. Her gaze rested on a leering face, set within a ram's skull and horns.

"Where do you keep it these days?"

Michelle pulled a black string necklace from under her gown. At the end of it swung a small key. She stooped and unlocked a liquor cabinet and withdrew an ornate wooden box draped in purple satin. She placed it on the table alongside the knife.

Trish pulled a box of black candles from a cabinet and set them equidistant around the table. Michelle pulled out a lighter and lit them in turn. The two sat drinking in the scent, contemplating the silence.

"I think he deserves another year of remorse," Michelle broke the silence. "Would you agree, sis?"

Trish nodded.

"Even though they abandon and forsake us, they never leave us empty handed." Michelle intoned as she flipped the box open and tipped its contents onto the table. From within, an almost spherical object, blackened and shrivelled with age, rolled into view and settled beside the knife.

"They always leave us their hearts."

The sisters exchanged a glance.

"Shall we begin?" Michelle asked.

Trish smiled. They joined hands.

LEAVE OF ABSENCE

Robert is taking the family on holiday. Marching them rote style he piles them into the car on the allocated morning, wife, boy, girl and luggage, in reverse order. It seems harsh but Robert knows that it is the only way to get them moving. Lord knows they would never achieve anything without him prodding them along. They probably wouldn't even get out the front door, period. Not just to go on holiday.

Heading out on the open road, Robert is relieved to leave the clamour of the office and city life behind. He can practically feel the layers of stress peeling off the further away they get.

Beside him, Anne, his wife of fifteen years, sits faithfully, emitting a half smile. No holiday for her this, not with the children along. Motherhood is a full-time unpaid career. Sometimes more like a sentence. She looks across at her husband. She'll play along with this for him. He needs this break, more than any of them.

Thirty minutes into the journey and the children are restless. Carla, five years old and impetuous, wants an ice cream. Tommy, aged ten and filled with the impatient spirit of adventure, joins in the mantra. Not just any ice cream, it has to be Maccas. "Wanna ice cream," the boy mocks his sister's baby voice. "Wanna ice cream, Daddy." They concur in unison.

A bead of sweat runs down Daddy's face, he thinks absurdly of an episode of the Simpsons, Bart and Lisa berating Homer from the back seat of the family vehicle. "Are we there yet? Are we there yet? Are we there yet?" The wife smiles across at him, offering tacit support.

"No ice cream. You just had breakfast," he says.

"We only just left the house," she adds. Marital harmony restored.

That wasn't the case earlier in the week, when she confronted him about that business trip with his personal assistant. "Explain to me again, exactly why she had to go with you." She had asked repeatedly. What right had she to distrust him, her provider of fifteen years? What did he do to deserve such a lack of faith?

Suddenly, the horizon fills with the figure of a man in a suit, waving them down. A stationary vehicle sits to the side of the road behind him, populated by a wife and two children, not unlike his own. The occupants eye Robert with a look of desperate hope.

Robert steps out of the car and the man encloses on him with a wave and a smile. "Hey buddy. Thanks for stopping. Having a bit of technical trouble with the car. You couldn't take me to the next town, could you?"

Robert takes a perfunctory glance at his watch. The man's eyes follow him down to his wrist and back up to eye level, causing a slight twinge of guilt. He motions with an arm toward his own vehicle, filled to the brim with family and possessions. Reassured, he composes a response.

"I'm sorry sir, but as you can see, we're pretty much full up." The man looks downcast. Robert searches desperately for another solution to the problem. As if by magic, he pulls a mobile phone from his pocket. "Why don't you ring the town up ahead, or the town back there, and ask for help?"

The man, who Robert notices is around his age, stares dumbly at the phone tendered before him. "What sort of help, chum?"

"I don't know… mechanical… assistance?" Robert responds, a little taken aback.

The man ponders this suggestion for a moment. "Who would I call, pal?"

"Well, I don't know," Robert admits with a defeated shrug. He glances through the open window at Anne, who shrugs.

The two of them stand facing one another in the middle of the road. Neither speaks for a couple of minutes. Anne leans out of the passenger door. "Is everything alright, Robert?" He waves her away abruptly. Tommy begins to drum on the rear window in a rhythmic pattern. Carla picks up the beat on the one opposite.

"Sorry," Robert says to the man, folding the phone away and secreting it back in his pocket, returns to the vehicle. They all watch the stranger, still smiling, as they pull away, receding in the rear-view mirror. Robert raises his voice, telling the children to stop their damn drumming.

"Directory assistance," Anne breaks the silence.

"What?"

"You could have let him ring directory assistance," she repeats.

"Now you tell me." He snaps angrily.

"Honey," she says softly, perhaps with a hint of condescension, "Remember your temper. Did you bring your pills?"

"Yes," he replies shortly. Not wishing to be reminded of his weakness. "In the glove box."

"Good," she says. He glances askance at her, sitting with her hands folded in her lap. *Doesn't trust me*, he thinks. *Every boss took his personal assistant to the seminar. Couldn't do all that work alone. What does she think I am? It's not like I'd even have time to…*

The thought is interrupted by the vision of a man standing in the middle of the road ahead, signalling frantically. Robert pulls over, steps out of the car as the man approaches, smiling gratefully.

"Thanks for stopping, chum. Having a few technical problems with the car." At this, Robert glances across, knowing already that he will see the wife and two children sitting patiently inside.

"You look familiar." Robert interrupts the spiel. "Have we met?"

The man looks at him strangely. "No, I don't think so, pal. Anyway…"

Without hesitation, Robert produces his mobile. "Call directory assistance," he says firmly.

The man looks almost disappointed, but takes the phone Robert proffers. He prepares himself to dial, pauses, his finger hovering above the button uncertainly. Robert thinks of an American President wavering over the launch missile button in a half-forgotten Cold War movie.

"There's no signal." The man holds the screen up, it catches the sun and dazzles Robert, who shields his eyes.

'Sorry,' the stranger says, and hands back the phone.

'Well,' says Robert, waving his arm to indicate his full load. "I'm sure someone else will be along." He walks slowly back to his vehicle. The man watches them drive away.

Further down the highway, Robert tries to entice the children into a camping song. They aren't having it. Fingers drumming on the windows. "Wanna ice cream", Carla grizzles. Robert glares at Anne. *You could at least try to help.* He says with his eyes.

"Stop that bloody noise," he shouts at the children through the mirror. Tommy reddens. Carla starts to sob. "Honey!" Anne admonishes, reaching for the glove box.

"Don't!" He demands. 'I'm fine.' She looks accusingly at him and retrieves a box of tissues from the compartment. Leans back and wipes their daughter's eyes and runny nose, comforts her.

Robert stares at the road ahead, leans on the pedal a little more. Makes it the focus of his anger. Eyes widen as a mirage like image gradually comes into focus. A man in a suit beckons them to stop. Puzzled, Robert pulls over. Steps out before the man can reach them. "Thank God you came along, friend."

"Having some technical problems with the car." Robert finishes the sentence for him.

The man flinches, a look of confusion momentarily crosses his face. Then the smile returns. "Yes. Don't suppose you could give me a ride to the next town?"

Robert looks aghast, sweeps his arm at the family and belongings. Surely, he should know. "Oh!" The stranger acknowledges. "Got a full load. Okay then buddy."

A thought occurs to Robert. "Why don't you pop the hood? Let me see if I can have a look for you."

"Oh no," the man says hesitantly. "That won't be necessary. I wouldn't trouble you, not in this heat."

"It's no trouble, friend," Robert insists through gritted teeth.

The man steps between Robert and the car now. "Really, it's okay. You wouldn't... It's not mechanical. I think it's a computer thing."

"A computer thing?" Robert repeats.

"Yes, a computer thing." The man says. "I'm sure someone will be along soon."

"Okay then." Robert agrees, withdrawing.

"Thanks anyway", the man smiles, waving them off.

As the solitary vehicle and its occupants recede into the distance, Robert turns to Anne, looking for collusion. "Did you see that?"

"Yes of course I saw it, Robert. Poor man. Those poor children."

"Poor man?" Robert splutters incredulously.

"Yes, poor man," she repeats, looking at him with a hint of disdain.

Doesn't trust her own husband, he broods. *As if I would. Twelve hours a day I put in.* Like a drum beat in his head it goes on.

"Tommy, stop it!" he yells at his drumming son.

The boy withdraws his hand from the window, hunkers back on the seat, sulking. Carla sits quietly now, consoled with a sweet from Mummy's purse.

Inevitably, the road ahead is populated by a familiar profile. Robert slams the car to a halt, throws the door open and hurls the mobile phone into the man's chest before he can speak. The stranger's smile flickers for an instant, then returns. He looks down at the phone, glinting in the afternoon sun on the tarmac, then back at Robert as the car disappears rapidly over the horizon.

The children are both crying now. Robert stamps his foot down on the accelerator. He won't even look at Anne, but she glowers at him. "Robert, really!"

"Don't!" He shouts.

Too late, she reaches into the glove box, retrieves the pills. Proffers one with some bottled water. "Come on. You know you have to," he entreats him like a child.

He snatches them from her hand. After everything he's done for her and those kids, he thinks. Swallowing the pill and water. Christ, all those clothes.

"What the Hell?" he stammers, slamming on the brakes. The car shudders momentarily, as if threatening to flip. The children scream. "Robert, for God's sake!" Anne cries.

Ignoring her, Robert flings the door open and runs up to the smiling man. "Look mister, what the Hell do you want from me?"

The man is taken aback, but the smile returns instantly. "Having a spot of technical trouble, pal. Can you give me a hand?"

"Listen, you." Robert prods a finger to the man's chest. "What on earth are you playing at? Why are you doing this to me?"

The man looks hurt. "There's no need to be like that, sir. I'm just looking for a Samaritan to help me and my family." He sweeps an arm behind him.

Robert takes in their pleading faces, the wife and two children, then looks desperately off into the surrounding desert. "How are you doing it? Going off road and overtaking me?"

The stranger maintains his air of calm, which only serves to inflame Robert. "Look, buddy, I only need a ride to the next town."

Robert tears at his hair. "I've told you and told you. I'm not taking you to the next bloody town. There's no room."

The man looks helplessly at Robert's full car, confirming the veracity of the statement. Robert closes in on him. "Listen son, I don't know what your game is, but my family and I are trying to go on holiday."

The man raises his hands and backs away slightly. "Woah! Easy there, fellah."

The passenger door of the stranger's car opens, and his wife steps out. She approaches the men. Robert thinks, My God, she looks just like...

"Hey, mister." She cuts him off. "Don't you point your finger at my husband. He's a good man, a damn fine man and a good provider."

Robert is bewildered. She continues the sudden tirade. "Fifteen years he's given me. Fifteen years of joy."

"What did you say?" Robert's eyes widen in terror. "Fifteen years?" he answers for her. Then, backing slowly away, not taking his eyes off them, he returns to the car, scrambles inside and screams away over the horizon.

Foot pressed to the metal, Robert softly bangs his head against the wheel. The children are too terrified to even cry now. Anne tries to console, proffering a pill and bottled water. "Honey, come on, take your pills."

"Fifteen years I've given you," he says softly into the steering wheel.

"Please, Robert. Do it for me, for us," she continues.

"And you accuse me and her," he says bitterly.

"I think we'd all feel a lot better if you took your medicine," she says, her voice wavering a little.

With a sideward swipe he knocks the pill and bottle of water flying from her grasp. "A man is not an island!" he roars.

Now Anne starts to weep quietly, her head on her chest

"Christ almighty!" *It's not my fault, he reasons. Fifteen years, two kids, and she closes up like a clam. Is it any wonder I had to look elsewhere? A man has needs for heaven's sake.*

He looks up, just in time to see the familiar face looming up ahead, the arm flagging him down, the resolute smile. Well not this time, pal, Robert thinks, planting his foot firmly. Anne screams. The children wail. "Not in my house!" Robert bellows as he cannons into the be-suited body, sending it flying over the bonnet and roof of the vehicle.

Careering into the distance, Robert looks back in the rear-view mirror to make sure. Sports a wild grin at the battered frame lying in the middle of the road. The woman flies from the stationary vehicle and sprints to its side.

Sobbing audibly, Robert guns the car along the road. Anne spits wildly at him. "Robert, stop the car! You're going to kill us all!"

He ignores her. "We are going on vacation," he states firmly, the voice wavering just a little. The tension is broken by a horrible cracking sound from the engine, and inexorably, the car shudders, lurches, and comes slowly to a halt. Robert motions it to the verge with the last vestiges of his strength. Looks around him desperately at their blank, hateful faces.

"I just want to go on holiday." He sobs forlornly. Beaten down at last. They sit there resignedly, not speaking in the fading light.

Gary is taking the family on holiday. His wife sits politely alongside, two children in the back. It was an effort to get them organised, but he's really looking forward to the break. Winds down the window, enjoying the feel of the wind in his hair. The car hurtles along the open highway. Then up ahead, a figure steps into the road. Gary slows the vehicle to a halt in front of the man in the suit who waves them down.

SINS OF THE FATHER

I pulled a beer from the fridge and sat on the battered old couch. The front of my sweatshirt was soaked through. I didn't think clearing up the old man's estate would be so tough. *Arcadia*. That was the name on the old wooden sign out front. Dad's idea of a joke, though he was never big on irony.

It would have been useful in these circumstances to have a sibling who could have given me a hand, but life doesn't always work out that way. On the other hand, being the only child meant dad left the place to me. Mom didn't get a say, having bailed out over thirty years ago.

Now it was mine to do what I want with. I could choose to move in for good, or just clean it up and sell it off. I had been leaning toward the latter after five days of dirt, sweat and tears.

That was until I found the box.

Dad died a couple of months ago, just as the November chills came sweeping down off the mountains. I sat with him those last few weeks in the hospital, watching him slide in and out of consciousness, watching him slip away. In the moments he was cogent he would talk to me in the hoarse whisper the cancer had left of his voice box, begging me for a smoke.

He often reminisced about the old days, the years it was just the two of us in the house through my teenage years. Mom walked out for good when I was fourteen. She had been practicing for years. Most times I would stand at the front gate and watch her walk away, pulling her suitcase along behind her. Dad would sit on the porch drinking beer, swearing, refusing to go after her.

Other times we would jump in the truck and trawl the streets until we found her, shuffling along with her case. She would be crying and he would get in her ear until she gave in and climbed in the car.

Lying in my bed at night I would hear them through the cracks in the wall, fighting and fornicating. His voice getting louder, then the sound of stuff being thrown around, both of them screaming in either pain or pleasure. Sometimes it was hard to tell the difference between the two.

Then one night she left and just never came back. I remember Dad got a real bad drunk on, worse than usual. He was yelling stuff at her about being a whore and he laid into her right in front of me. He bloodied her up real good and though I didn't know what they were yelling, it kinda sounded like she deserved it that time so I kept my lip shut.

He went off up the street again, and when she got up off the floor she just packed up some things and left. I tried to stop her but she shoved me aside, her eyes and lip all swelled up. She didn't say a damn thing.

He found out where she was staying and used to go around there and reason with her. Later on she told me his idea of reasoning mostly consisted of threats of violence.

Dad grew more bitter after that, but he never lacked for female company. Often times I would get up for school and there would be a new woman there. None of them lasted too long. I would sit at the table opposite them. They all seemed to have that same bewildered look on their faces, like rabbits in the headlights, like the faces of them lost kids on the milk cartons I poured on my cereal.

When I got older, I tracked Mom down myself and made it up to her. She and I still keep in touch to this day. Dad never knew that. Just like she never knew I resented her for walking out—for her weakness.

He always treated me right though, I give the old bastard that. Dad never raised a hand to me after I grew as tall as him and did his best to raise me right. Practiced positive parenting in his own way, like when he would come home from his carousing and find me up late in front of the television on a school night and pass comment.

"Jesus, boy, your eyes are like piss holes in the snow. Get to bed."

Gave me my first drink on my eighteenth birthday and he even set me up for my first time with a woman. She was years older than me, but she knew her way around. After dealing with her, I found girls my own age a lot easier to figure out. Dad was always there with his homespun advice.

"Son, don't ever let a woman do you wrong. Keep 'em in their place."

It's true what they say about acorns and trees. Neither of us could keep a marriage intact. Suze walked out on me and took the kids with her. That was three years ago now. Can't say I blame her, brought it all on myself. She came home early from her shift at the canning factory and found me in the sack with Linda from down the street. That was the one she found out about, but one was enough. Even then my immediate response was to lay another beating into her. Guess that was something else the old man and I had in common.

In his final months Dad started to lose the plot. He was forgetting things by the day, and quite often he would tell me or the nurse or anybody who would listen the same thing over and over. On account of this I didn't pay attention to a lot of what he said, but one thing resonates with me now.

One night as I sat by his bed he reached out and pulled me in close. It took all of the breath out of him to do this.

"Make sure you clean the place up good, boy, if you wanna sell it."

"I know Dad, I know. There's no way I could sell it in that state anyway. We've been through this."

"The shed, son, you gotta clean out my shed."

I shrugged. "Yeah, of course I will, Dad. I'll do the whole place, like I said."

After we buried him, I did just that. Mom came to the funeral, which was good of her. The people from the home dropped her off but they let me take her back afterwards. Then I packed a case full of stuff and set up home in our old place to clean it out.

It felt weird at first staying in the house I grew up in. Even though I had visited once or twice a year it was different being there day in day out. It was like the whole place had faded and shrunk and somehow diminished. I knew a part of that was just me growing up and leaving my boyhood behind.

I started at the front of the house and worked my way back, sorting the stuff I could sell from the crap that had to be thrown away. I did the basement and the attic, and then after several days I got out back to the shed. I had about forgotten Dad's words.

I sorted the tools and pulled out the mower. There was stuff in there had seized up and would never be used again. I was digging under the work bench when I discovered what appeared to be a small man-made compartment back there.

That was where I found the box.

I dragged it out. It was just an ordinary cardboard carton, but it sounded like there was a fair bit of stuff rattling around inside. I took it out on the lawn into the light and pulled it open.

When I saw what was in it, I took it inside the house and locked the doors.

At first I was puzzled. There was a whole bunch of jewellery and several items of clothing. It was all women's stuff, lingerie and panties, and some of the jewellery was engraved with names. A bracelet with 'Cindy' etched into the reverse, a heart shaped locket with an inscription, 'To Emma with eternal love', and a silver cigarette case with 'Rose' scratched on the lid, among others.

I figured it was Dad's secret stash of mementos from his philandering years, that was the reason Mom walked out. I remember a time when I was about thirteen, Mom went across state to visit her folks for a couple of months. Dad didn't go with her on account of her people never being sold on him in the first place. I never paid much heed at the time, but Dad went out a lot and left me alone in the house, and when he came back late one time, he came into my room and started talking. There was whisky on his breath and most of what he said went over my head but one sentence stuck in my mind and came back to me after I reached manhood.

"Son, when you get older you might come to realise that

sometimes, one woman just ain't enough."

But the longer I sat there in the lounge, staring at that box, sucking on a beer and a Marlboro, the more something nagged at the back of my mind. I couldn't fathom what it was at first, but after several hours and several beers, it hit me.

It was the names of those women.

The next day I drove over to the rental I had been living in since I lost the house to Suze, and I stopped in for more supplies and picked up my laptop.

Back at Dad's place I set it up there in the sitting room on the coffee table. Acting on a hunch I started checking missing persons' cases going back thirty odd years. I focussed on the name Cindy and when I came across this piece it started coming back to me.

Police Baffled by Case of Missing Mother

State police are calling for anybody who might have seen missing thirty-seven-year-old mother of two Cindy Bishop on the night she disappeared, while walking home from a party in downtown Alberson a little over two weeks ago.

The article, dated February 1986, went on to detail the case and drop some not very subtle hints about the missing woman's unhappy domestic situation. It all but pointed the finger at the husband.

I remembered the case well from my teens as it dragged on over the course of one summer. The woman lived in the same town as us not six or seven blocks away. She was never heard from again but they never could pin it on the husband. In the end the police just accepted she had run away and made a new start somewhere, with a new name.

I tried the next one, Rose, a bit harder to pin down. There was a Rose Anderson, aged twenty-nine, who disappeared on her way home from work in 1977 in the next town along from us. This one raised suspicion on both the husband and his brother, and the article seemed to imply that some sort of tryst had been going on. She was never heard from again either. There was also a Rose McGee, aged nineteen, waitress and known party girl, found raped and murdered on the dunes at Cutters Beach in

1990, about an hour's drive from our place.

I fingered the locket and typed in Emma. Took an hour to pinpoint this one but the nearest I got was a story about an Emma Price, aged thirty-two, known alcoholic, disappeared in 1988 on the way home from one of her benders. No husband to pin this one on, though there were a string of men who could have been described as boyfriends.

I sat up half the night and by the end of it I had tied up the stories of seven missing women over the past forty years, all of whom could potentially be linked to my father by an item of jewellery sitting in that cardboard box stashed in the shed.

I collapsed on the couch with my head spinning.

The next day I sat and thought back over all the jobs Dad held over the peak years of his life. He never had a career as such, nor did he stay in one place for too long. He spent some time in an auto shop, did a stint as a delivery driver, worked in office supplies, hauled building equipment long distance. Whatever angle I approached it from, it seemed Dad spent a lot of time out on the road and moved around the state and across county lines in the course of his work.

It got to a point where I knew it wouldn't be too hard to pinpoint the movements of all these women and the whereabouts of my father and find that they all coincided at a certain point and place in time.

Jesus H. Christ, I never saw it. Nobody did.

Not even Mom.

Still, I had to make sure.

Mom was sitting out the back of *Shady Springs* in a large wicker chair. She had on the pale green shawl the old man had given her years ago in one of his lighter moods. The wind was teasing the branches of the cypress trees in the yard. I pulled my coat tight around myself as I sat down opposite.

"It's a little cold out here, Mom," I said.

"I like the fresh air," she said, as she took a drag on her Marlboro and set it down in the ashtray.

"Careful, Mom, those things'll kill ya."

"Hardy ha! So, what brings you down here? You wanna talk

about the asshole, I suppose?"

I nodded and began to probe her for information about Dad's habits and his movements back in the day.

Mom ground the cigarette out hard and set her jaw firm.

"If you mean his fancy women, I knew all about those, he never bothered with secrets."

"Yeah, I'm not so sure about that, Mom."

"Bullshit! He used to enjoy rubbing my face in it. I knew about all of them, that filthy whore, Loretta Baker!" Her voice rose an octave and it was obvious I had hit a sore point, but I had to know.

"Who else, Mom?"

"What?"

"Who else was there? What about Rose? Emma?"

It was like re-opening an old wound.

"Sharon Gates, and that barmaid bitch, what was her name?" she asked.

"Cindy?" I offered, more in hope.

"You're enjoying this, aren't you? Tormenting me?" Mom's voice turned into a high-pitched wail.

"I'm sorry, Mom. I can't explain. Please keep your voice down."

"Bitches and whores!" Mom yelled, slamming her fist onto the glass topped table.

Nurses and security guys in white coats strode toward us.

"Was there ever a Carolyn, a Stephanie? Think, Mom."

"Bastard! You're just like him."

A heavy hand gripped my arm and pulled me away from her.

"Mr Bridges, we can't have you coming here upsetting your mother…"

"I know, I know. I'm sorry, Mom. I didn't mean to… Look, I'll just go, okay?"

"Just like him!" Mom yelled as they pulled her away.

My mother died the following week, and it bothered me I never let her go on happier terms. Suze and the kids never showed for the funeral, just as they had skipped Dad's as well. That also upset me.

I decided to keep the old place after all.

As for the box and its contents, I knew I had two choices. It seemed Dad was smart enough to keep his business and pleasure separate.

One thing puzzled me though. Why did Dad want me to know?

Suze and the kids weren't coming back, I knew that now. I moved on as best I could. Took up with a married woman from work, then moved on to a widow I met online. That didn't stick either. The more time passed the more I was reminded of something my mother had said when I was a bachelor.

"All these women, Darrel, and not once do I see love in your eyes."

I don't miss Suze, but I miss my children. Sometimes I drive around by the high school in the morning when the kids are going in, in the hope of catching sight of them.

Like today, I'm cruising along, feeling sorry for myself. It's after nine, and a light drizzle starts coming down. I see her at the bus stop. She looks like she should be in school. There's no cover and she's getting wet.

When I pull over, she gets in without hesitation. We drive along in silence, exchanging glances.

"Not in school today?" I ask.

She doesn't answer.

"You got a cigarette?" she finally speaks.

"Sure, in the glove box."

She pulls out my Marlboros and lights one up.

"Got some rum and cokes in back if you want one."

She reaches over the back seat and pulls a can from the stash I had picked up the night before.

The rain sets in heavy. She takes a drag of her smoke and a slug from the can. She's got her head back on the seat rest and her eyes closed. A lick of dirty blonde hair falls over one side of her face.

"You got a name, honey?" I ask, as I turn off the road, down a dirt track.

THICKER THAN WATER

It all started in the blood. At least that's what we were told later when they began to get it under control. Get them under control. No one knew how it began, a medical procedure gone awry, or a military experiment that spiralled out of control. Even in the looped broadcasts the authorities seemed reluctant to elaborate on the actual cause.

The virus spread fast, but it was not quite the apocalypse we feared. As irony would have it, the zombie mythos of popular fiction had us well primed for the event. The military response was well organised and effective. They managed to contain most of the trouble with just a few major cities being over-run, and they were working on taking those back as well.

We lost a lot of people at first. We all had to adjust. We all had to make sacrifices, but now that the worst of it seems to be over, people like me can carry on with our lives without too much trouble. Sure, you have to keep your wits about you. There are still large numbers of the undead roaming around in rural areas. But in the major towns, the street sweepers are pretty vigilant. They complete a wide arc of the entire metropolitan zone every day. You see their trucks with the insignia everywhere and hear the drone of the helicopters. So, people are starting to feel safe again.

The company I work for assumed a significant role in the re-building process. We analyse, assess and package a range of foodstuffs for human consumption. There isn't a whole lot of fresh produce around, for obvious reasons. The undead are partial to any kind of meat, and most animals were too dumb to realise the danger before it was too late. It became impossible to farm on open land because of the swarms, and the stupid buggers trampled most of the crops. That is something we are attending to now: moving our fresh food production into protected areas.

Still, as much as I appreciate the shelter afforded by our guarded suburbs, there is something exhilarating about getting out on the open road and taking a few risks. It makes me feel more alive. That's where I find myself this Saturday afternoon, behind the wheel of my four-wheel drive, enough height to afford a sense of security. I'm heading for the old hometown. The occasional chopper buzzes me but I flash the lights to let them know I'm okay. Ditto the road checks, a salute sees them wave me through.

No matter how old a man gets, and I'm getting up there, I don't think he ever forgets the streets of his youth, or the old family home. My birthday is as good an excuse as any to indulge in a nostalgia trip.

The sun is still high in the sky as I turn into the familiar street, the sign pock marked with bullet holes, and ease up the slight incline. It is not the steep hill I remember from my childhood, but then my mind was small and the world was big, not the shrunken shell I see before me now. I pull up in front of the old place, relieved that it is still intact. It is a bit run down these days, but it will always be home to me. Mum and Dad never sold the place.

It's funny how it's the little things you remember. Like the way mum would stand at the end of the porch and wave us off to school, always waiting until we had rounded the corner. Or how every pay day dad would collect his envelope and stop off at the toy shop on the way home and buy Keely and me a toy each, a piece of furniture for her dolls' house, and a Matchbox car for me to add to my collection, a different car every week. I still had most of them to this day, even after all this time.

I ease the car door open, scan the horizon and step out onto the footpath. The streets are empty, though there's a meat wagon just up the block. A bunch of guys in overalls are pitching corpses onto the tray. One of them notices me and waves. I swallow and wave back.

What if they got loose?

I hurry up the familiar path, remembering every crack. Pull the key from my pocket and ease it into the lock. I push the door open. It creaks like something out of a horror movie. I make a mental note to oil the hinges.

I peer into the cool shadows as my eyes make the uncomfortable adjustment from the brilliant afternoon sun.

"Mum? Dad?"

The guttural response in high and low tones is enough to ease my concern. I walk through to the lounge room and they are still tethered up where I left them.

"Mum, Dad, thank God you're okay."

They grunt through lipless mouths and I busy myself picking up after the mess they have left in my absence.

"You guys had me worried there," I say, as I give the house a liberal spray of air freshener. "I thought you might be outside on the meat wagon."

Mum lurches as far as her shackles will allow and reaches out to me. I squeeze her bandaged hand. I pulled the nails off both of them months ago to stop them scratching, as well as removing their false teeth. Heck of a job but you can't be too careful about infection.

I stay for a couple of hours, making small talk. Give Mum and Dad an update on Melissa and the kids. Tell them how much we all miss them. It's sad the way things turned out. The kids are too young to understand why they can't visit grammy and gramps anymore.

Sad for me too, but I figure I owe them this much. It was me that kept them safe after they turned, couldn't bear to let them go. The street cleaners would have shown them no mercy. I still remember how they brought me up, taught me right from wrong. Christ I even tried to finish them myself, out of mercy. Put the gun up to Mum's head, but the way she looked at me, I could tell she knew.

What's a guy to do? They're still my parents. I pull out the old photo albums and reminisce with them a while, until I see the sun start to dip toward the horizon through the window.

"Okay guys. I better be getting home now."

I stand up to leave, then stop dead when I see it, sitting on the coffee table, smack bang in the middle of a cleared space I hadn't noticed.

I walk over and pick it up—a brand new Matchbox car.

I turn to them with tears welling in my eyes.

"How?"

They respond in unison, and I swear I can make out the words, 'Happy birthday'.

That's about the same time as I hear a noise from the other end of the house, something bumping against a wall. I freeze, look at mum and dad. They heard it too. Their ears are cocked and they are both looking down the hallway toward the bedrooms.

My first thought is the undead, and then all of a sudden it clicks. I stride down the hallway to the last bedroom, Keely's room, and fling the door open. It smacks back against the doorstop.

My sister sits on her old single bed. Her hair is unkempt, like she just woke up. "Happy birthday, bro," she says with a smile.

"How long have you been here?" I ask once I pick my jaw back up off the floor.

"A couple of weeks," she says as if it means nothing. "Saw your handiwork on the folks, figured you'd be back sooner or later."

I join her on the bed and take her hands in mine. "Jesus, sis, I'd given up on you, I thought you were dead."

"Nope. I survived," she says, squeezing my hands. "My old place got overrun though."

"I know. I checked."

"So, I thought I would hole up here for a while, brought you a present. You like it?"

I pull the Matchbox car from my jacket pocket and turn it over in my hands. "Yeah, I love it, sis. Thanks."

"So, um…" Keely says at about the same time I notice her hand has strayed onto my knee. "Would you like a special birthday treat, for old time's sake?" Her eyebrows jut back up her forehead on the last word, and she turns her head sideways and looks up at me, just like the way she used to.

I feel my face redden. "Oh. I... What about Mum and Dad?"

"Don't be a pussy, they're just dumb animals now. They won't even notice," she says, rubbing her leg against mine.

The touch of warm human flesh, even through corduroy, feels so good, though I try to flinch away. Keely stands up and walks across the room.

"If it makes you more comfortable, I'll close the door. There, now we're alone."

I should have got up right then and left the house. I should have gone home. I should have left the past in the past.

But I didn't.

It was pitch dark when I left, never a good thing to be on the streets after dark now. My mind was spinning the entire journey home. To my good fortune the traffic was sparse and the patrols packed up for the night. I turned on the radio for company. Still nothing but conflicting government propaganda reports and static, "...the virus is under control...stay in your homes...a cure is imminent..."

Forty-five minutes later I heard the familiar crunch of gravel under the wheels as the headlights swung over the threshold. I eased the window open a crack and let the cool night air reawaken my senses. I was just about to hit the remote to open the garage door when I saw it lurch out of the bushes in the front yard. I was reminded of the repeated media warnings that noise and light can attract them after dark.

I sat still and scanned the vicinity. Thank God there was just the one, a stray. I took a deep breath and fished around under my seat, retrieving the cricket bat. I had learned this one from American movies, though they tended to favour a baseball bat, being Yanks. I wasn't too worried. I'd had some experience with the bat. Still you never quite get used to it. It is a small blessing the things move so damn slow.

By this time it was scratching at the window, hissing at me, eyes bulging out of its female head. I did a quick mental calculation to work out the required velocity of my swing. Women are lighter than men. This one was petite. I unclipped my seatbelt and slid over to the passenger door, released it and stepped out before the thing had time to get around.

By the time she rounded the bonnet I was ready and I let her have it with the open face of the willow. There was a sickening CRACK! And she went down and out for the count. My eyes flew to the horizon toward an imaginary boundary and I sung sotto voice an old refrain from a telemovie I once saw, "Come on Aussie come on, come on; come on Aussie come on."

Sniggering like a schoolboy I shouldered the bat and whipped out my door keys. Had the five locks sprung in no time and shut the door behind me. Then I took a deep breath.

The house was cold and empty. I lit the gas heater and pulled a six pack from the fridge. Popped the top of the first can and sat in my armchair. Picked up the remote and stared at the television, leaving the sound on mute. Nothing but re-runs of programs from the old world when it was safe to go outdoors. One channel in a fit of irony was screening back-to-back zombie flicks. I settled on a government head in a suit and tie mouthing words over back images of the street sweepers doing their thing. The bodies piled high on the trucks. I had heard all their patter before and the mantra never changed. "We've got it under control (but we still haven't found the cure)." I took a swig from the can.

I stayed away from the old house for several weeks after that. It wasn't that I wanted to avoid Keely, it was more my general unease about what she told me that night, and the things she showed me in the freezer.

"You know they have to eat," Keely had said, nodding at Mum and Dad as she joined me on the couch. She had pulled a couple of cans from the fridge and tossed one at me. She ran a towel through her shower fresh hair.

"Don't talk about them like they're not here," I said, depressing the lid of my soft drink. "They're still human beings."

"Are they? Not any more they're not. Get real, Nick. Not unless they find a cure."

"What do you mean they have to eat? Isn't that all they do?" I said, as Mum echoed my words with a low moan.

"No, you're not getting it. If they don't eat, they starve, because they're not quite dead."

"Bullshit!"

She took a pull from her can and let rip a gassy belch. "Nup. S'true. Don'tcha watch the news?"

I sucked the dregs from my can and squeezed the life out of it. "I don't watch much television. I find it too depressing. Nor do I read the papers any more. Not since the obituary column started to take over the whole newspaper." I pointed at our parents, straining at their manacles halfway across the room. "Well, they've been chained up like that for yonks. Why aren't they starving?"

Then Keely gave me her lopsided smile. It was kind of like the smile she gave me when she put her hand on my knee, but not quite the same.

"Because I've been feeding them." Her eyes sparkled as she said it.

I took a close look at her, saw every little perforation in her skin, and even though I somehow knew the answer before I asked the question, because I could read it in her eyes, could smell it oozing from every pore of her skin, I went ahead and asked it anyway.

"What have you been feeding them?"

That was when she showed me the freezer.

"Oh, don't look so shocked." I heard her voice across the room as I sat with my head in my hands. "I only take the ones nobody misses. Christ, it's easy enough these days... just go hunting after dark. That's when you find those who are looking for trouble."

Something thumped heavy on the table and I looked up to see her reach into a large canvas bag and pull out a bloody great crossbow. She pulled the string back taught and winked at me. All I could think was it was me who bought them that bloody freezer. It was way too big for the two of them, but I got a great deal. "Mum, you can stock up for the whole winter, like you did in the war. The meat will never go off." I had joked.

So, I hadn't been back since. I knew I would though. Blood is blood. Mum would be asking after me.

It was the phone call that made up my mind for me. It came in the middle of the night. I raced out of bed to shut the noise up.

Too much noise can wake the dead.

"What the … who…." I said down the line.

"Hey bro," she said.

"Keely. What the fuck! How are you calling? The phones have been dead since…"

"Battery, bro. The lines are coming back. Jesus don't you watch the news?"

"You know I don't," I said, rubbing the sleep from my eyes.

"Enough small talk, bro. Where the hell you been? I need you to come over."

"What, now?" I said. "Aw Keely. Can't this wait until morning?"

"No it can't wait… oh I get it. That's not what I want you for, loverboy. Christ! Don't flatter yourself."

"Well, what do you want then? I can't just up and leave Melissa and the kids in the middle of the night."

The line dissolved to static and I could picture Keely giving me that lopsided look again.

"How is Melissa, by the way?" she asked.

"She's fine."

"Is that right?" she said in a voice which suggested the opposite. "Could you put her on? I'd like to say hello."

I hesitated. "She's asleep. I don't want to wake her."

"What, I can't say hello to my sister-in-law?" came the exasperated reply down the line. "Okay, put one of the kids on."

"No." I swallowed. "Why are you doing this, Keely?"

"How long have they been gone, Nick?"

I tapped the phone against my temple. "Three months… I told her not to go out without me. She insisted… she wanted the kids to see the outside world. Took them to the market, but there was a swarm…"

I heard her swallow as she searched her vocabulary to select the right words. Keely never did sympathy very well. "Fuck! I'm sorry Nick, but it's fucking vital that you get your arse over here now, please!"

I was chastised. "Is there something wrong? Did Mum and Dad escape…hello?"

I was talking to dead air.

I walked into the bathroom, splashed warm water on my face. Went back to my room and threw on some warm clothes. Unlocked and re-locked the door as quiet as possible. The night was still. I jumped in the car and fired it up. As I pulled onto the tarmac a couple of undead appeared in the headlights, the bastards are stealthy sometimes. I recognised one of them as Tony, the mechanic from the local garage. He was still in his tattered overalls with his name sewn into the breast pocket. I recalled how the prick had ripped me off on my last service. I revved the engine hard and the wheels showed them no mercy.

Keely was waiting at the door when I got there, with a machete in her hand. She lowered it as soon as I crossed the threshold and bolted the door behind us.

When she turned around I saw the wound on her forearm. I took a huge gulp of air and sat on my arse. Mum and Dad pulled at their restraints. They could smell the blood oozing from their daughter's arm.

I ran the implications through my brain as she gave me an expectant look. "Shit! Keely. How did you…"

She pawed at the wound, a sheepish look on her face. "Dad bit me."

"What?"

"I was feeding them, you know."

I looked back and forth between our parents and my sister. "They haven't got any fucking teeth," I said.

"I put them back in so they could eat."

"Fuck's sake!"

"I know. I fucked up. Pretty stupid huh?" She waved her bloody arm around in front of her, sending delicate spatters across the carpet. "Oops! Sorry."

I kicked the coffee table, sending a half frozen severed limb sliding onto the floor on a bed of slimy flesh.

"Well what the fuck are we going to do now, genius?" I shook my head and bit down on my lower lip.

She gave me that look. "I think we both know the answer to that one, bro."

I followed her gaze, and that when I noticed the third heavy chain bolted to the far wall of the lounge room.

"Oh Keely. No!"

"Yes bro. You know it's the only way. I've done all the hard work for you." I shut my eyes but I couldn't block out her words, or the sense she was making.

"I calculate I've got about three hours until I turn. You gotta do it, bro…if you love me. It's either this or… or you put me out of my misery altogether."

I rubbed my thumbs into my temples and let it all pour over me. She handed me a stubby from the fridge, took one for herself– Dad's favourite brand. She clicked her glass against mine, took a pull. I did likewise. Dad looked at us as if to say, "Leave me bloody beer alone." I toasted him. Alcohol couldn't make the situation any worse. It could even improve it.

"Oh man! This is some pretty messed up shit," I said and took another swig.

Keely belched and sat down on an armchair. She began to pick bits of lint off the armrest. "Come on bro. It's not that bad. Christ, who knows, they might still find a cure."

I looked into her hazel eyes, my kid sister. She picked up the metal collar and placed it in my hand. "I love you bro. Always did. You know that." She took another hit from her stubby.

I held the collar in one hand, the bottle in the other. I looked from Keely to mum to dad, I sculled the rest of the beer.

"Fuck's sake!"

Afterwards I sat and watched them. Keely, her pretty eyes glazed over, edged closer to Mum and Dad. They sniffed her up and down, but they soon realised she was one of them. She hugged them, but they didn't return her affection. She was dead to them too now.

She looked toward me. "See, they're just animals, Nick, empty vessels. But they recognise their kin."

I popped the lid on my second beer, or perhaps it was my third. "I'll move in." I said. "I'll take care of you all."

"I knew you would bro. Don't forget to feed us, eh?"

I shuddered at the thought of it, but tried hard not to show it. "You got it, sis." I fingered the crossbow she had passed on to me, admiring the craftsmanship. Damn the thing was put together.

"I'm going to lie down now Nick, get some sleep. Maybe you better go into your old room. Come out in the morning. It should be over by then."

"You want a pillow, or some blankets?" I asked, at a loss for words of comfort.

"Nah bro, the floor is good enough for me now." Keely smiled. I was going to miss that smile.

She was right, she was always right. I did move in and take care of them. I brought a load of supplies over from work for me, and I made the food in the freezer last as long as possible, but I was just delaying the inevitable. When the white bottom of the freezer yawned up at me a gaping chasm, I went out after dark to hunt like she told me.

Keely was right about that too. They were out there, the ones who were asking to be taken, and nobody cared. There were the survivalists, the ones who thought they heard voices from God, telling them to rid the world of the undead. There were those who enjoyed the sport of it, the danger of risking it all to bring home a scalp. Then there were those who liked to torment the undead for their own nefarious reasons. I felt no remorse taking those types out of circulation.

I was fascinated by the appetites of my undead kin. In some way they compensated for mine. I didn't much care for food any more myself. Watching them eat was enough for me beyond mere subsistence, and just grain, fruit and vegetables at that too. No more meat for me.

After a while I started to look like them too, my flesh drawn and pressed hard against the bone. Though mine was malnutrition by way of choice, for them it was brought on by a lack of circulation and the impossibility of nutrition. I needed a bare minimum of fuel to hunt, and I even grew to love my instruments of death, the silent efficiency of the crossbow and the dull thud of the machete, the sound of its impact on willing flesh. The living came to sicken me as much as the dead. Family was all I had left, all I ever wanted. The government still failed to find the promised cure for the virus. I gave up hope that they would ever find it.

Time passed until I no longer kept a record of its passing. I abandoned the concept of time itself. Then I made my choice. It seemed the one remaining logical path left to follow. I sat on the couch until late one night, sucking on a beer. The wind was howling in the eaves. My kinfolk were groaning and pulling at their restraints. I knew they were starving. I was letting them down. The place was a mess. I had long ceased cleaning it. I turned toward Keely. "You were always the strong one, sis. You would have seen it through." I saluted her with my stubby.

She watched as I hurled the machete at the opposite wall. It cut into the plaster with a loud THWACK! And wavered there at eye level. The freezer was almost empty again. I couldn't bear the thought of preparing any more livestock. I had long cut all ties with the outside world. Now it was time to get myself ready.

I showered and shaved. I put on my best clothes and cleaned the house from top to bottom. These were the rituals which linked me to the rest of humanity. I wanted to experience them again. I put on one of Mum and Dad's old LP records and let a dead crooner serenade me. I pushed the front door open for the first time in years. I blinked into the rising sun, feeling its warmth on my face. I hadn't even noticed the night pass by.

I left the door wide open. Then I took the keys from on top of the freezer and walked into the lounge room. I unshackled mum, then I unshackled dad. I told them both that I loved them. They stood there dumbstruck at first, as if not quite believing they were free at last. It was as if they had forgotten even the limited function they had left. Perhaps it had been cruel to chain them all along.

Keely watched my every move with a keen eye. She was looking at me with that lopsided grin. We both watched Mum and Dad stumble around until the realisation set in that they were no longer tethered to the wall. They moved toward the door and the light. Mum turned and took one last look at me. I liked to think she recognised me. Then she was gone.

"Bye, Mum. Bye, Dad." I said to their departing shadows.

I turned back toward Keely. I smiled and said, "Do you still love me, sis?" She strained at her tether and made a shrill keening noise. The LP had finished and the needle was making a repeated scratching sound on the ancient record player. I walked across and lifted it off the album.

"What shall we have to play us out, Keely?" I asked, flicking through our parents' substantial collection. "I'm afraid mum and dad didn't move with the times. What about Englebert Humperdink? No? Shirley Bassey? Frank Sinatra?" Then I found the right one. I wiped the dust from the cover, unveiling the taught tanned flesh and the swarthy complexion, the cream slacks drawn ever so tight over muscular loins. "Aha!" I said. "You'll remember this one."

I lifted the stylus and lowered it into the groove. After a short crackle of static Tom Jones began to croon the opening bars of mum's favourite tune, *The Green Green Grass of Home*. I turned the sound up as high as it would go.

It started with the blood, and that is where it should end as well. As the music serenaded us I swayed over to the wall and unleashed my sister. Her chains thudded to the floor. She didn't turn away, just stood and watched me. Then I spread my arms wide and walked into her loving embrace.

LOVE THY NEIGHBOUR

Shayna groaned and reached for her headphones. Jamming them over her ears, she cranked the stereo up full blast onto some heavy rock. Anything to drown out the sounds of passion oozing through the walls from the bedroom next door, or maybe it was the couch in the lounge room, or the laundry.

She chewed on her upper lip hard enough to draw blood. She tasted it on her lips, bitter and coppery, but not as bitter as she felt about the little love nest over the fence. Fuck Kat. Some mate she turned out to be, and fuck Brendan too, the rotten bastard. She rued the day she let him park his throbbing, baby-shit yellow, V8 ute in her driveway.

Emma and Larissa had tried to warn her that he was a love rat, but she hadn't listened, dismissing her hairdressing salon mates as jealous bitches. They tried to tell her the rumours circulating about Brendan round the Leopold, their local watering hole, but she had closed her mind off to the negativity. She even ignored the stupid love-heart inked on his chest with some other bitch's name in it. Hard as it was to do when he was on top of her, pumping away. But he assured her it was a mistake he had made in his wild youth, and anyway, as soon as he had the dough, he was gonna get the name altered to hers.

"Fucken liar."

Kat was even worse. Sucking up to her and pretending to be mates, when all the while she had her eyes on Brendan. She even had the nerve to bad mouth her man as she comforted Shayna that one time Brendan drove over a bit too shitfaced from the pub and backhanded her when she asked him what he was upset about. Turned out his footy team had lost, but fuck, Shayna wasn't to know.

Still, she forgave him though, cos he was real sorry the next day when he sobered up. It wasn't his fault his team lost. She should have been a bit more sensitive to his needs. Should have seen how much he was hurting. His pride dented. He said he'd make it up to her though, and she believed him. He even bought her a carton of her favourite smokes.

The smokes were another thing. That time she came home from work and found that strange butt in the ash tray on the bedside table. Brendan swore blind one of the blokes had given him a new ciggie to try, but she was adamant there was a faint hint of lippie on it. Couldn't prove it though, because when she went to check again, Brendan had emptied the ash tray, destroying the evidence. All rather convenient she thought.

Then a few days later, when she had put it behind her, and she was over Kat's place having a gossip, she saw it on the table by the telly. An ash tray with those same butts in it.

Shayna went ape shit. She chucked the ashtray at Kat, smacking her fair on the scone and let rip with all sorts of accusations.

"Why don't ya get ya own man, Katherine?" Kat hated being called that. "And get a fucken job too, ya lazy slut. Then maybe ya wouldn't have time to root my bloke."

To her chagrin, Kat didn't deny it. In fact she admitted it. "Yeah, Brendan and I have been on for months, Shayna. He's fucken sick of you. Reckons you're a boring lay. He has to come 'n see me to fulfil his needs."

Kat went on the describe how Brendan would pick her up at the phone box outside the corner shop and take her out into the scrub, where they would climb in the back seat of the king cab and go at it like horny teenagers. It was at that point that Kat made a gesture that sent Shayna spinning over the edge, rubbing her crotch through her jeans while telling Shayna how much she loved rooting Brendan.

That was it for Shayna, she leapt on Kat like a cat, biting, scratching and pulling chunks of her hair out. When Kat fought her off and started screaming back, Shayna bolted, and chucked a pot plant through the window on her way out for good measure. Probably not the smartest move, because Kat called the cops and threatened to take out a restraining order, and she had to pay for the window. Almost a whole week's wages.

So, she and Kat weren't on the best of terms, to say the least. Shayna knew she and Brendan were deliberately turning up the volume on their love making just to torment her, and it was working. The bed slamming into the wall just over the fence. Why did they have to build houses so close together these days? One night they even did it in Kat's back yard, up against the fence. Shayna got 'em that time though. She turned her hose on the pricks. They yelped like a pair of scolded dogs. Kat swore like a trooper and hurled half a brick over the fence.

"Fuck off, Katherine!" Shayna had yelled, egged on by the sound of Brendan's stupid giggle emanating through the asbestos.

Now, as Kat's squeals went into overdrive through the thin plaster, Shayna lit a smoke and cranked the Metallica up a bit higher.

"Fucken arseholes!" Still at least Kat's three kids would be home from school soon. The bitch would have to stop sucking Brendan's cock for a few minutes then. She amused herself trying to guess who had fathered Kat's awful spawn. Each of the little bastards looked totally different.

That train of thought led down a dark hole though. It wasn't Shayna's fault she couldn't have kids. She had told the story to plenty of blokes over the years, about her childhood bout with a pelvic inflammatory disease which had left her incapable of conceiving. She knew it was what drove most of them away. Shayna never would have thought that the thing which had proven such a great source of protection against pregnancy in her teens, would go on to become such a curse in adulthood. Shayna would give anything to be a mum. Sometimes, just hearing Kat's kids squealing as they ran up the path and slammed the door open was enough to bring her to tears.

Shayna stubbed out her smoke and flicked open a porno on the laptop. She kept the music cranked up loud and eased her pants down. At least she could entertain herself while she blocked the whole world out.

On Friday night Shayna stood in front of the bathroom mirror for a good hour. She'd let the girls do her hair that afternoon at work. She figured it was about time she got back on the horse and found a new bloke. She had to admit it didn't look like she'd get Brendan back, as much as she still wanted the ungrateful bastard.

She was planning to call an Uber and go into town. Fuck the Leopold. Then a funny thing happened on the way out the door. She popped into the bedroom where she'd left her smokes, and a book was laying on the bedspread. She didn't remember leaving it there. So, she picked it up and started flicking through the pages.

Larissa had given it to her as a bit of a joke. "Just in case you wanna come over to the dark side," she had winked as she handed it over. The title stood out bold and red across the top of the page in capitals, *SATANISM AND DEMONOLOGY*. A mock parchment adorned the cover, yellow in colour, adorned with a green dragon and two little red horned figures with wings.

Shayna was intrigued. She'd never read a whole book in her life, but Larissa said it wasn't necessary, just look up the bit you wanted and run with it. Larissa was a funny chick, with her tatts and piercings and all that ornate jewellery. One day in the bathroom at the beauty shop, Shayna had walked in on her topless. Larissa covered up, but not before Shayna saw the deep red scratches all up her back.

"Jeez, looks like you had a good weekend," she had joked, but she noticed the pained look on her mate's face as she quickly pulled her top on.

Before Shayna knew it two hours had passed by in a flash. The Uber guy must have given up and gone. She had blocked the entire world out as she read. She pulled a bottle of bourbon out of the kitchen cabinet and sat in her battered armchair with the book in her lap. The clubs would still be there tomorrow night. Maybe there was something to this voodoo shit after all? Shayna hadn't read this much in one sitting since high school.

Crazy ideas ran through her head as she flicked through the pages and sipped her bourbon. Strange notions of finding a perfect alibi to kill Kat and win Brendan back, only this time, putting a spell on the prick so he actually respected her. By the time she nodded off, Shayna was fixating on a plan.

A banging on the door snapped Shayna out of the weird and vivid dream she was having. She was walking on a dark, ornate, elevated archway above a boiling black sea. There was someone by her side and they were deep in conversation. Yet on waking, Shayna realised she could not remember a word of what was said, and what's more, she had no idea who the other person was, or what they looked like. It was as if she had been talking with a shadow in a grey colourless world.

The heavy fist on the door grew more urgent. Shayna shook the shadows out of her head and rose unsteadily to her feet, stumbling over the half-empty bottle on the floor.

"Alright, alright, I'm coming!" she said to the door as it reverberated in its frame. *Can't be the cops*, she thought. She hadn't seen her dealer in a few weeks, and it was only weed.

"What kinda time d'ya call this..." she said as she jerked the door open. Then Shayna froze, mouth agape.

Kat stumbled over the threshold, threatening to collapse in a heap.

Without hesitation, Shayna's motherly instincts kicked in and she engulfed her wayward neighbour in her arms and guided her toward the couch. "Fuck's sake, Kat, what happened?" The flaming red egg under Kat's left eye had already given her a hint as to what had transpired, but Shayna wanted to hear it in words.

She grabbed a box of tissues off the table as she eased Kat down. Then put a gentle consoling arm around her former friend's heaving shoulders. Their tatt sleeves complemented one another. She handed Kat a wad of tissues which she used to dab at her eyes.

"It's Brendan," she said. "He's...he's pissed off with another chick."

Shayna was stunned into silence. She expected to learn about the hiding Brendan had probably given Kat, was even looking forward to hearing it. But this was unexpected. It had simply never occurred to her that Brendan would treat another woman the same way he had treated her.

"Aah, luvvee," she said, pulling Kat in for a hug, swallowing down all her bile and hatred. "C'mere." Kat lay her head on Shayna"s breast and wept. When she had let it all out, Shayna grabbed a six-pack out of the fridge and solicited the whole sorry tale.

An hour later they were laughing like they used to, all their animosity forgotten. They had found some common ground again.

"Where's the kids?"

"At mum's. Aah shit, Shayna, I'm sorry, 'ey?"

"For what, luv?"

"You know…"

"Yeah, I know. It somehow doesn't seem as bad now he's done the dirty on you too."

Kat gave a lop-sided grin and winced as the taut skin pulled against her swollen eye. Her foot kicked against something and she reached down and picked up the book on demonology.

"What's this?"

Shayna shuffled across so they could spread the book on their laps. "Larissa at work gave it to me. It's got all sorts of magical shit in it. Even tells ya how ya can conjure up demons and get them to do stuff for ya."

"What sorta stuff. Like go down the seven-eleven and buy some smokes?"

That set them off again.

"No, ya silly bitch. For revenge and stuff, you know."

"Revenge?"

"Yeah." They eyeballed each other.

"You thinking what I'm thinking, Shay?"

"Yeah… But we couldn't, 'ey? It'd never work, not for chicks like us."

"Ah come on Shayna. Let's at least find out what's the go." Kat cracked open another can and the two of them sat and read through a range of demonic spells.

By the time Shayna woke from a slumber, stretched and yawned, the lounge floor was littered with empties.

She nudged a dozing Kat, who lay slumped over on the couch with drool hanging out of her open mouth. "Geez, I need to get some sleep, 'ey?" She tapped the solid cover of the text. "Let's pick this up again tomorrow."

Shayna escorted Kat to the door, hugged her and pecked her on the forehead. "Hey, before ya go, let me get a nice piece of blade steak for that shiner. Gonna be sore in the morning."

She saw Kat off down the path, both of them checking in case Brendan's ute came into view. "Hey Kat. What was the bitch's name again?"

"Jade."

"Righto, get some sleep luv. See ya tomorrow."

The following days saw Shayna and Kat pooling their resources to track down Brendan the love rat. It wasn't too hard; gossip flew around freely in their down-market suburb. Social media was always within the price range of the downtrodden—their connection to the world.

So, it was on a dark and warm evening the two women crouched in the bushes across the road from a rundown duplex. Brendan's ute conspicuous in the driveway.

When the door opened and a slight figure in a tank top and cut-off shorts pranced out to throw some empty bottles in the bin with a noisy crash, Kat had to restrain Shayna from jumping up to confront the girl.

"Lemme go. I'm gunna strangle the mole."

Kat yanked her down by the seat of her pants and gave her an incredulous look. "Don't be a farken idiot, Shayna. Carn't ya see what's happenin' here? It's HIM we need to take out, not her. This is a pattern that will just keep repeating if we don't do something."

Shayna stared open mouthed as an epiphany hit. "Aw yeah... Fuck! Ya right, Kat. I never thought of it that way. It's him who deserves to suffer for what he's done to all us women."

"Now ya getting it, Shay. And if we don't do somethin', he'll do it to her next. She's the victim here, just as much as we are."

They watched the lithe girl move back inside the duplex.

"Hey, Kat," Shayna gave her neighbour a mischievous grin, "I just had a fucken great idea."

The interior of Larissa's apartment was conspicuous by its collection of unusual religious icons. She explained the origin of a few of them to Shayna and Kat before she sat them down to listen to their tale of woe.

"Well, I dunno girls. Yeah, he sounds like a prick and he probably deserves a hiding, but conjuring up a demon is not something that should be entered into lightly."

"Yeah, but with your help..." Shayna said, sipping from the glass of cheap wine their host had offered.

"What makes you think...?"

Shayna eyeballed the rows of books on the shelves over their host's shoulder, imagining they were all about magic. "You've done it before, haven't you? I'm sure I heard ya talk about it a while ago."

Larissa swallowed. "But there's so much preparation. You chicks wouldn't understand. It takes a great force of collective will."

Shayna looked from face to face. "Yeah, but...the three of us, together."

"You have to research," Larissa continued. "It's important to pick the right demon. You have to get the mood and setting right, you need incense, candles, and they have to be the right scent and colour. You need to draw the demon's sigil."

"Squiggle?" Kat repeated.

"No, sigil. It's a magic symbol."

"Like the ones in me book?" Shayna re-filled her glass from the bottle.

"Yes, Shayna, like the ones in that book I gave you. There's more... You have to chant the name over and over, you have to focus your will. You have to recite the demon's prayer."

"What's that?" said Kat, sipping from her glass.

"I know it. It's okay."

"Far out," Shayna sighed. "Anythin' else?"

Larissa glanced toward the ceiling. The girls followed her gaze.

"Yes. You have to offer something in return...a tithe."

"A what?" Kat tabled her glass, almost spilling the contents.

"A tithe, an offering. The demon will expect something in return."

"Cripes, like what?" asked Shayna.

"That you'd have to wait and see."

"Well, what did the one you conjured up ask you for?" Kat put her empty on the table.

Larissa made a show of collecting the empty glasses. "Look, I made it up, okay?"

Kat and Shayna followed her into the kitchenette.

"Whaddya mean?" asked Shayna.

Larissa spun around. "I made it up. I never conjured up a demon, alright? It's too scary."

"Well why did ya say you did?" Kat put a restraining arm across Shayna's chest, and the three of them stood in silence in the tiny room. The only sound the rubbing of cicada wings coming through the small window.

"Shit!" Shayna broke the silence.

"So, ya can't help us then?" asked Kat.

Shayna glared at Larissa, silently goading her into a response.

"I never said that," said Larissa quietly.

"What's that?" Shayna leaned in.

"I'll help you."

Shayna beamed and punched Larissa on the arm. "Aw ya won't regret it, sister."

"I might not, but someone will," Larissa swallowed.

"Where will we..." Kat started to ask before Larissa cut her off.

"Here. In my back room. I got it mostly set up. I need to buy some stuff..." Larissa pulled another bottle of wine from the fridge and pointed it at each of them in turn. "...and youse two have to chip in."

"Right."
"Right."

Shayna slept fitfully the night before they were due at Larissa's place to conduct the ritual. She had the dream again, about the grey world and the faceless companion. This time they wandered through great cavernous buildings with winding stairwells, and then down through endless catacombs. Always passing numerous grey featureless figures, but the thing she remembered most from the dream was the complete and utter silence of the colourless void.

She shared her agitation with Kat when she picked her up in her buggered old Getz once they had dropped Kat's chattering kids off at her mum's for the night.

"Christ, Kat, me guts've been churning all day."

"Mine too." Kat lit two ciggies and passed one over to Shayna. The highway opened up before them, ill-lit, black and foreboding. They smoked in silence, lost in their own thoughts, then parked up outside Larissa's apartment block on a quiet street not far off the main road.

Shayna reached across and squeezed Kat's hand. "Well, this is it."

"Yep."

When they knocked on Larissa's door there was no answer for a long time. Shayna looked at Kat with a palpable sense of relief, and they were turning to leave when the door finally opened. Larissa ushered them in.

"Come through, girls. It's all set up."

Shayna grabbed Kat's hand again as they followed their host into the back room. They stood at the doorway and looked around. The entire space had been painted black from floor to ceiling. A large oak table sat in the middle of the room, covered in dark purple candles and burning incense, the aroma sweet and almost overbearing.

Larissa sat them down at the table and clenched her hands in front of her. "I gave it some thought. I think the demon who can…assist you with your problem is called Isacaaron. He's the demon of blind lust. I think he will fully appreciate Brendan's little problem." Larissa's eyes wandered around the room, to such an extent that Shayna began to feel uncomfortable. A shadow passed over them and the flames on the candles flittered.

"Larissa, what's going on?"

Larissa turned to the doorway, as did Shayna and Kat. The latter let out an involuntary yelp. Shayna leapt to her feet and backed against the wall.

A tall dark figure stood in the doorway observing them with abyssal eyes. He was dressed roughly in faded jeans and a battered sleeveless leather jacket. His arms were well muscled and etched completely in black ink—a range of swirling intertwining patterns, dark leaves through which grinning human skulls poked. His face was half covered in a scruffy black beard, so thick and unkempt it fully hid his mouth.

"Larissa, is that…is that him..? Did you already do the ritual… without us?

Larissa shook her head slowly. "No…no. There's not gunna be a ritual."

Kat sat and shook violently. Shayna put her hand on her friend's shoulders to try and calm her. "I don't understand."

"I told you, those rituals are too dangerous. You don't want to mess with that shit." She nodded toward the figure in the doorway. "This is Mick. He can help us."

A smile appeared amidst the hairy bristles. The lips parted. Long yellow teeth glinting in the candle light.

"Howdy."

"He's not a demon then," Kat said, finally composing herself.

"No, he's an…old friend of mine," said Larissa. "But he can help us."

"How?" Shayna asked.

Mick grinned. "Well, I can make people disappear. You might say it's my special skill."

A strange scrabbling sound filled the air, and something small and dark limped into the room, poking its head between Mick's legs. Shayna saw with some relief that it was just a mangy dog. A mutt with only three legs. A neat suture showed on its chest where the phantom limb should have sat.

"This is Zack," Mick grunted. "He's me best mate." He scratched the dog's rough head, and it responded by nuzzling and licking his thick, greasy fingers.

"Wait a minute," Kat interjected. "Are you saying you're gonna kill Brendan?"

Mick spread his arms wide. "Well, if that's what you want?" Man and dog scrutinized them.

The girls looked at each other.

"I've already paid him, with the money youse chucked in," Larissa added with finality.

"I work cheap," Mick added.

"But what if we get caught when Brendan disappears? What if they trace it to us?" Shayna asked.

Mick shook his head. "Trust me, they won't suspect you. They never do." The candles undulated in the breeze, and Shayna could see their flames reflected in Mick's eyes. For a moment she felt mesmerised, her feet nearly gave way under her. She gripped the back of the chair in front of her and shook the image out of her head.

"So, ladies," Mick looked from one to the other in turn. The dog let out a sharp yip. "Do we have a deal?" He held out his calloused paw.

After some hesitation, they each shook. The dog gave them a lop-sided grin, tongue lolling out of its mouth.

Shayna stared into the reflected eyes of Kat in the mirror as she worked on her hair in the studio. Neither of them willing to speak of the turn of events for fear of somehow implicating themselves.

Eventually, the silence got too much for Shayna to take.

"What did the papers say killed him again?"

"Hang on," said Kat, fishing around in her pocket. She retrieved a scrap of paper. "I looked it up and wrote it down… *Bal-an-i-tis*," she spelled it out, "a severe inflammation of the penis." She stifled an involuntary giggle.

Shayna slapped her gently on the head. "Fucken severe alright. He was so far up that chick, they had to cut him out of her. She's bloody lucky she survived. Poor Brendan though, 'ey?"

Kat's reflection met her gaze. "Yeah, poor Brendan."

They discussed it more openly that night at Kat's place once the kids had gone to bed. "I thought the prick said he would make Brendan disappear?"

Kat scratched an itch on her arm and shrugged. "Well, he kinda did, in a way. I mean, Brendan's gone now. Dead and buried."

"Yeah, but, Mick had nuthin' to do with it. He couldn't possibly have caused Brendan's dick to swell up like a balloon...could he?"

"I dunno," Kat shrugged again. At least they can't pin nuthin' on us. All I know is that Mick bloke promised Brendan would be gone, and now he's gone. He won't be fucking over any more chicks."

"Yeah, I guess so." Shayna paused.

"What?"

She scratched at her forearm. "I'm gonna nick off down south for a bit, Kat, go visit me mum for a while. Just until this whole thing blows over. I feel kind of weird."

"Yeah, I don't blame ya, Shay. Probably do ya good to get away for a bit. When ya leavin'?"

"Tomorrow." Shayna nodded.

Kat nodded back. She saw her neighbour off at the door. Then carefully locked it and padded back to her bedroom. She pushed the door open. Three-legged Zack sat looking up at her. Mick lay on the bed, naked, erect, hands behind his head. He winked at her.

"She gone?"

Kat was already pulling her top off. "Yeah."

Shayna wound down the window, stuck a metal CD on and cranked it up. She felt she had made the right decision to get away from the city for a bit. Even she had noticed the unnatural lull in conversation between her and Kat. Like they were suddenly keeping secrets again, like when Brendan was around.

It was true. Shayna hadn't told Kat how she found Mick and his dog on her doorstep late one night a few weeks earlier, after the Brendan thing went down. How he had talked his way into her house, then into her pants.

"Ya owe me, Shayna," he had said. "I want something in return."

Not that Shayna was complaining. She was in dire need of a good length, having hit a dry spot after Brendan. Mick gave her that and more. She was taken aback by the ferocity of his love making, and all the while, that damn three-legged dog sat and watched them. Then he was gone, just as suddenly as he had arrived. Leaving her with a warm glow, and a series of bites and welts all over her body.

That wasn't all he left behind either. She still shook her head at the uncanny turn of events, which she was itching to share with her mum. The kit she got at the chemist had confirmed it. Her eyes nearly popped out of her head when she saw it turn blue.

She had asked Doctor Rasmus how it was possible, and he had just raised his arms and shrugged.

"Sometimes, Shayna, these medical miracles do occur. The good lord smiles down upon us and shares with us his bounty."

She smiled, imagining how thrilled her mother would be to learn she was finally going to be grandma. She already knew it was going to be a boy, somehow, and she had already picked a name. It came to her in one of her dreams and stuck.

Shayna placed a hand on her belly and depressed the accelerator as the road opened up into a three-lane highway. "Just gonna be me and you, Isaac, my little man."

PROTÉGÉ

I first met Sally Burns in the summer of '07. School was finishing up, and I was set to drive my old Plymouth from Chicago State to New York. A buddy said he knew this chick who needed a ride and we could split the gas. It helped that we both originated from the South.

She was a tiny thing, I recall. Petite is the polite word I guess, with a bob of brown hair, and dark eyes. We met in the cafeteria. She wore a pair of tight jeans and was clutching a journal to her chest. A little on the chubby side but cute with it. Not quite my type, but hell, gas money is gas money. Conversation's a bonus.

"Pleased ta meet yew, ma'am. The name's Harry Deville," I said in a mock Southern drawl while dipping an imaginary hat her way. "Hell girl, if you ain't as purty as a lil pixie." Then I reverted to the more sophisticated tone my college education had afforded, and that squeezed a laugh out of her.

"Charmed ah'm sure," she said in her best Scarlett O'Hara and took the hand I proffered.

Turned out her journal was a text from her major in journalism. She was heading back to New York to start an internship with a minor newspaper. I was headed there to start a similar position in a law firm. My daddy's connections had sweetened that deal.

On the long drive we get talking and it transpires that the girl I am dating at college, Amanda, is an acquaintance of Sally's. So, we spend a good few hours dissecting my girlfriend's character from the male and female perspective. I mention that Amanda is staying on in Chicago but I have every intention of visiting her on a regular basis to maintain the relationship. This leads to another long discussion on the viability of long-distance romances. Sally opines that they don't work out in the long term. She also suggests that it isn't possible for men and women to just be friends.

"Why is that, honey?" I ask.

"Well, you know," she says all wide eyed. "Cos of the sex thing."

"The sex thing?" I feign ignorance.

"Yeah, because you men can't keep that thing in your pants is all."

"Horseshit!"

"It's true," she insists, crossing her arms over her chest. "I guess I'm an old-fashioned girl in some ways."

"Now what makes you so certain that men and women can't maintain a platonic relationship without getting all sweaty and pawing at one another?"

She steals a sideways glance at me and folds a little deeper into the seat. It seems she's about to unburden herself of something that's trying to claw its way out of her. I allow myself a little smile.

It isn't until a while later, when we pull over and sit opposite each other in the booth of a crusty old diner with the steam from two cups of fresh brew curling up over our faces that she lets it go.

She leans forward and blurts it out in a whisper.

"Couple years ago, I got raped by a man I knew."

I swirl the black stuff around in my mouth before swallowing.

"That so? And this was a guy you trusted?"

She nodded and took a sip. "Uh-huh."

"Was he your boyfriend?"

"No, sir. He was a friend of my father."

"Aha I see. Honey, can I be a little blunt?"

"I… I guess so."

I nodded and pushed on. "When you say he raped you. Do you mean rape…or was it something else, like say, seduction?"

She seemed taken aback by the question.

"It felt like he did…"

I cut in on her, like a good prosecution counsel, "Well, which was it, girl? You mean you let him have you, and you decided after the fact? Did you lead him on? Stir his blood with your innocent flesh? Were you just curious 'bout the ways of the world, huh? Maybe afterwards, when it was done, why, you found he weren't gonna sweep you off your feet and take you away to his mansion after all, huh? No sir, he just scrunched you up, another notch on his bedpost, and threw you away. Went on back to his wife and kids no doubt." I slammed my empty cup on the table, as if to say I rest my case, your honour.

Sally lowered her cup. "No…"

I had her trapped like a deer in my headlights. "Well, what did you do about it?"

She back-pedalled. "Why nothing. What could I do? He had all the power. I…I was just a stupid little girl."

"You didn't tell anybody?"

She inhaled and let out a sigh. "I told my mother."

"And?"

"She slapped my face, told me to stop telling lies… I think she believed me, but she had my daddy's reputation and position to maintain. You know how it is."

I knew how it was alright. She looked up at me with those big brown eyes and after a long pause she said, "Well?"

"Well what?"

"What do you think I should have done?"

I smiled. "You should've taken a blade to that asshole's balls. That's what you should've done. Held them up before his face and then shoved them down his throat. Christ, get a grip, take control of your life."

Now, in retrospect I admit that was perhaps not what the girl wanted to hear. Sure as Hell made the rest of the journey a mite uncomfortable. By the time we hit the big smoke we weren't saying much and did not part on the best of terms. So all things considered I thought that would be the last I ever saw of Sally Burns.

That was until that whole mess with Amanda went public.

I maintained a long distance relationship with Amanda and visited her as often as I could. But to be honest the whole affair was on the rocks well before she disappeared. The police kicked in my door to ask me a few questions. Questions like *who put the seventeen stab wounds in her and sodomised the body after she was killed?* That type of thing. Stands to reason the boyfriend or husband is always the major suspect, and I understood that with my background in law. Did they honestly believe me the kind of monster that could do that to another human being? I loved her for Chrissakes! Thankfully my profession also gave me a good grounding in building a case for the defence.

The trial went on all through summer, and it was while I was sitting in court that I spotted Sally up in the press section hunched over a laptop. I acted like I hadn't seen her so she never knew I was watching her watch me, but she was there for the entire duration, right up to my acquittal.

Once again, I thought that was that until one day a year later. I'm loitering around the news stand at La Guardia waiting to catch a flight up-state to defend a con-artist when I hear a voice calling my name. I turn around and there's Sally standing before me looking all grown up and a little svelte too.

"Thought it was you," she says.

I give her a good look up and down and revert to stereotype. "Well, lookit yew, honey, all growed up and pretty."

We swing by a tavern and catch up over a beer or two. I tell her about Helen, my fiancée, and she tells me about her latest beau.

"You might even know him, Harry, Randy Pepsacone from back at Chicago State?"

"The college ball player?"

"One and the same."

I whistled. "Sure you know what you're doing? As I recall it that boy had a mean streak a mile wide."

She looked down at her brew and whispered, "Don't I know it."

We talk a little about Helen, and she professed her surprise that I would ever settle down. We touch on the Amanda case and I pretend to be none the wiser about her covering the story for her paper. I swing the conversation back around to Randy, and then godammit if I don't mess up again by telling Sally to take control of her life and grow a set. I even offer to give her some relationship advice, which is about as welcome as a crack whore knocking on your door and telling your wife she wants the money you owe her.

I thought that was it for sure with Sally, but two years later I'm walking out of a drugstore and just about bump heads with her. This time she's looking very slender, her hair is longer and peroxide blonde. I notice she's taken to smoking these long menthol cigarettes which can't be good for her health. After a couple of minutes' persuasion, she agrees to accompany me to a nearby coffee shop.

We discuss our previous relationships, hers with Randy and my engagement to Helen, and how they ended. Later when we take a stroll out along by the Hudson, I notice Sally's more confident poise. I can see from her stance that she's got something to reveal, so I wait for her to light up another menthol and spill her guts, which she does through a mouthful of smoke.

"So, I took your advice, Harry."

"What advice was that, darlin'?"

"I decided to take control of my life like you said."

"No kidding? Well good for you, girl. You look better for it too."

"I do?"

"Yeah, ya know, you look more self-assured."

I got to admit I'm intrigued by this new version of Sally. So, I persuade her to keep in touch and we swap numbers.

"Just friends you mean, no funny business?"

I raise my hands in self-defence. "Platonic, like I always said."

And that was that. We had phone conversations, the occasional dinner. All the while we maintained our romantic liaisons with other people. As time passed I noticed that Sally's once divergent views on love and sex were now more conversant with my own. Hell, we got to be such good friends that we set each other up with a couple of mutual acquaintances. Cindy and Jeff were their names. We even double dated. Everything seemed swell, until one night I get a call from Sally. I can tell she's been crying from the tone of her voice.

"It's Jeff and Cindy, Harry… I think they're having an affair."

This was news to me. I'd been dating Cindy over three months. Then again, I didn't have a woman's intuition.

"Don't you care, Harry? She's your girl."

"Sure, sure, of course I care, honey. I'm as upset as you are. Just a little shocked is all. Listen, I'm coming over there right now, okay?"

"Okay."

I was close to boiling by the time I got to her apartment, but experienced enough to reign it in and think it through. I hugged Sally and calmed her down. Sat her down on the couch and handed her the cell phone.

"Okay, honey, this is what I want you to do. Call Jeff and act as if nothing is wrong, ask him to come over."

She looked up at me with those big wide eyes and started tearing up again.

"But Harry…"

"Trust me, Sally. This is the best way to go. We'll both confront him."

She put the phone down.

"No, Harry, you don't understand. I already called Jeff. He's in the other room."

This time I have to admit she threw me. I looked down the hallway.

"He's already here, in your bedroom?"

She nodded. I took her by the hand and led her into the bedroom, and lo and behold, there's Jeff, sitting in an armchair, arms and legs trussed up with gaffer tape. I smiled at him.

"Hey, Jeff. Long time, no see."

Jeff's eyes rolled around in their sockets then widened in recognition. He gave me a look of desperation tinged with gratitude like the cavalry had just arrived. Sweat poured down his brow over the ball gag in his mouth, and he thrust at his bindings, trying to tip the chair over onto the roll of plastic sheeting Sally had laid over the floorboards. *Clever girl*. I turned to her.

"Now how did a little thing like you get ol' Jeff here in such a compromising position?"

She smiled and produced a small packet from her jeans pocket. "I slipped him a roofie, Harry. Been done to me before. Now I'm turning the tables."

"Well, shoot, this looks like a bit of a pickle, honey. What are you gonna do now?"

That's when Sally picked up the kitchen knife from her dresser and held it up toward me. Jeff damn near had an aneurism. I waved her away.

"Christ no, honey, don't go at him with that. What the hell are you thinking?"

Sally looked downcast. Jeff heaved a sigh of relief

"I...I'm sorry, Harry. I'm just not thinking straight."

"Damn straight, girl. You won't make a scratch with that thing. Use this instead."

I whipped out my trusty hunting knife from the holster secreted inside my coat and handed it to her, hilt first. I swear the girl's eyes about lit up the room.

"Oh Harry. It's beautiful."

She caressed the thing like a newborn infant.

I lay back on her bed and folded my hands behind my head. "Mind if I watch?"

She looked apprehensive. Jeff looked ready to shit his pants.

"You don't mind, Harry? You wanna join in?"

"Hell no. Knock yourself out, girl. It's your show... Word of advice though."

"What's that, Harry?"

"Take your time, girlie. Enjoy the moment. Don't go at it like a bull at a gate. Carve your name in that fucker, make sure he feels every last bit of it."

Sally approached her lover with the reverence of a Satanic initiate at their first black mass. She used the tip of my knife to pick the buttons off Jeff's shirt one by one. The shirt fell open to reveal the flesh of his torso. Jeff tensed up in anticipation much like I did. He shook his head, moaning behind the gag, tears running down his cheeks. I felt my cock grow hard in my pants.

Sally started to carve grooves into Jeff's body like a butcher's apprentice. He was screaming into the gag. I was up and across there in an instant, my hand eased over hers. "Easy, honey. Take your time." She flashed a look up at me, smiling hesitantly. I felt her gaze drop toward the bulge in my pants. "You're an artist now, girl. Shut the fuck up, Jeff!" I kicked him in the leg.

"Like this, Harry?" she whispered, drawing the blade across Jeff's abdomen, causing a flood of intestine to pour forth in a bloody stream. Jeff looked at his own unravelling guts with a sense of wonder. I could see him straining at the tape, trying to free his arms so he could push all that viscera back in, like a GI in 'nam who just stepped on a mine.

"Oh, God, yes, honey," I hissed back at her.

Later I helped her bundle what was left of Jeff into the trunk of my car. Told her I knew just the place to get rid of the body. Just had the one shovel in the trunk but we could take turns. On the ride out toward the boondocks I notice Sally had gone a little quiet. I knew she was stewing on something.

"Well?"

"Well, what, Harry?"

"Come on, girl. I know you're just itching to spit it out. Don't hold out on me now."

She shifted in her seat, stubbed her menthol out on the dash, squished the butt and threw it out the window.

"It's just... How is it, Harry, that you know a good place to bury a body?

I smiled. The cat was out of the bag at last.

"Ah shoot, honey. Can you keep a secret in that pretty little head of yours?"

She glanced back toward the trunk.

"I think we're way past that stage now, Harry."

Had to admit she had a point.

"I killed Amanda."

She let out a laugh.

"You find that amusing?"

She pulled another cigarette from the pack on the dash and lit up.

"No, it's not that, Harry. It's just that I always suspected you did."

"Does it bother you?"

"Hell no. I never liked that bitch anyway. No doubt she had it coming. Besides, your defence was brilliant."

I swelled up at that. "I pride myself on my work, honey."

"I swear Harry, when I saw you up on the stand, and I thought about what you did to that girl, it kind of excited me. Made me all tingly downstairs, you know."

I let that one swill around in my gut for a while.

The unravelling dawn was just threatening the last stars when we got back to Sally's apartment and parked the car. We went upstairs and stood in her bedroom facing each other, all covered in mud and filth and blood.

"Tell me how it felt, when you watched me up there on the stand in court."

"You wanna shower first, Harry?"

"No."

I pounced on Sally and wrestled her onto the bed. I tore her sopping blouse clean off, the buttons flew across the room, clattering across the wooden floor. Then godammit if she didn't scratch and claw and bite and force her way right back on top of me. As she lowered herself upon me she let out a predatory growl. My mind flashed back to the image of my hand sliding over hers on the knife as we carved into warm flesh together.

When we woke up the sun was high in the sky and forcing its way through the shades right into our faces. We didn't speak as we showered. I put on some of Jeff's clothes out of her closet. We exchanged pleasantries as she made us coffee and soon after that I left.

For the next two weeks I didn't call Sally and she didn't call me. It was almost like the sex had spoiled it, ruined a good friendship. But it was more than that. I think we both realised we had given away an incriminating secret, something each of us would have preferred to take to the grave. A secret shared can be a major burden. I went back to Cindy. She even asked me if I had seen Jeff around. She was good, I'll give her that.

Soon enough Sally came knocking at my door. I let her in and she sat herself down on my couch with that look on her face again. I fixed us a drink, scotch and water, set them down on the coffee table.

She took a sip and let out a deep sigh.

"Christ. Whatever it is that's gnawing on you girl, let it go."

"I can't take it, Harry. I can't take all the lies. I can't stand being so alone. Sometimes I feel like turning myself in."

I took a sip of whisky, felt the knife pressing against my ribs, resisting the urge to reach for it.

"Now come on Sally, honey. Let's not be rash. Let's think this through. We both have a lot to lose here."

She started to tear up, sitting there, looking all lost and small, like that little girl I first met in college.

"I can't do it by myself, Harry. I just can't!"

I sat and put my arm around her. "You don't have to do it alone. Not anymore. I'm here. Harry's here for you, baby."

I turned her pretty face up to mine and kissed her. She kissed me back.

I wiped her tears away with the back of my hand. "Let me let you in on a big ol' secret, girl. This whole world is a game park, full of prey, and a few of us are the hunters."

She sniffed. "If…if we're gonna make this work, you're gonna have to get rid of Cindy."

I smiled and took her by the hand and led her outside to the garage. I popped the trunk of the faithful old Plymouth, let her peer inside at Cindy's body, trussed to the neck in plastic wrap. Sally squealed with delight, clapping her hands.

I walked over to my tool-rack, which hung along the wall of the garage on neatly arranged hooks. She stood looking into the trunk with her back to me.

"I killed Randy," she said over her shoulder.

"Yeah? What did you do with the body?"

"I cut it up and threw the bits in the East River."

I snorted. "Smart thinking, cops would have put it down as another mob killing."

I lifted the item I was looking for off a hook, turned back toward her.

"I offed Helen too," I confessed. "She was a royal pain in the ass."

I stood behind her. She didn't turn, just kept looking down at Cindy's body. Then she reached down and smoothed a wisp of hair back off the corpse's forehead.

"I'm glad you did, Harry… There's one more thing I need to tell you."

I raised my arms and stopped dead, a sudden sharp pain clawing at my guts. Several thoughts ran through my head and they all arrived at…the Rohypnol. Damn this girl was good. I swallowed.

"What's that, honey?"

"Jeff and Cindy weren't having an affair. I made that up because I wanted you for myself. I hope you can forgive me."

She turned around and reached for the shovel, grabbing it from me as I fell to my knees.

"Damn you're a cold bitch, Sally," I grunted before collapsing in a heap.

"I know, sugar," she said.

I lay on the cool concrete, helpless as a babe. I heard the sound of a lighter firing up and the scent of menthol permeated the air.

"How…how the hell did you spike me?" I flicked my tongue across my lips, finding it difficult to form words, and was it just my imagination or godammit was I hard again?

"Oh hush now, Harry. You rest up. We got some driving to do." Her voice seemed to come from a distance.

I heard the shovel being thrown into the trunk, then felt two strong little hands grab me under my arms.

"Damn you, Harry," a sweet voice breathed into my ear. "Now I gotta dig two holes."

OINTMENT

Cody Wyatt sat on a park bench overlooking the river, watching her breath condense in front of her face. She tried to convince herself it was too cold to be out. It was a bad idea. She should just walk away now. She belched and the hint of ethanol on her breath told her otherwise. She rubbed her bleary eyes, half raw from drink, the other half her angry tears. She knew she was in for the long hall. Too late to turn back.

Try as she might Cody could not stop her brain re-visiting that awful grey afternoon. Bursting into the house, shopping bags under each arm. Calling out to Nikki to get downstairs and give her a hand. Putting stuff away and her ears gradually tuning in to the sound underneath her daughter's teenage music, the spatter of running water.

Anxious, taking the stairs two at a time as the first wave eased over the top of the stairs. Calling Nikki's name more urgently, bad thoughts flooding her mind. Slamming the bathroom door open to find the body slumped over in the tub and...all that blood.

Cody stopped balling her hands into fists just before her own nails began to draw blood.

"Jane?"

At first she didn't respond, then she remembered the name she had given. Cody looked up at the man standing over her.

"Jesus! You look like shit, lady." He sat beside her, uninvited. He was skinnier than she had imagined. Salt and pepper cropped hair dotted his scalp. Dark, hawkish eyes flitted around, looking everywhere but at her. The accent she couldn't place. It was either Irish or Scots, she could never tell the difference.

"You're not exactly beauty pageant material yourself," she said, pulling her cigarettes from a coat pocket and shaking one loose. She lit up with a shaking hand. "Do you mind?"

"It's a free world. They're your lungs," he said, shaking his head. Cody saw droplets of ice formulating on his close-cropped scalp. She wanted to brush them off.

"You look a bit thin for this sort of business," she said, taking a lungful of tar deep inside her chest and savouring it. "I expected you to be more…robust. If you don't mind me saying."

He snorted and spoke sotto voice. "Lady, you got it all mixed up. I'm just the messenger. The delivery boy. The perpetrators of this sort of deal don't do their negotiating in person. Christ. *They're* not fucking stupid. Just like Jane isn't your real name, unless you are?"

Cody blew a plume of smoke out of her nostrils. "So, why was I asked to come here?"

"Cos I got something for you. Something you need, and the sooner we get down to it, the sooner we can get out of this shitty weather, and you can get back to drowning yourself in booze."

"Fuck you!"

He smiled. "So, down to business. You contacted a certain person, and that person put you onto another person, and so on until you reached an associate of mine…"

"It was a friend of a friend…"

He waved her away. "It doesn't matter who did what or who said what. Just listen, okay?"

Cody nodded, sucked her cigarette down to the filter and tossed it aside. Her brain ached for the next drink, anything to blot it all out.

He paused as a jogger, young and male, pounded past them, turning to check them out. Cody guessed they looked like any forty something couple. He closeted in dark garb and a thick coat, the stubble on his chin matching that on his head. She caught the young man's eye for an instant and read his disdain at her bloated face and puffy eyes. Her long red hair swept messily away from her forehead, showing tinges of grey where, in the lingering malaise brought on by her grief, she had neglected to keep up her grooming.

As the runner disappeared around a bend he continued his story. "Your tale of despair reached the right ears. A certain person is sympathetic to your plight, and offers the ready solution to the retribution you seek."

Cody coughed and cleared her throat. "So, what happens now, Mr...?"

"No names." He reached inside his coat and withdrew a small khaki holdall, from which he lifted a little plastic container.

"What's that?"

He passed her a slip of paper. "If you would just forward the deposit to the account number written there."

"Now?"

He nodded.

Cody pulled out her mobile and did as he instructed. He smiled as she clicked *send*.

"The balance falls due as soon as our little matter is attended to, and you return the item to me." He tapped the transparent plastic container. Cody could see something small flitting around inside it. A black moving speck. He handed it across to her. She held it in her lap.

"Don't open it here," he said.

"It looks like a school lunchbox." She cackled, which became a rasping cough.

He ignored the comment. "Listen carefully to what I'm about to tell you."

Cody inspected the container. "...Is it a fly?" She went to lift the corner of the lid, and was surprised by the suddenness of his response, the ferocious grip on her wrist.

"Do not open it here."

"Jesus! Alright. What is it?"

He turned his dark eyes on her. "Are you familiar with the Curse of the Pharaohs?"

She looked puzzled. "I guess so. I've seen enough old movies."

He lowered his voice even further. "What you hold in your

hands is a plague worse than the ancient prophesies."

Cody flushed. "Are you kidding me? It is a fly, isn't it? Ten-fucking-grand to lease a house fly."

"Your daughter was tormented to the point of suicide. Am I correct?" He cut her short.

Cody's breath caught in her throat. "Yes... I found her in the bathtub."

He avoided her gaze. "I know how these things go. These days, our tormenters cannot just reach us in person. They have learned to use new technologies to oppress us twenty-four hours a day."

"They were relentless. On Facebook, Twitter, Instagram. I didn't know until it was too late... The police showed me." Cody spat the words with venom. "Telling her...she was worthless, ugly, that she should kill herself. Posting doctored images of her."

He glanced at her. "There was one ringleader in particular. There always is."

Cody shook another cigarette from the pack and lit up. "Yeah. Danny Grimes. They suspended him—"

"He was involved with your daughter."

"They suspended him!" Cody said with bitter emphasis. "Can you believe it? My kid fucking dies, and he gets a suspension."

"We did our research. Relationship gone bad. She gives him the flick. He posted those pictures online, even if it couldn't be proven. Family ties. Legal obfuscation. Slap on the wrist. It's not enough, is it?"

She studied the glowing tip of her cigarette. Pictured grinding it into Danny Grimes' eye. "He deserves to suffer."

"So, you sought out my associate, and here we are." He looked at the object in her lap.

Cody held up the container. The thing inside made small clicking noises as it bounced off the walls. "What is this exactly?"

"It is what you seek: vengeance. Are you prepared for the consequences?"

"Do I have a choice? I've come this far. So, what do I do with it?"

"All you need do is get yourself within a few feet of the one you wish to punish and open the lid. It will do the rest."

"That's it?"

"Yes."

"How do I get it back in the box?"

"It will return when the job is done, don't worry. Now if you don't mind, I'd like to get out of this pissing weather."

He stood up to leave, turning up his collar. "Hey!"

He turned. "Yeah?"

She swallowed. "Will he suffer?"

"Oh yes. They all suffer."

She sat and watched him walk away, finishing her smoke.

Cody sat in her bedroom, the television blathered quietly behind her, her only companion. The house was cold and empty. All she had left from a broken marriage. The bottle sat inviting on the dresser next to her cigarettes. The mobile phone signal flickered in her hands. She dialled.

"Hello?"

"It's done."

"… I hope you get what you want."

"Rach?"

"Yeah?"

"Thanks for pointing me in the right direction. I mean it."

A snort came down the line. "Yeah, forget it. When you move in the circles that I do, you meet all sorts. So, what happens to Grimes? When do they…and how? Did they say?"

Cody poured a draft from the bottle and told Rachel about the fly. When she finished, the bottle was dry.

"What happened? How did you get close enough?"

"I tailed him around the city. He didn't notice. He was wrapped up in his own world. Funny thing…"

"What?"

"Well, he just seemed kind of lost, empty, alone… I've never seen anyone so alone."

"He deserves it."

"Yeah…I know. It just wasn't how I pictured is all. I imagined him surrounded by friends, laughing at getting away with it.

Enjoying my suffering. But instead, he looked haunted. I almost didn't go through with it."

"But you did."

Cody reached for her smokes, gripped the pack. Fought back the cravings. "I waited for the right moment. He went into a food hall, like he was looking for a crowd. Just to be surrounded by humanity. I followed, took the next table. Made sure he had his back to me. I lifted the container out of my bag. I opened it and the thing came out. It looked like a regular fly."

"So, what happened?"

"Well, it flew out and buzzed around my table for a minute, circling. It was kind of weird."

"How?"

"Well for a few seconds it stopped dead, right in front of my face, and it hovered there, and it looked right at me."

There was a pause until the voice came back down the line "Right."

"Like it was examining me. Then it flew right across to the other table and landed on his ear."

"Did he notice?"

"Oh, yeah. He brushed it off, but it came right back. It landed on his ear, his nose, it just kept coming. He was waving his arms around. People started to notice, and they were laughing, pointing, making comments behind their hands. After several minutes of this, he totally lost it. He started yelling and stabbing at the thing with his fork. Made a real scene. I quietly moved away."

"So, it's working then?"

"I guess."

"So, you wanna go out this weekend?"

"Out? Me?"

"Yeah you. All due respect, honey. You can't mope around forever."

"Gee, Rach, I don't know if I'm ready."

"Look at us, Cody. Couple of washed-up spinsters and we haven't hit fifty yet. One bad marriage apiece. Trust me, we can't afford to be picky. Especially you. After Sean."

The words Rachel left out cut deep. Cody winced, but she knew it was true, and only her best friend could get away with dragging it up.

"Yeah, alright. I'll go out with you. Do me good to get out of this place."

"That's the spirit. So, where is the fly now?"

"Well, the container is empty. I guess it's still with him."

Danny cursed and climbed off Mrs Duxton. His neighbour recoiled, closing her legs and swatting the buzzing insect away from her face. "How did that thing get in here? Did you leave the window open again?"

"No," He sat on the edge of the bed, bathed in sweat. When he heard the fly buzzing in his ear he swore and batted it away.

Roslyn sat up and reached for her cigarettes, lit up. "Damn that fly. I was just about there." She blew a plume of smoke and the fly buzzed through it. "I thought they bloody died in winter."

"Not this one." He snatched the smoke out of her hand and took a drag. The fly landed on his face. He flinched and stabbed at it with the hot tip of the cigarette.

"Hey." She reached for it.

Danny got up. "Gotta take a piss."

Roslyn watched as the young man stomped out of the room. The fly following like a puppy dog. "That's too weird," she said to the empty room. She glanced at the dresser, saw her husband's photo eyeballing her, reached across and turned it over.

In the bathroom, Danny sighed as he emptied his bladder while it flitted about his head. He looked at all of Roslyn's make up and medications dotting the cabinet shelves. He stood in front of the mirror, examining his bloodshot eyes. She was twice his age, but just as lonely as he was. A husband who no longer cared and often worked away. This is what he had come to. A long way down since Nikki.

The fly buzzed across his face, and somehow he knew.

It was the same damn fly.

It had been five days straight that fly had been following him around.

After the mall it followed him to the bottle shop, causing him to drop and smash a bottle he had to pay for.

It trailed him to work. Tormented him all through his shift. Even flipping burgers is hard with an insect buzzing around your head. Sanjib, the night manager wasn't too impressed either.

"Can't have that thing in my restaurant," he said.

Yet no matter how many times they chased it out the door the bloody thing came back and landed on Danny again.

"Is that your bloody pet?" an exasperated Sanjib said.

In the end Danny was sent packing two hours early. First the damn thing cost him money he badly needed, now it was impeding his sex life.

Noticing the sudden absence of insectoid drone, Danny looked around for the fly. He was distracted by Roslyn's voice, calling him back to the bedroom. He strode toward the sound on a wave of desire, his cock growing more rigid with every step.

When he entered the room his eyes widened. She lay spreadeagled before him, teasing herself with lacquered fingers.

"You dirty bitch!" Danny groaned and moved toward her. She gazed between his legs, and her smile turned into a scream.

He looked down to see the fly perched on the tip of his glans, like an unwelcome cancerous growth.

Roslyn leapt to her feet and started grabbing his discarded clothes and throwing them at him. "That's it, I've lost the urge now."

"But Ros," he protested. "Can't we just finish?"

"No thanks," she said, tugging a bra over her breasts. "You piss off and play with your friend. You seem well acquainted."

Danny looked down his nose as he felt it disappear up his nostril. He waved his arms and snorted, and the fly came out on a trail of mucus.

"Gross, Daniel. Go home and take a fucking shower or something. My hubby's coming home in a couple of days anyway... Maybe we should call it quits."

"What about when he buggers off for work again?"

Her silence was all the answer he needed. He swept the fly away and pulled on his pants. "So, that's it? You're dumping me?"

Roslyn stood up, started straightening the bed. "Don't sound so surprised, hon. We both knew this was a short-term thing."

It didn't make Danny feel any better to know she was right. He pulled his shirt over his head and sneered. "Yeah, well who needs you, you old slut!"

"Get out, Daniel!"

"I'm going, bitch."

It got worse over the next few weeks. He couldn't do anything without his constant companion buzzing in his ear. Couldn't eat, couldn't work. Even Roslyn told him to sling his hook. Danny got to thinking that it wasn't much fun being tormented

Cody saw Rachel waiting at a table in the quiet café. She smoothed down her hair. Popped a mint in her mouth. She saw Rach's face drop as she sat.

"Jesus, Cody, you're as white as a ghost. What happened?"

Cody stuck her mobile phone in front of Rachel without a word. Her friend's eyes narrowed as she took in the picture and headline on the screen. She picked it up. "What's this?"

"He's dead."

Rachel read as she talked. "Who's dead?"

"Danny Grimes."

"No!" The words on the screen gave the lie to Rachel's words. "Suicide?"

"That's what they say, but was it?"

Rachel kept her eyes glued to the online article. "It says he ran onto the road right in front of a speeding car."

"Like he was being chased. Keep reading."

"Yeah." She handed the phone back and looked into Cody's pale face and lowered her voice. "So, he killed himself. Isn't that what you wanted?"

"I didn't think it would go this far."

"Oh, come on, Cody. Yes, you did. It's exactly what you wanted."

"Rach, we murdered him."

"Don't be stupid. We did nothing. He did it to himself. Besides, you did it, not me."

"You put me onto those people."

Rachel's gaze swept around the empty café. "Because it was killing you. I wanted to help you." Rachel reached out and put her hand on Cody's arm. "Cody, it's over. You got what you wanted. Just let it go now. Nikki's been gone five years. Move on.

Cody chewed on her lip, slowly withdrew the plastic container from her bag and placed on the table. Rachel saw the thing flitting around inside and looked around in panic.

"Don't bring that fucking thing out here," she hissed. "Get rid of it."

"I thought you could take it back."

"Me? You're kidding."

"You're in this just as deep as me."

Rachel pushed the object back across the table at Cody. "Oh no, you're not dragging me into this." She stood up, the chair scraping across the floor. "I can't fucking believe you, Cody. Get a grip. Don't call me."

Cody watched her friend walk away. She grabbed the container and put it back in her bag. Her mobile buzzed. The flicked the screen across. An anonymous message gave a familiar rendezvous.

Cody was still distracted when she got home. She put her bag on the table, went to the kitchen cupboard and poured herself a drink. She went upstairs and changed. The sound of a police siren made her rush to the window. She flicked the blind open to see the lights flash by up the street, felt a tinge of relief. Maybe Rachel was right. She didn't kill Grimes. They'd never pin it on her. All the same, she couldn't sleep with that thing in the house. She'd be glad to see the back of it.

Cody slipped off her shoes, went back downstairs to the kitchen. She lit a cigarette and stood by the window, deep in thought. By the time she noticed the subtle change in the atmosphere it was too late. She failed to notice the figure lurking behind the door.

"Cody."

She wheeled around in shock to be confronted by her ex-husband.

"What the hell are you doing here? You're not allowed." She backed away, her brave façade crumbling as all the old fear came flooding back.

Sean's face creased in a smile. "Just got back into town. Thought I'd come and see my house. Why is it such a mess? Don't you fucking clean?"

"It's my place now, Sean."

"And what's this?" He picked up the bottle. "Jesus, you've let yourself go, girl. When did you start smoking?"

"None of your business."

"You know I hate that smell."

Cody blew smoke toward him. "You're off your head."

Sean's eyes glazed over. He reached out and grabbed Cody by the hair. "Don't talk to me like that!"

"Get off!"

He dragged her across to the sink, stooping to pick her dropped cigarette off the floor. The sink was full of dirty water and a few dishes. "You wanna smoke. I'll show you what I think of that." He tried to cram the smoke in her mouth but ended up stubbing it out on her face. He yanked her head down into the water. Turned the faucet. Cody kicked and yelled.

"This is what you get, bitch, when you give me lip."

The words were muffled by the water pouring into her ears. Cody felt her strength waning, until it occurred to her that it might be better for everyone if she just let go. She stopped resisting, but just as she felt herself drifting away, the pressure on the back of her head dissipated.

She pulled her head out of the tepid water, coughing and gasping for air. She looked around. Sean was gone. Cody felt her legs go and she slid to the floor, sobbing.

Her cheek still stung from the cigarette burn as she sat on the same park bench on Saturday afternoon. Every step made her wince, but through make up and will power she dragged herself across town to keep the appointment.

Stubble man was already waiting this time. He eyeballed her as he sat down.

"Jane. Nice to see you again."

"Cut the shit. What sort of game are you playing here?"

He looked perplexed. "I'm not sure what you mean?"

"You know exactly what I mean. I asked you to help me exact revenge on Grimes. I never said I wanted you to kill him!"

"I didn't kill him. He did it to himself, aided by our little friend. Besides which, you asked for retribution, but you never insisted what form it should take."

"Don't try and turn this around on me." Cody yanked the container out of her bag and thrust it at him. "I never said I wanted him dead, for fuck's sake!"

He shrugged. "I say you got just what you wished for."

"You can keep the money, just take this monstrosity back."

"What happened to your face?"

"I'm fine."

He shook his head. "That foundation barely disguises it. Maybe you had a visit from someone you didn't want to see."

"What would you know?"

He smiled. "More than you think."

She thrust the container at him again. "Are you going to take this thing back?"

"No. I'm not."

"What?"

"I think we both know what happens next. Our deal isn't complete yet. In fact, we may need to extend it a little."

Cody felt a cold wind pass through her. She saw herself take out her phone. Then she saw herself log onto her account and send another down payment.

He watched her do it, then rose to his feet. "Have a nice day. We'll meet again."

Cody lit a cigarette. Her hands were shaking.

She knew she was taking a huge risk following Sean into the bar. She recalled it was one of his favourite haunts. Fortunately it was busy enough for her to slip in unnoticed and find a place in the shadows toward the back. Cody spent an hour nursing a drink, hating the atmosphere, loathing the merry banter. Watching her ex shooting the breeze with his obnoxious buddies. There were streamers and balloons around his table. She remembered it was his birthday. She just wanted to get back to her cold empty house and shut the world out.

Finally, when the Dutch courage kicked in, and she was sure Sean and his friends had drunk enough to throw them off their guard, Cody stood up on uncertain legs. She pulled the container from the carry bag under the table and slipped across the crowded, dimly lit bar.

When he suddenly wheeled around on her Cody was shocked into a stupor. She froze. He sneered. "What, thought you could sneak up on me, wifey?" He laughed, his mates joining in. "I saw you creep in here over an hour ago. Wondered what the fuck you were up to. Thanks for not calling the cops on me the other week. So, what is it? Can't get enough of me, eh?"

His mocking tone snapped Cody out of her state of shock, and she stuck the container in front of his face and went to lift the lid.

"The fuck is that?" Before she could react he smacked it out of her hands and sent it spinning across the room. It hit the edge of a table and fell to the ground, the lid jarring loose in the process.

Nobody but Cody noticed something small and dark fly up into the air. Then a strong fist closed on her wrist and jerked her around.

"Well, what the hell are you doing here?" Sean yelled into her face. A bouncer made his way toward them.

As he spoke, a small black object flew right into his open mouth. Sean let go of her arm and took a step back. He hacked and coughed and managed to dislodge the fly. It buzzed around his head, looking for a place to land.

Cody forced a smile. "I just wanted to say, happy birthday honey. I got you something."

Before he could respond, she strode away from the bar, stooping to collect the empty container. Sean looked at his friends, then started after her, but something buzzed inside his ear. He stopped to scratch at it.

Outside in the cold night air, Cody watched him through the window. Then she turned and walked away.

BLACK VINE

"Start at the beginning, Jim. Let me get my head around it."

Jim Donahue took a breath and looked at the motley bunch of survivors dotted around the old church. Bob Baxter, the local police Sergeant and the town's only surviving copper, pulled a mini recorder from his top pocket.

"Ya mind, Jim? This might be useful down the track."

Donahue took a deep breath and sat down on a pew. The congregation drew closer to listen.

"Okay, um, as I remember it…me and Pete Hannigan was out looking for roos. We always go roo shooting on a Saturday evening. So, we're out on Hangman's Plain just east of town, when in the distance up on the ridge, we spot something glinting in the setting sun. It almost made me lose control of the truck."

Jim paused to drain a plastic cup of ice-cold water Liz Squires, the young barmaid from the pub, had thoughtfully set down for him. They watched him swallow, the Adam's apple in his wiry neck bobbing like a cork.

"Pete wanted to phone it in, but curiosity got the better of me. I insisted we check it out. As we get a bit closer, we see it's a big four-wheel drive, parked up right on the edge, overlooking Dead Gully Gorge. We make out the silhouette of someone inside at the wheel.

"Pete looks at me and I toot the horn. Try and get the driver's attention…nuthin'. So, we drive up there and pull alongside."

Jim paused again and put his head in his hands. His audible sobs were the only sound echoing around the high walls and stained glass for the next few minutes. Jesus looked down on the small congregation from his perch. Baxter rubbed Jim's back.

"Take ya time, mate. I know it's not easy."

Baxter cast his eye around the holy place dotted with the town's ragtag survivors. The big wide doors blocked as best they could with the materials at hand.

"This town's gone to Hell," he said to no one in particular, though his eyes met Father Brian's.

Jim pulled the truck up next to the four-wheel drive. The vehicle looked in good nick, fairly new. It was coloured a pristine white. That was what had caught the waning sun and dazzled them on the dirt road down below.

Pete shielded his eyes and looked though the side window.

"There's a bloke in there, mate... Shit!"

"What is it?" Jim strained to see across Pete.

"He's slumped over the steering wheel, Jim. Bugger! Ya reckon he's...?"

Jim killed the engine.

"Ah, fuck. Well, he hasn't moved since we pulled up. We better take a closer look."

They got their answer as soon as Pete opened the vehicle's door. The stench of death rocked them back on their heels.

"Jesus! Been there a couple of days I reckon." Pete slammed the door shut again.

Jim shielded his eyes and looked in the passenger side window. "Suicide?"

"Looks it."

"You see a gun? What did he use?"

They looked for signs of gunshot wound or knife marks, until Pete blinked and cleared his throat.

He cracked the door open again, covering his nose with his hand. He grabbed the dead man by the shoulder and pulled him back against the seat.

"Awww!" Jim made a choking sound.

Pete slammed the door shut on the terrible sight, spat a wad of bile into the dirt and wiped his mouth. "Judging by the marks around his throat, and the way his tongue's stickin' out. Looks like he was strangled."

"By who?"

"Buggered if I know."

"Doesn't make sense," said Jim. "You can't strangle yourself, can you?"

Pete cast his gaze across the ravine.

"Great view, I guess. Nice place to bid the world farewell."

"You know him?"

"Nup. Out of towner."

Staring across the gorge, trying to avoid looking at the corpse, a subtle movement caught Jim's eye.

"What the hell is that?"

He pointed downward to a spot on the opposite rock face. At the opening of a dark cave, something dark and spiderlike crawled out of the wide opening. Long black tendrils snaked forward from the darkness, crawling along the face of the rocks. Several appendages raised themselves off the surface and probed the air. A couple of them seemed to point toward the two men.

"Bugger me," said Jim. As if responding to the sound of his voice, the fingers retracted backwards and disappeared into the dark fissure again.

Pete clamped both hands around his ears. His knees buckled slightly.

"Pete? You okay?"

He straightened up again and shook his head.

"Yeah mate, I just got this weird...buzzing in my ears. Thought I was gunna black out for a sec there."

Pete looked at Jim. "Mate?"

"What?"

"Your nose."

Jim instinctively brushed his hand across his nose. It came back wet and red.

"Damn! Nosebleed. Ain't had one since I was a kid."

"It's a gusher, mate."

Sure enough, the trickle of blood quickly became a stream. Jim pulled a hanky from his breast pocket and dabbed at it. The flow quickly receded back to a trickle again.

"Seems to be stopping now," he said.

"We should call this in. Get the cops up here to clean up." Pete pulled out his mobile, held it up to the sky.

"No service."

Jim did the same. "Me either."

Pete shook his phone.

They both turned toward the cave.

Jim shoved his phone back in his pants. "This bloke ain't going anywhere. I reckon we should drive over there and check out that cave."

"Now? Can't it wait?"

"Nup. I wanna know what that thing was. I know that cave. It's accessible by foot. Kids used to go there, back when kids was curious about stuff that wasn't on a screen."

"Righto, mate. If ya think we should."

They jumped in the truck, Pete behind the wheel, and headed back down and around the other side of the ravine. Jim dabbed at his nose.

"I sometimes forget you didn't grow up here, Pete. You moved out here, what when you was about thirty?"

"Yup. Best thing I ever did was buy out the lease on that servo on the cusp of town, catching the passing road trains. I never looked back."

Jim knew all about this once famous gold town they called home. Just off the main interstate highway, it pulled in tourists from both sides of the country. Jim had lived here all his life. Pete wasn't familiar with the myths and legends. Jim and the other beer sodden locals filled Pete's head with stories in the solitary pub, the Coolies Spit, on many a cold night.

"Coolies was what me old man and his old man called the islanders they brought across to do all the hard yakka, and the Chinks who came looking for riches," Jim had said. "The spitting thing is a reference to one of their dirty habits. They never used to let 'em in the bar in them days, ya know. They had to go to a special window out the side with the abos and get takeaway grog. Not that they took to the grog much, them Chinkos. Never seen a harder working mob."

The truck bumped awkwardly across the rocky terrain and climbed up the adjoining ridge, until Pete pulled up at the roughly hewn track that led down and around to the as yet invisible cave mouth.

The sound of the doors slamming shut echoed down the valley. Shouldering their hunting rifles, they moved down the path, scattering a few loose stones before them. Jim looked around, noting the absence of bird life.

They hesitated at the mouth of the cave.

"After you, mate." Pete smiled.

Jim peered into the darkness, searching for movement. A brief slithering sound snapped them to attention. "Hello?" Jim called.

He looked at Pete and edged into the wide mouth of the cave.

"Keep it quiet in here, just in case."

About fifty metres in they came to a juncture, where the cave split into two passages. With a nod they took one each. Jim headed right. As he rounded the first major bend in the darkness he stopped in amazement as an incredible sight met his eyes.

The kitchen of his house unfurled before him. Everything in its place. The stove, the table and chairs, the ceiling with its lights, and there, stirring a pot, Rosemary, his wife. She turned as he stepped onto the linoleum floor.

"There you are, Jim. I was getting worried about you. Come on, put that gun away and sit. Dinner's almost ready."

Puzzled, Jim laid his gun against the rocky wall by his side and moved toward her.

"Rose?"

"Jim, you could at least wash your hands." She smiled and started to ladle stew onto a white China plate. A rich aroma filled Jim's nostrils. He began to salivate.

He peeled off his cap. "Where are the kids, honey?"

"They're outside playing. Go on, sit. I'll go round them up."

"Jim?"

Jim turned to see Pete standing at the edge of the darkness. Rocky walls peered out over Pete's shoulder in the dim light.

"Pete? I found Rosemary."

"Jim…come away from there. Come on, mate."

"Stay for dinner, Pete."

"Yes," said Rosemary, "You'd be welcome, Pete. There's enough for everybody." She dropped a plate on the Formica table with a noisy clatter.

"Jim, come on!" Pete reached out and grabbed Jim by the collar.

Jim resisted. "No, mate!"

A scuttling sound made them look to their right. Black spiny tendrils edged rapidly along the kitchen walls.

Pete yanked Jim towards him. "It's trying to surround us. Come on, Jim."

Jim turned and reached for Rosemary. She stood by the stove as black creepers started to crawl over her shoulders, covering her yellow cardigan.

"Rosemary!" Jim yelled.

She opened her mouth to speak, but instead, inky black fingers erupted from inside her and crawled across her face.

"Jesus!" Pete dragged Jim along, away from the black vine. Jim came to his senses and they both ran toward the mouth of the cave. The sound of tiny feet came from either side and above them.

"Don't look at it, Jim."

They ran blindly. The exit seemed to be much further away than the distance they had walked coming in. But Jim saw the light approaching. They ran past a small child; Jim gave it a cursory glance. Pete refused to acknowledge the little girl.

They crashed out into the fresh air, gasping for breath.

"What the hell?" Jim said. Pete yanked him to his feet and pulled him toward the truck.

"Come on."

As Pete fired up the engine, they saw the vine burst forth from the cave and snake toward them, skittering along the dusty ground.

"Shit!"

Pete swung the truck backwards in a violent arc. They shot off down the hillside. Jim cranked the window and glanced behind.

"Faster, mate, its coming."

Pete swore under his breath and planted his foot. Jim crossed himself.

By the time they hit bitumen they seemed to have outrun it. Pete looked dead ahead.

"We gotta get to town, warn everyone."

Their breathing subsided as the immediate danger passed. Jim retrieved a small bottle from the glovebox, took a hit and passed it over.

"Pete. When you pulled me outta there, who was I talking to?"

Pete shook his head. "It doesn't matter, mate. You were hallucinating, that's all."

"But she was right there, large as life."

"Don't dwell on it. It was trying to trick ya. Probably what happened to that bloke in the four-wheel drive."

"Pete…"

"Rosemary's dead. You know it. The cancer took her four years ago."

"But she was so real."

"No, she wasn't mate. None of it was real."

"What about you? You saw something too, didn't you?"

"Nup! I didn't."

"You did," pressed Jim. "I saw her too, mate. We ran straight past her. Your little Emily."

Pete slammed the brakes on. The truck shuddered, spun sideways and came to a screeching halt in the gravel.

Pete glared at Jim, his eyes wild with rage.

"It wasn't her, okay? She's fucken dead, Jim. They're all fucken dead."

"Jesus! What the fuck was that thing?"

"I dunno, mate." Pete turned the engine over. It failed. He tried again, and again.

Jim glanced up the road behind them.

"Shit!"

The engine kicked over and they sighed with relief.

"Come on, let's get to town and warn them."

"They won't believe us. A couple of ghosts tried to smother us in black vines? They'll think we've been hitting the bottle." Pete tossed the empty miniature out the window.

"Yeah, but we have to try."

The truck roared onto the main strip of town straight into a conflagration. A few stray figures ran down the street, yelling and screaming. Jim ducked instinctively as rapid-fire gun shots roared in the night.

"Ah, fuck! I think we're too late."

They saw black tendrils running along the top of buildings, threading themselves around lampposts. Pete gunned it to the police station. Jim jumped out, but Pete sat tight.

"Pete, ya coming?"

He leaned out the window. "I better check the fuel station. Whitey Brown is out there by himself."

Jim nodded. "Be careful, mate."

Jim ran inside, just as one of the younger coppers held out a phone to Sergeant Bob Baxter.

"Sarge, its Davey Ricketts. Said his old man went crazy and shot the wife and the rest of the family. He was lucky to get away."

The old school copper looked at the phone, where a voice could still be heard shouting.

"Something about a black creeper?"

"The black vine!" Jim yelled.

All three station phones were going off, people were talking across each other.

"What the shittin' hell is goin' on?" Baxter yelled, as the window shattered and a Molotov cocktail bounced along the floor.

"Take that, piggies!" a voice yelled from outside.

"Christ! Get down!" Baxter roared, throwing his ample body headlong to the ground.

Everybody hit the deck as the bottle exploded. Flames swept across the walls. One officer ran screaming out the door, hands in the air, his upper body alight. As he went out a thick set man in a biker jacket ran in.

"Ya fucken pigs," he bellowed, waving a machete around his head.

"Muggsy?" Baxter yelled at the solitary member of the town's bikie gang. "Whaddya fucken playing at?"

"Look out, Sarge!" a constable barked as the crazed bikie screamed and ran at the solid six-foot copper with the weapon raised. Jim saw black tendrils crawling out of the man's nose and mouth. "He's got the plague."

"Fuck this." Baxter pulled his service revolver, but a shot rang out taking the bikie down from the rear. The big body hit the deck. His momentum caused him to slide a few feet across the station floor. The bikie corpse began to shake as little black spikes started to penetrate through its skin.

They all swung around to see the local priest, Father Brian Mulcahy, at the end of a shotgun.

"Fuck me, you blokes. Let's get out of here."

Outside under the sparse streetlights, pandemonium reigned. Seemed like everybody in town was in the main road, trying to kill themselves or each other.

Raymond Feather, the local hairdresser, ran up to Father Brian and took a swing at him with a big pair of scissors. "Bless me Father, for I have sinned."

The priest ducked and kicked the barber in the balls. "Fuck you, dickhead!"

The barber pushed himself back up onto his knees again, spreading his arms in supplication. "Well, if that's the way you want it." He jammed the scissors forcefully into his own throat, hitting the jugular. A fountain of crimson pumped forth, and the barber slumped on his side.

Brian made the sign of the cross.

"I forgive you, my son." He turned to the others. "Let's get to the fucking church, quick."

More stragglers joined them as they barrelled into the town's place of worship. Brian slid the heavy wooden bolt across the door. He nodded to Baxter and a couple of others who helped slide the back row of pews across it for good measure.

A sharp sound from the rafters caused them to turn. Baxter had his gun raised.

Neil Primrose, the parish organist, perched on the thick central beam running across the middle of the church, a noose curled around his silver haired head. The lens on one side of his glasses was cracked.

"Neil?" said Father Brian. "What the Hell are you doing?"

Liz Squires pressed her fist against her mouth to stifle a scream.

Primrose chewed his lower lip as tears streamed down his face.

"I've sinned, Brian. I saw his face. His little face."

"Neil, don't do it, mate," said Baxter.

"It's too late, Bob. Too late. He was just a little angel. They all were. I couldn't help myself. Now it's time to atone."

This time Liz did scream, as the organist leapt from the beam, the rope unfurled till it broke his fall and his head snapped back with an awful crack.

"Ah, fuck!" Father Brian said as he leapt back out of the way of the swinging corpse, which immediately voided its bowels and bladder.

Jim led Liz away to the other side of the room.

"Anybody got a knife?" the priest asked, steadying swaying Primrose by the legs. "I better cut him down."

After a while, the screaming outside died away. The night grew quiet. The group sat near the altar to collect their thoughts, and Baxter scratched his bald head. "Now, can *somebody* fill me in, please? What the bloody Hell is going on out there? And what's that black shit crawling all over the place?"

Jim stepped forward to tell the tale. As he broke down with the emotion of it and Baxter rubbed his back, a huge sound thudded against the door, reverberating through the wooden pew.

Baxter jumped up. "Christ, something's trying to get in. Grab your weapons everyone."

A parishioner pulled on Father Brian's sleeve.

"Will the door stop them, Father?"

"If it doesn't, then this will," said the priest, pulling his rapid repeat shotgun from under the pulpit.

One of the others scaled an upturned pew and looked out the stained-glass window.

"It's Pete!"

The name reverberated around the congregation.

"Pete!" Jim yelled.

"Hold your fire, everyone," said Baxter. "Is anyone else out there?" he asked of the sentry.

"No. Looks like he's alone."

"Get the door open."

They pulled the pew aside, opened the door, and dragged Pete inside. Someone handed him a bottle of water, which he sculled. Father Brian tossed him a flask of whisky, eliciting a look from Baxter.

Brian shrugged.

Pete took a hit. Jim grabbed him by the shoulders.

"What happened, mate? Where's Whitey?"

Pete shook his head. He took another belt from the whisky bottle, pulled something out of his jacket, and threw it on the floor.

Baxter regarded the charred black object. Father Brian crossed himself.

"What is it?"

Pete wiped whisky off his lips. "The vine… I think I found a way to kill it. I need a couple of blokes to help me. We gotta get back to the station."

Baxter picked up the charred, shrivelled object and sniffed it. "Petrol!"

"I'll go," said Jim.

"With ya," Baxter echoed. "Barricade this door good behind us, and don't open it for anyone else."

"Wait," said Father Brian. "You're going in your truck? Is that gonna hold enough tins of fuel?"

"What are you thinking, Brian?" Pete asked.

"I got the church's hearse out back. That could take a few more."

Baxter grinned. "Righto, I'm with you, Brian. Meet you two there. Be careful." The copper threw Pete a spare gun. He caught it.

"Cheers, but we'll need more than bullets."

The two vehicles beat a hasty path down the main street into the rising sun. Daylight revealed the extent of the previous night's devastation. Around them, the black vine raged and stretched its tendrils towards their fleeing wheels. Pete and Jim led the way in Pete's truck. Father Brian's hearse tailed behind, the burly copper riding shotgun.

Pete turned off onto the tributary road leading to the station. As Brian swung the hearse around to follow, the rotund figure of Barry Jonas, boisterous town drunk, lurched across the road in front of the funeral car.

Brian slowed the hearse. As they drew closer, Jonas raised his arms and sprinted toward them emitting a primal scream. As he ran, his copious beer gut erupted and a stream of black vine sprouted up in all direction.

"Jesus H Christ," Baxter spat. "Sorry, Father."

"Don't be a cockhead, Bob," said the priest, as he planted his foot and ploughed into the Jonas monstrosity. The body seemed to split and fly in all directions. Baxter swore under his breath.

"Never liked that prick anyway," said Brian.

The two vehicles roared into the station without any further impediment. Pete ran toward the storage unit and the others followed. They formed a daisy chain, tossing tins of fuel along and storing them as best they could.

They had almost completed the task when a woman's voice cried out.

"Oh, Father Brian."

Brian swung around to see a heavy-set middle-aged woman staggering toward him.

"Christ, it's Mrs McCarthy," said Pete.

They all recognised the woman as a keen regular church goer, but they had never seen her quite like this. Betty McCarthy wore a very low-cut top, over which her large, usually restrained bosom, blossomed. She had topped it off by squeezing into a very tight black leather mini-skirt.

"Brian." She fluttered her heavily made-up eyes. "I've come to take my regular confession. I can't seem to find the confession box, but I guess I can kneel right here for you."

Mrs McCarthy's lips parted wide. She ran her tongue around the rim of her mouth seductively, then two forked black tendrils shot out of her throat and formed the sign of the devil in the air.

"Move, Brian!" Pete yelled as he jumped in from the side and threw a bucket of fuel over Mrs McCarthy. She roared in disapproval. Pete patted his pockets desperately. Catching on, the others did likewise. All shook their heads.

Shaking her petrol-doused blonde head, Mrs McCarthy set off in a run toward the Father, arms outstretched. Black vines burst through the tips of her painted fingernails.

The other three looked on incredulously as Brian almost nonchalantly upturned one of the tins and poured petrol on his embossed handkerchief. He jammed the hanky onto a stick, pulled a lighter from his cassock and lit the makeshift torch, then threw it at the advancing sinner.

Mrs McCarthy let out a pained scream as her whole body went up in flames. Black fingers lunged out trying to escape the conflagration, to no avail.

The body of the former parishioner toppled over and curled up into a charcoal ball, spitting and smoking.

They all stood motionless, holding their noses, looking at Father Brian.

"What?" He pointed at the mess. "I've never seen that woman before in my life!"

"Come on," ordered Baxter. "Let's just get to the bloody cars."

"You reckon youse two can handle what's left of town?" Jim directed the question at the Sarge and the vicar.

"I guess. Why?" said Baxter.

"Pete and I are gonna go back to the cave, try and take this thing out at the root."

"God be with you, my sons," said the priest.

Pete eased the truck back up the solitary dirt track toward the cave entrance. The two of them sat in solemn silence.

"Pete?"

"Stow it, mate."

"Nah, I gotta say this. Mate, no matter what you see in there, just ignore it, okay? Like you told me before. It's not real."

"Yeah. You too, mate. You too."

They pulled the truck as close as they could and started offloading the tins. They stacked several up close to the mouth of the cave. They made two makeshift flaming torches with petrol-soaked rags, lit them with the truck lighter, and walked down toward the forbidding gaping mouth where the vine lay in wait for them. Inky tendrils thrust out from beneath the roof of the aperture like daggers. Pete slung the fuel around and Jim waved his torch at it. They both hit the dirt and the conflagration was instant. The vine let out an unholy, high-pitched scream.

They got to their feet as the initial wall of flame subsided, leaving black death curling in its wake. They walked into the mouth and heard the stuff slinking away into the darkness. Day turned instantly to night in the murky depths, but each man had his torch. They splashed petrol onto the walls as they moved further in and down. Soon enough, they came to the place where the cave split into two separate passages.

"Split up here again," said Pete.

Jim nodded. "If we don't make it out, I want you to know, you've been a good mate."

"Fuck me, Jimbo, it's not like we're goin' to war." Pete gave a toothy grin, but his eyes gave away his terror.

"Aren't we?"

"I love you, buddy."

"Back at ya, mate."

Jim strode into the hell mouth, holding his flaming torch in front of him to light the way. Almost as soon as he rounded the corner, he found the light was unnecessary.

He felt polished tile beneath his feet. It shone white in the artificial light of his hallucination. An antiseptic smell filled the air.

"Jim?"

He tried to look away, but felt compelled to turn towards the croaking voice.

He almost dropped the torch.

"Jim, how could you? How could you leave me here to die?"

Rosemary looked at him from the confines of her hospital bed. Her face was slack and pale, her head almost bereft of hair. He had a terrible flashback, and his heart felt fit to split in half.

"Jim. Please."

"Rosemary," he sobbed. "I'm sorry."

A slight movement caught his eye, and just beyond Rosemary and her bed, he saw a figure lurking in the shadows. A black, almost human shaped mass.

"I'm sorry, Rosie, but…you're not her!" Jim said and launched the torch at the bed.

It erupted in flames, and Rosemary and the figure behind her screamed.

She sprang out of the bed, merging with the black thing. Jim backed away. Her dissolving face gave one last cry of despair as flames engulfed it.

"Sorry." Jim swept the tears away from his face and turned and fled. The flames started to swallow the entire scene before him.

Jim ran, cursing himself for losing the torch, but the light from the chasing flames gave him vision enough to see ahead.

"Pete!" he yelled as he reached the split and paused. Hearing murmuring voices above the lick of the approaching flames, Jim ventured down the other passage.

It didn't take him long to find Pete, kneeling on the floor, weeping. His shoulders heaving.

Jim touched him gently on the back.

"Pete? Come on buddy, we gotta go now."

Pete moved back and as he did Jim saw the little girl he had been cradling in his arms.

She looked up at Pete with opaque irises. Her black mouth split wide, and she hissed at him. "Leave my daddy alone. He's *mine* now."

Pete turned and looked at Jim through black eyeless sockets.

Jim recoiled. "Hell!"

Pete rose to his feet and moved towards him. Jim backed up.

"Where ya going, mate? Come join us. It's beautiful in the dark," said Pete.

193

"Fuck!" Glancing around, Jim saw Pete's torch, jutting out from a crack in the cave wall. Thankfully it was still alight. Jim snatched it and waved it in front of them, jostling them back.

"Hey, love to join you, buddy, but I kind of like it in the light. So, fuck you, and fuck you too, kid."

Jim threw the torch at Pete, anticipating there would be enough spilled fuel on his mate.

He was right. Pete went up like a medieval heretic. The small childlike figure screamed and threw herself at Pete as if by instinct.

Turning, Jim saw the light at the juncture from the approaching flames. He ran as fast as his middle-aged legs could carry him, choking on the smoke as he saw the light at the end of the tunnel. He ran towards it while all around him, the black vine tried to fight its way through the flames. It hissed and whispered things in his ear. It put images in his head. Half-buried suppressed memories resurfaced in a rush of regret and despair. He felt blood dribble down from his nose.

"Fuck off!" Jim screamed and ran as if he was in a fever dream. His legs seemed to move in slow motion. It felt like he was running in tar. Every person he had ever wronged yelled at him to give in, told him he was useless, a failure.

Jim saw the light approaching but as he got closer, the roof of the cave seemed to slide down. The floor rose upwards, and the walls closed in on either side, threatening to cut off the light and enclose him.

"No!"

"*Yes.*" A voice spoke from the darkness. "*Stay. Mine. Forever.*"

"No. It's...not...real..."

Jim ran at the tiny circle of disappearing light, closed his eyes, and threw himself at the black wall, expecting to smash his head into the rock face.

It dissolved in front of him and he tumbled out into broad daylight.

He sat on his arse and hugged himself, aching all over. "Pete," he said. "I'm sorry, mate."

Behind him the cave spat and hissed, and he rose unsteadily

to his feet and stumbled toward the truck. For one terrible moment, he thought Pete might have taken the keys with him, but as he swung the door open, they sat in the ignition. *You're a fucken champion, Pete.* He smiled through his pain.

Jim rolled the truck down the main street into what looked like the aftermath of a war. Most of the buildings were burning or smoking burnt out relics. Bob Baxter, Father Brian, Liz Squires, and a handful of other survivors hailed him. He stopped and got out.

Baxter glanced at the empty passenger seat. "I'm sorry, Jim. He was a top bloke." Jim nodded sadly.

"You stopped it though?" Father Brian asked.

"Think so, yeah."

"Same here." Brian looked down the street past the alien visage of smoking, dead black vines toward his ruined church and sighed. "Well, the town's fucked, but at least we beat the bastard."

"We can always go somewhere else, start over," Liz said.

"Yeah, Brian," said Baxter, slapping the priest on the back. "I'm sure there's another town that needs a lay preacher."

Jim looked down the road off into the shimmering desert. "The important thing is we stopped it. Whatever it was."

Jenny Carlisle glanced at her Fitbit as she jogged though the park on the cusp of the city. Still half an hour until she needed to hit the shower and get ready for work. Couldn't afford to miss the train again. Those reports had to be on the manager's desk by nine on the dot.

Ahead and to the right, she saw a large group of people gathered together and pointing at something. She veered off the path to get a closer look.

A small child stood in front of the group, dancing up and down on the spot. "Mummy, Mummy, look at the dancing flower."

Jenny looked across the manicured grass toward the flower beds near the man-made pond, where a strange looking black vine seemed to undulate and snake over the ground toward them.

NOT LIKE US

Ben knew it would be a long time before he got the stench of Vietnam out of his nostrils. It was a fetid combination, a mixture of exotic spices, rotting vegetables and burning flesh. He rolled a smoke as he sat with his back to a log in the makeshift bivouac the boys had set up and looked through the haze at the sky, listening to the sounds of the jungle.

On one side of him sat his rifle, the still warm SLR, within easy reach. On the opposite side of the clearing, the others lingered. Cliff Nankervis, his NCO stood whispering with Dougie Ramsden, the sarge's best mate. Cliff flipped back his giggle hat and wiped the sweat from his brow with the back of a hand. He made a sweeping gesture in the air. Both of them stole an occasional glance toward Ben, and he lowered his head to avoid their gaze.

Ben knew the other blokes weren't keen on him, the rookie. They were all five or ten years his senior, and even though they relied on his medical knowledge, at the same time they resented his university status. "Smartarse little prick!" the sarge had spat at him when he tried to enlighten their medieval attitudes.

Ben knew where he stood.

The other blokes hovered, looking busy. Chook and Slim occupied themselves handing out the Dapsones and preparing their meagre Jack rations, while Chimney lit up his umpteenth rollie of the day and blew a carcinogenic plume into the oily night air. They were eight hours into a twenty-four-hour cordon and search operation.

Slim leaned over Chook's bully tin and peeled one off. Chimney almost spat his cigarette into the fire. "Dirty mongrel," Chook said as he cuffed the laughing farter. Tears rolled down the cook's chubby face. Ben thought his crinkled eyes made him look like a laughing Buddha. Despite the therapeutic nature of the banter, Ben knew it paid to keep your wits about you during these sweeping manoeuvres. But sometimes at night when he looked around their creased-up faces, he wondered if they considered him their real enemy, and not the Viet Cong.

Local legend said Charlie always knew where you were.

"He can smell the stink of white men a mile off, just like the red Indians could in the Wild West," was one of the first things Ben was told when he got posted. Cursing his luck when the luck of the draw saw his birthday come out of the hat, setting the wheels in motion to send him into this fresh kind of Hell.

Ben learned all about Charlie's inscrutability: his secret tunnels too well hidden for the eye to detect, his dirty booby traps. Although the news was always suppressed, Ben heard stories, like the one a fellow medic told him about the Yank who stood on a Punji Bear Trap.

"The devious mongrels dig two holes, a bigger one on top of a smaller one. When an unsuspecting sapper treads on the grass covering, his weight takes his boot through to the second trap and sinks into a bear trap set over the top of it. The weight of the descending foot springs the jaws of the trap shut on the lower leg. Sometimes for special effect, they leave a poisonous snake down in the pit, or they lace the spikes on the jaws with poison, so the cuts become infected. Poor bastard lost half his leg." The medic had shaken his head in disgust.

Then there were other stories of assaults on soldiers by wild animals, and the strange mutilations of the local water buffalo population. All unconfirmed of course, but enough to put the shits up the men. It seemed the Cong would do anything to gain an advantage.

Ben slapped at a platoon of mozzies grazing on his forearm, and, against his better nature, edged closer to the boys. He watched Doug lean in toward Cliff and bark in a hoarse whisper,

"Got a letter from the missus the other day."

"Yeah?" said Cliff, taking the smoke his mate proffered with a nod. "Cheers. How're things in Sydney?"

Doug sucked on his cigarette and exhaled a mouthful of blue-grey smoke. "One of Deb's girlfriends has been slipping it to a GI."

"Don't say. Does her old man know?"

"Nup. He's over here somewhere, poor prick, while his missus is canoodling with a uniformed Septic. Plenty of sheilas at it too, Debs says. The Yanks are all over the local bars."

They both stole a glance Ben's way. They knew about the letters he exchanged with his own sweetheart back in Melbourne, Louise. In his early days, Ben had made the mistake of showing them a photo. Ever since, they had ragged him that the curvy blue-eyed blonde would do the dirty on him the first chance she got. "Yeah," Cliff had snorted, winking at Dougie. "I know the type. Looks like she bangs like a dunny door."

Cliff nodded, the rollie bouncing on his lower lip, encouraging his mate to go on.

"Too many of the bastards are over there on the prowl. And they've got plenty of money, the mongrels. The local sheilas are all over 'em like flies round an outhouse dunny."

"It's the thrill of the exotic, Dougie." Cliff ground his cigarette into the dirt.

"Eh?"

"Viva le difference."

Doug bore the same puzzled expression. Ben knew what the sarge was getting at, but kept quiet.

Cliff sighed. "To our sheilas, those Yanks are something different, something new, with their funny accents, fancy hair and shiny uniforms, not to mention all the readies. They're fanny magnets mate."

"Bastards! Why aren't they over here with us, like the rest of Uncle Sam's mob?"

Cliff shifted position and fiddled with the ring on his index finger. "More to the point cobber, did it occur to you to wonder what your missus is doing in pubs frequented by Yank servicemen on the pull?"

There was a pause as this revelation sank in, and Doug's face slowly turned a shade of crimson.

"What the fuck… I'll batter the fucken cow! If I find out she's been slipping it to some other mug, above all some fucken jumped-up Yank …"

Cliff leaned in a little closer and spoke into Doug's ear, but loud enough for the rest of them to hear. "Hold ya horses, mate. You lined up with the boys outside that brothel in China Beach on bangers the other week. So, you know, what's good for the goose…"

Slim looked over and gave Doug an evil wink, his fat face creasing up. Chook punched Slim on the arm.

"That was fucken different," Doug said. "That was fucken R and R. I earned that. I needed that release, after all we been through. Besides, it's not the same, Gooks ain't real people."

Cliff placed a restraining arm on his mate's chest. "Keep it down." He hooked a thumb over his shoulder toward the jungle. "Charlie's always listening. But I know what ya saying. Like them sheilas that time, by the river."

Ben looked at their faces around the fire. He had heard snippets of this apocryphal story before. Some minor atrocity the platoon had committed before he came on the scene. One by one they all looked away. In his mind's eye Ben saw the women lined up along the riverbank, hands behind their heads, heard the thump of cicadas' wings, and smelled the burning straw huts.

"They're not like us," Doug said, staring into the ashes of the fire pit. Their collective silence was all the confirmation needed. Except for Ben, who couldn't bite his tongue.

"They are like us."

"Aw, here we fucken go. Another lecture," Cliff grunted.

Ignoring the sergeant, Ben pressed on. "They bleed like us. They have mothers, fathers, siblings, wives and children, just like us. They're human beings."

"Didn't stop you killing 'em," said Chimney around the tip of his cigarette.

"Only because they were trying to kill me," said Ben. "I had no choice."

"Didn't stop ya gettin' up some little yellow bitch on bangers, did it?" Cliff said through a low growl.

Ben remembered the rudimentary brothel on China Beach. The one they had dragged him along to, against his will. They'd packed him off to a squalid little room with some poor wide-eyed girl. Ben shuddered at the thought of how young she must have been. The room, if you could call it that, was the size of a large cupboard, with a solitary fold up bed, dirt floor and a couple of chickens scratching around in the damp soil.

There, satisfied that the cacophony of contrasting voices coming from similar spaces nearby, and the hawking of callers on the dirt roads outside would drown out their conversation, Ben had taken the girl's hand and reassured her that she didn't have to sell herself for him. Instead, he had listened to her whisper in broken English when he asked her about her life, pulled out the photo of his sweetheart and told the girl about Louise, how she waited for him back home when this nightmare ended.

Ben hoped he had done enough to fool them, but it didn't stop them referring to him as a 'faggot', a slang term for queers they had picked up off the Yanks.

Sometimes, when he lay in his bunk late at night, thinking about her, the seeds of doubt sewn by their words hit home. Ben wondered if Louise was still true to him. He tempered these negative thoughts by memories of the bolt of electricity that rushed through his body every time he held her in his arms, and the way it felt like coming home every time he was inside her. He was comforted in the knowledge that they were soulmates. Louise had said the same herself. Nothing could come between them.

Ben glanced over his shoulder from his position at point and saw Cliff gesticulate toward the clearing. The jungle had thinned over the past few hundred yards and the patrol knew from Recon that another village lay just ahead.

Ben tensed, as he always did in anticipation of contact with the enemy. He slapped a feasting mozzie away from the back of his neck. *Only another six weeks*, he thought, *and I'm out of this shithole.* If it wasn't Charlie, the insects, or the heat, it was those jungle telegraph stories about-

A short high-pitched groan cut the air.

Ben tensed and looked behind him. The others heard it too. Cliff scurried ahead, paused, and waved them over. The sound came again, high and nasal, but distinct.

"It sounds human...like a woman," Cliff whispered. He motioned the small group onward, and they proceeded with caution until they reached the outer huts of a burnt-out village in a clearing. It seemed to be abandoned, but they didn't need to be reminded how deceptive the local villagers could be: man, woman or child. Sometimes they were with you, other times not. Sometimes, you go to pat a smiling kid and the little bastard would pull out a grenade.

At the lip of the jungle, before the first of the ruined husks, they found themselves faced with a large stone effigy. They stood before it, dumbstruck.

"The fuck is that thing?" said Chimney, prizing the rollie from his lip and casting the butt aside. The carved idol glared down upon them as it sat coiled on its haunches, its elongated snout and serrated teeth sitting beneath a set of large, cat like eyes.

"Fucken gook mumbo jumbo," Cliff spat on the effigy and motioned them on.

The sporadic cries were coming from a pit in front of the main huts. They edged toward it. As they drew nearer, the moans segued into broken English. "Help me, GI. Please...help me!"

Cliff peered over the edge, followed by the others.

They discovered a young Vietnamese woman lying in the wide trench, her white Ao Dai covered in filth. Then they noticed the source of her discomfort.

"Christ, look at the mess," said Slim.

The girl's eyes widened as she looked from face to face. "GI! Morphine! Please help."

"Lady, we're not GIs." said Chook.

"She can't tell the difference, ya mug," said Ben.

"This doesn't add up," said Chimney, prizing the smoke away from his lips. "Who abandons a village and leaves someone behind? This isn't Charlie's normal form."

"Maybe she's not Cong?" said Cliff, oblivious to the suffering of the woman at their feet. The Ao Dai was split from her heart to her left shoulder, and from within pulsed a bloody wound, staining the delicate fabric.

"It's gotta be a trap," said Chimney.

"Maybe she just crawled in there to die," said Slim, swallowing.

The girl was muttering in her own language along with the broken English.

"I've butchered pigs on me farm neater than that," said Chook as he spat on the ground.

"Fatal?" asked Doug.

"Looks it", said Cliff, pulling his KA-BAR from its sheath and running his fingers along its edge.

"Pity" said Doug.

Ben recognized the look in Cliff and Doug's eyes as they took in the contours of the girl's body beneath the native garb. Her facial features were easy on the eye. His mind drifted back to that night in China Beach. One of the bar girls had sat in Doug's lap, her arms around neck, as the boys knocked back a few cold ones. With the others laughing and egging the pair on, Ben watched her tongue probe Doug's ear, while her hand slid down between his thighs and she explored him with painted long nailed fingers. She was whispering in Doug's ear. Ben was familiar with the bar girl behaviour. Telling a GI how much she loved him, leading him on, while her real interest was in the contents of his wallet, rather than his fatigues. Dougie was too far gone to care though. His mouth had nuzzled the girl's throat, probably feeling for a tell-tale Adam's apple.

Ben saw Doug glance toward the sarge, then his eyes hardened. He clenched his teeth and declared. "Hey, you think we can fuck her before she dies?"

"What?" said Ben as his face dropped.

Doug stifled a grin. Ben looked toward Slim for some moral support. The cook wiped a chunky hand across his brow. "Jeez Dougie, I dunno. We done some shit we ain't proud of, but this is pushing it."

Doug spat on the ground and slung his SLR aside. "Christ! Nobody's gonna tell the missus. What happens on tour stays on tour, eh Cliff?"

The grunts looked up at the sergeant, as he rubbed the dull edge of his knife over his bristled chin, deep in thought.

"Cliff?" said Chimney, casting the stub of his cigarette aside.

"Right fuck off you blokes. Chook, Slim, flank right and check the huts. Chimney, Benno, go left. Circle formation, back here in twenty."

"Sarge ya can't..." Ben pleaded. He glanced down at the girl, still whimpering in the pit.

Doug shoved him aside. "Fuck up, Benno. It's ya first tour. You don't get a say. Fresh out of bloody school when ya number came up. You just about learned how to unhook a bra when we dragged ya into that knocking shop." Doug sneered as he turned to the others for moral support. "Remember that dopey looking Gook we set the kid up with?"

The sarge let out a raspy laugh. "I said fuck off! No one's asking youse to join in."

The boys all recognized the tone and they saw the sarge's eyes glaze over. Saw the way he caressed the KA-BAR. Ben swallowed. He had seen that look before, around the fire when Cliff told them stories about his civilian life as a butcher, killing and dressing the meat.

The men shouldered their SLRs and disappeared into the darkness of the village, the sound of their voices fading in the dying early evening light. Except Ben, who shouldered his medical kit, swallowed, and jumped into the pit next to the suffering girl.

The sarge swore. "Benno, I gave you a fucken order, boy."

Ben turned and saw the sarge swing his SLR around to train it at his chest. He shook his head in defiance. "I'm the medic here, sergeant. I say let me at least examine this girl before we decide what to do."

Without waiting for an answer, Ben turned back to the girl and squatted before her. "It's alright," he whispered. "I'm gonna try and help you, okay?"

The girl's eyes were like saucepans. Ben had no idea if she even understood any English, aside from the rote sentences she spoke to draw their attention, but she seemed to understand when he set down his kit and took out some gauze and a bottle.

He smiled at the girl and nodded shyly. She gave a half smile back. Tears ran down her oval face. Cliff's harsh voice cut in like staccato fire.

"Benno, so help me I will fucken gut you."

"Let me do my job." Ben turned to look up at the NCO, who's finger still hovered over the trigger. Doug stood at the sarge's side, wordlessly egging him on. He gave Ben a look that would have cut him in half.

Swearing under his breath, Ben turned his attention back to the girl. Gripping the bottle in his sweaty fingers he prized the lid off, the antiseptic smell momentarily clearing his head. He poured a little on the cloth and as the girl shied away, he whispered, "I'm sorry, this might hurt a little."

She let out a low whine as the antiseptic hit her wound, and then, Ben blinked. He thought he saw the wound start to turn in on itself, like it was retracting back into the girl's skin.

He looked up at her, and that was when he saw her eyes flicker, and her face began to twitch.

"The fuck's goin' on down there?" he heard Dougie exclaim.

"Get the fuck out of that hole now, Benno. Last warning," said the sarge.

Ben sensed he must be obscuring their view. Before him, the girl opened her mouth and let forth a stream of some local dialect, her voice growing distinctly deeper with every vowel. Then she locked eyes on him and whispered, in perfect English.

"Run."

She reached out and squeezed his hand. Gentle, but he felt a hint of tensile strength, hovering beneath the skin.

Ben didn't need a second invitation. As soon as she released his hand, he scrambled out of the pit.

"'bout fucken time," the sarge said in a low growl, handing his gun to Dougie.

Ben looked at Cliff out the side of his eye, not daring to look back into the pit as the sarge edged his way down.

"Gimme some more light down here," he ordered Doug.

Doug pulled the torch from his rucksack and lit the hole. The girl trembled before the hulking figure leaning over her. Cliff probed for traps with the point of his knife, then he started to cut the girl out of the tight-fitting garment. She gurgled in discomfort, and the sergeant grunted with anticipation.

"After you mate," Doug called down. He turned to Ben. "Go on, get the fuck out of here, faggot."

Ben motioned to go, but crouched at the lip of the jungle, transfixed. He sensed something major was about to go down, and he was torn between loyalty to his platoon and fear for the girl.

Cliff stuck the knife between his teeth and started to pull down his fatigues.

A sharp cry broke the air, followed by another. Ben and Doug jumped to attention.

"What the hell was that?" Doug reached for his rifle and saw shapes forming and merging with the jungle off to the edge of the huts. Ben felt something brush past him like a ghost. Then a short burst of delicate laughter drew their attention back to the pit.

Doug directed the light onto the girl's face. There was a smile edging across her features, as she reached toward Cliff and pulled him down toward her. "Hey we're in luck, Dougie. She fuckin' wants it."

The girl's placid oval face blurred in the torch light, yellow eyes shone like the moon, and then the entire visage seemed to elongate, the mouth now filling with serrated teeth jutting outwards at oblique angles. As if acknowledging the display, the gaping maw clacked open and shut, huge globs of saliva dripping between the vicious fangs. Ben froze. Doug raised his SLR but couldn't aim with one arm. Then Cliff began to scream, as a splintering sound rebounded off the walls of the surrounding huts.

"Jesus!" Doug said as he swept the torch beam across the ditch. The girl's body rippled and tensed, lithe features expanding and tearing through the stained Ao Dai. She let out a low moan filled with hunger and rage, peppered with a stream of invective in a foreign tongue, somehow emanating from that monstrous mouth. Cliff's body was being folded back upon itself. Ben heard a slick crack which cut off the sarge's scream. Doug dropped his SLR and the torch shook in his hand. They saw the obscenity before them tear at the sergeant's flesh. Doug backed away from the pit and its awful contents.

Half hidden in the undergrowth, Ben heard a twig snap behind him and froze.

Turning, he made out silhouettes gliding from between the huts with uncanny stealth. Three more of the monsters, their cruel eyes focused, hideous mouths gaping and dripping with hunger. They ignored him and fanned out to flank Doug.

"Benno!" Doug cried as the monstrosities circled him. Ben fingered his KA-BAR and edged further back into the foliage.

Doug turned as the other one crawled up over the edge of the pit. It carried Cliff's upper torso in its claws and placed the stump upright in the dirt. It looked like the Sarge was half buried up to the chest. Ben and Doug stared at Cliff's bloodied face.

Doug fell to his knees, holding the torch before him like a weapon, and clawed the ground with his other hand, muttering, "Shit, where the fuck's me rifle?" He saw that he was unzipped and had also soiled himself. The creature before him caught the scent of his excrement and licked its lips and leered at Doug.

Ben heard Doug whimper as he raised the torch toward the thing creeping toward him on all fours. Lithe muscle rippled under the flank where the wound no longer dripped. Beyond it, Cliff's eyes flickered to life, and the dead torso addressed Doug, blood spattering his lips.

"Don't sweat it cobber, every man creates a Hell of his own imagining. Whether it's a rat-infested jungle, or a house in the suburbs where your old man comes home shickered from the six o'clock swill and redecorates the lounge with your mum. Shit. Pretty soon you figure that's how all women like it, eh Dougie boy?"

"I just gave her a slap, once or twice," Doug whined, "When she was asking for it."

Against his better nature, Ben edged out of cover, the knife firm in his grasp. He wished to Hell he hadn't set aside his rifle, not that it would do much good now. He watched them encircle Doug. Cruel calloused paws began to explore the terrified soldier's body, tender at first, then with more urgency.

"What the hell are you?" Doug asked, his voice breaking, as the first one rose on its hind legs and lifted the torch from his hands with stained long-nailed claws.

The beast smiled at Doug, uncomprehending.

"It's no use mate," Cliff said. "They don't speak our language. They're not like us. Told you as much, didn't I, Benno?" The dead sergeant winked at Ben. "Smartarse uni faggot."

That was enough for Ben. He dropped the knife and ran through the jungle in the fading light. Lingering long enough to hear Doug's agonized screams. He kept running, as far away from those things as possible.

When some villagers found him several days later, ragged and raving, Ben kept his counsel. They took him in and nursed him. Even when they handed him over to some passing Yanks, Ben never talked about what he saw, or spoke of what happened to his platoon.

When they shipped him home, Ben maintained his silence, and in the years that followed, he swallowed it all down. The shithouse reception and lack of appreciation they got for their service was bad enough. Fucked if he was gonna let them lock him away as a lunatic as well.

Then, on their tenth wedding anniversary, after they tucked the kids into bed, spurred on by a shared bottle of wine, Ben finally confided his dark secret to Louise, in front of the fire.

She listened intently, taking his hands in hers, giving him that familiar pulsing surge of power with its subliminal tensile strength.

And she understood, like he always knew she would.

SHE AIN'T HEAVY

Colin Jonas peered through the damp foliage toward the ancient ruin of a mansion. He had heard the rumours that the old rock legend had let the place go to pot, but this was worse than he expected. The manor house seemed to ooze and sweat a slimy discharge. Perhaps leftovers of the occupant's legendary decades of booze and pills, night sweats and DTs—or maybe Jonas was thinking more about himself.

The weather didn't help either. A thin sheen of rain pattered Jonas's face. Drops hung from his lashes. It pattered off the leaves and ran down the dark murky walls of the two-story relic before him. He pulled his coat tighter. Hugging it to his wiry frame in a futile attempt to stave off the effects of the fast-approaching English winter.

The house hadn't always been a ruin. He had seen it featured in a prominent hard rock magazine in its eighties' heyday. Like its occupant, it had once been a glowing example of British achievement. A fine piece of seventeenth century architecture, built to last, a bit like the metal god who dwelled within its walls—the fallen idol Jonas intended to pay a visit to tonight.

The large ornate stone driveway, only slightly overrun with weeds, was conspicuous in its absence of vehicles. Where once, Jonas remembered from those same old rock magazines, sat a plethora of limousines and the shiny black edifice of the Devil's Gate tour bus, there was not a motor in sight. Surely the old boy wasn't that hard up he had to sell them all? Still, the absence of limos didn't necessarily mean the place was empty.

He crept up to the imposing front door, wide enough to admit a hospital gurney, and chancing his luck he gave the handle a twist. It opened with a creak. Jonas shrugged and slipped inside, closing it behind him. He found himself in what looked like a boot room.

From there he snuck around the lower floor, checking the kitchen, scullery, various sitting rooms and a small library, to ensure there were no staff still in attendance. The absence of chatter suggested there were none. No cooks, no cleaners, no gardeners. How far the mighty had fallen.

Jonas spent a few minutes enjoying what was clearly the occupant's trophy room. Several dust-coated framed gold disks adorned the walls. Pictures of the band in their pomp with various hangers on. Devil's Gate, all gone now to that great rock heaven in the sky, or, in the Gate's case, perhaps the one down below for heavy metal bands. All gone bar the subject of this little visit.

He flicked though the LP record collection and smiled at the memory of some of the band's disks, recalling how, when and where he had first encountered them. Many through his old man's stories. Jerry Jonas had introduced his son to the eighties rock legends.

Opening another door, he found a set of stone steps leading downward to darkness. Jonas quickly closed the door again. The basement could wait. He hated basements. He had watched too many horror movies, knowing full well that according to lore, cellars were invariably the gateway to Hell.

Finding a half full bottle of whisky on a cluttered dresser, Jonas took a sniff and had a swig. The burn was good going down his gullet. He took another belt, felt his skin glowing. He swaggered across to the bottom of the stairs, and yelled, "You up there, Mr Crowley?"

Getting no reply, he shrugged and took another swig of the burning malt. The guy might be a faded star, but he still stocked quality booze.

"Yo, Ace. You here?"

The only response was the sound of falling rain on the weathered shingles. Cackling to himself as the rich liquor took effect on his innards, Jonas started up the winding stairwell. The walls here were also encumbered with mementoes of the occupant's glory days. Posters from gigs played long ago, and more photos of the dead band and the sole survivor's subsequent solo career, which itself had flickered brightly until age wearied the man and he faded away.

Ace Crowley, a cliched but apt pseudonym for a wild haired rock god. Certainly more appealing than his birth name, Reg Smith. *Nobody was shelling out big bucks to hear Reg Smith belt out black metal classics eulogising Satan, that's for sure.*

Accessing the upper landing, he made his way from room to room, several dusty bedrooms revealing a sad lack of use, or a lack of groupies and various hangers on, the accoutrements of fame. The layers of filth also belied the absence of hired help. Two of the three upper bathrooms were similarly decrepit. The other just looked in need of a good scrub. The grubby vanity held a couple of empty bottles of scotch.

Finally, the worn carpet led him to what could only be the master bedroom. Jonas reached into his coat and pulled out the rusty filleting knife he'd found in the kitchen drawer of his latest doss-hole. Enough to terrify the occupant on the off chance he was in there, sleeping off a bender. He pushed the door open and crossed the threshold.

"Mr Crowley, I presume?" Jonas announced to the empty room. The dishevelled bed suggested recent occupancy, and the bottles on the bedside table confirmed he was in the right place.

He glanced around, taking in the contents. More gold records. *Might have to nab a couple of those. He won't miss them.* A combination safe, tall and solid, peeked out at him from an array of spandex and other remnants of a rock career from the depths of a large walk-in robe. Slipping the knife away, and cracking his fingers, Jonas made his way across to it, like a spider to a fly, when something caught the corner of his eye and he swung around.

"Holy fuck!"

The figure stood across the room from him, hard against the

wall. How had he not noticed it before? It seemed to blend into the garish wallpaper.

Jonas reached for his knife. He stared at the mute figure. It stared back.

The effigy had its arms raised toward him in a supplicating manner. Jonas squinted and looked closer. "Where the Hell did you come from?"

He wondered why it stood so mute and frozen. Jonas began to laugh.

"Well bugger me!"

He walked around the huge four poster bed to get a closer look.

He reached out and poked the woman, for it was definitely female, in its ample chest, marvelling at the give in the alabaster flesh.

Jonas reached up and pulled the dressing gown off the girl's shoulders. Beneath she wore only a flimsy negligee, which barely covered her generous curves and outsized breasts. The breasts were stuffed into an ill-fitting sheer black bra, almost spilling over the top.

She regarded him with large but lifeless mascara laden green eyes. Her full pouting bee-stung lips were slightly parted, revealing a set of gleaming white teeth. If she had lived, she gave the appearance of recent death. Yet live she did not, could not, never had. She was instead a perfect replication of somebody's ideal sexualised female form.

Jonas drew in a breath and shook his head. He reached out and squeezed her hand with its painted fingernails, marvelling at the verisimilitude of her touch. Just for a moment he imagined that she squeezed him back. He recoiled, and stepped back, but found the mild repulsion quickly subsumed beneath…what? Attraction, curiosity, desire?

"I know what you are," he said. "You're one of those new kind of sex dolls. Yeah, I've seen you on the Internet."

He sat back on the bed and admired her. In his regular solitary onanistic meanderings around the world of Internet pornography, Jonas had occasionally stumbled across advertisements for these new twenty-first century iterations of the old inflatable rubber dolls. However, he had never seen one in the flesh, so to speak, or the silicone, or whatever marvellous substance this work of art consisted of. He knew they were bloody expensive, only within the financial reach of the most well-heeled of perverts.

"Do you talk?" he asked her, to be met with her eternal silent stare. Her brilliant eyes seemed to observe him with a hint of disdain, her lips set in a fixed coquettish leer.

"No, I guess we haven't got that far yet, eh?" He smirked at her, glad to wrest back control of the monologue.

He stood and ran his fingers across her cheek and around the back of her silken hair.

"You can stand on your own two feet. That's impressive." He leered at her. "Still, I'm sure you're more useful when you're horizontal."

Jonas peered at her sheer black panties and reached out with a glint in his eye.

"Let's have a look at you then."

He pulled the nylon restraint forward and eased the panties down over her wide hips.

"Oh wow!"

The doll's sex organs had been skilfully and majestically crafted. The inner and outer labia perfect in the rendition of permanent arousal. The pudenda swollen and a darker shade of pink. Unable to resist, Jonas ran his fingers down her manufactured slit, flicking the doll a guilty look, expecting her to protest, feeling like a naughty teenager again.

To his surprise, she was damp.

"Oh!"

He probed and slid his middle finger inside her, seeking out and finding the perfectly rendered clitoris.

"Well. You're full of surprises." He withdrew. "I bet our rock god gets a great deal of satisfaction out of you."

He reached up and slid a sticky finger between her lips. Surprised to see the mouth widen to admit him. Even her tongue was exquisite in its craftsmanship. Whoever made these objects of desire certainly put their heart and soul into the work.

Jonas let out a squeal as he felt her lips close around his finger, and he jerked his hand back automatically, as if anticipating a bite.

"Jesus!"

She looked at him doe eyed, her mouth still forming a perfect circle. A look of recognition crossed his face.

"Oh, I get it. You're a godamn android! High functioning sex toy." He slid his finger back between her red lips and cooed as he felt her gently sucking on it. He felt himself begin to stiffen and withdrew the digit.

He took in her whole form again, head to toe. Almost shocked to find himself short of breath. "Jesus! I can see why blokes…"

Jonas reached out and pulled the doll toward him, pushing his body against hers. His erection straining at his greasy pants and rubbing against her bare rounded midriff.

"What the fuck are you doing?"

Jonas almost leapt out of his skin.

He spun to find himself confront by a legend. Ace Crowley in the flesh, or at least what was left of it. The rock god stood in the doorway, clad in an unforgiving pair of tight black leather pants and a faded black t-shirt promoting his European tour of 1991. The years had not been kind. The leather of the bikers' jacket hanging off his narrow, drooping shoulders looked as old and battered as Crowley. Jonas couldn't help but notice that above the sunken cheeks and bloodshot pin-prick eyes that the once lustrous flowing black mane had retreated back well over the ridge of his crown, and had turned an ashen grey.

"Mr Crowley," Jonas stammered. "I'm a huge fan."

"Never mind that bollocks," the rock legend growled in his native East End drawl. "What are you doing in my bleedin' house, and what were you about to do wiv my Lily?"

"Lily?" Jonas turned and gave the doll and accusing look. "This thing?"

"She's not a thing. She means the world to me. You keep your 'ands off her." The ageing rock god took a step toward Jonas, who raised his hands and backed away.

"Easy does it, old mate. It's not her I came for." He pulled out the knife. That stopped the angry rocker in his tracks.

Crowley backed away, raising his hands before him. "What do yer want wiv me?'

Jonas grabbed an old wooden chair from one side of the bed and dragged it across. "That's more like it, Ace, or should I call you Reg? Why don't you sit yourself down here, and we'll have a little chat."

The rocker reluctantly did as he was bid. Jonas took a closer look at the fallen idol. Hard to imagine this wasted relic once commanded audiences of tens of thousands of dedicated fans.

"What happened to your hair, Ace? Last time I saw you on stage, you had a beautiful head of hair."

Crowley scowled. "I got old, you muppet."

"It was only about eight years ago."

The rocker's eyes narrowed. "Eight years… The Fallen Angels tour? That was a bloody wig."

"Oh. I couldn't tell."

Crowley gave a half smile. "Tricks of the trade. Wigs, 'airpieces. I even had a weave at one point. Didn't take. Course the technology is much more refined these days. Look at Elton… Anyway, wot the bladdy hell are you doing in my manor?"

"I'll ask the questions, Mr Crowley." Jonas gesticulated with the knife. "You can guess why I'm here. You've got something I want. Cash, moolah, filthy lucre. I've heard all the rumours. How you never trusted the banks. Got all your money holed up here with you." He pointed the tip of the blade over Crowley's shoulder. "I'm guessing it's in that safe over there in the closet."

They both turned toward the closet. Crowley shook his head. "Nothing much in there these days."

Jonas gave a bitter smile. "Nevertheless, I would still like to take a look for myself. You see, Ace old chum, I've got myself into a bit of a pickle. I owe some nasty men rather a lot of money, and I figured you could see me right with a small donation."

The rocker snorted, "Here we go, another bleedin' sob story. Some things never change. Always somebody looking for a bladdy handout. Wot is it, gambling, drugs?"

"Bit of both," Jonas shrugged. "So, if you would just be good enough to give me the combination of that little beauty over there,

I'll be on my way and out of your hair…. What's left of it."

The old rocker shook his head. "How much do you owe these thugs, son?"

"Does it matter? About fifty grand, and I'll take a bit more for my troubles."

Crowley chewed his lip. "There ain't fifty grand in there, pal."

Jonas sighed. "Look, old man. I know you're stalling. Just give me the combo and let's get this over with, and you can get back to shagging the arse of your little mannequin missus here, to your heart's content." Jonas glanced at the doll as he spoke. Was she staring at him?

A sudden memory slid its way to Jonas's frontal lobe. "What did you call her? Lily? Wasn't that the name of that infamous groupie that used to follow you around on every tour?"

"Yeah. Lily the lush. I bleedin' loved that gal."

"I heard you all did, and half the road crew as well."

Crowley's face hardened. "You watch your mouth, pal. You don't know the first thing about love."

That drew a laugh from Jonas. He waved the knife in front of the rocker's nose. "Oh, that's rich, coming from a bloke who shacks up with a bloody doll."

Crowley sneered. "Yeah, look at yer, big lanky streak of piss. You've never loved and been loved, I can tell. You don't know nuffin' about women. Lily might've been a slag, but she had a heart of gold. Loveliest little gal I ever met. I should've married her."

"Oh please, Ace," Jonas laughed, "spare me the sordid details of your infamous gang bangs. Enough of the banter, sunshine. Are you gonna give me the combo, or do I have to start cutting?"

This time Crowley snorted. "You 'aven't got the bollocks, son."

Jonas's hackles rose. He juggled the knife from one hand to the other and swung his fist into the old rocker's face. Crowley's nose snapped with an audible crack.

"Oh, yew fucker!" Crowley raised his hands to his bloody nose and spat through a mouthful of blood.

"I'm sorry, Ace. I don't want to hurt you."

"You coulda bloody fooled me!" The rock god wiped his streaming eyes.

Jonas spied a box of tissues on the dresser and passed it over. "Here. Don't make this any harder, Ace, just give me the combination."

"Fuck you!" Crowley dabbed at his crooked nose.

Jonas sighed. He grabbed the rocker's left hand and yanked it toward him. He pulled the old man's digits out straight and poised the rusty blade over his index finger.

Crowley shook his head from side to side. "No...no...don't do it, son."

"How would it feel to never pluck a guitar again, Ace?" Jonas raised his voice an octave.

"No!"

"Don't make me do it!"

"I can't give yer the combo..." Jonas saw the old man's wild eyes flicker toward the doll and back.

"So help me I'll cut it off..." Jonas had a sudden thought and swung the knife around toward the doll. "I'll cut her. How would you like that? I'll gut her."

"Please, no...".

"Let's see what she got inside." Jonas yelled. He raised the knife and positioned it over one of the doll's erect nipples.

"Don't hurt her."

The words only further enraged Jonas. "Hurt her? She's not fucking real, you old goat. She's made of fucking silicone." He gave a bitter laugh. "She can't feel pain. Here, look." Jonas swung a roundhouse punch and knocked the doll off its feet. It crashed to the floor.

"NO!" Crowley screamed.

Jonas lifted his boot above the doll's face, ready to bring it down with force. He looked back at Crowley.

"1-9-5-9-6-6-6."

The foot hovered, then lowered.

"That's better."

Jonas pocketed his knife, and moved across to the safe, pushing rows of old mouldering stage clothes aside.

He looked back at the rock legend. "Don't you fucking move!" He gazed back from the safe to the rocker as he worked. "6 6 6. I should've bloody guessed. What's the first bit represent?"

"Year I was born."

Jonas smiled as the safe gave an audible sigh and clicked open. Somehow, he sensed it was the first time it had opened in a long while.

"Aha! Here we go. Let's take a little look…. Ooh!"

He pulled an object from a stand nestled inside. Brandished the gleaming black and white guitar before him. "Oh my God! Is this the legendary Gibson Les Paul? The one from *Kings of the Underworld*?"

Crowley nodded. "The very same."

Jonas marvelled at the beautiful object. "Jesus! This thing must be worth a fortune. Isn't this the one you supposedly had on your lap when you met the Devil at them crossroads? Obviously, that was just a story."

"Yeah. Stories sell records, son. But there's an element of truth in every legend."

"Yeah, well I didn't see you die at twenty-seven, though. More like a hundred and twenty-seven."

"Some of us make different deals, sunshine."

"That right?" Jonas tossed the guitar onto the bedspread. "Well, it's no good to me anyway. Cold hard readies are what I need to solve my problems."

Jonas turned and reached back into the recess. "Ah, here we go." He retrieved a smallish black tin and prised it open. Pulled out the wads of notes and flicked them through his fingers. He turned on Crowley.

"What's this? There's not even two grand here?"

The rock god sniffed. "Well, I did tell yer."

Jonas shook his head. "No, there's got to be more somewhere." He turned back to the safe and reached inside to something sitting further back, the last item held within. He pulled it out into the light. "What the fuck is this, a book?" He turned it over. There were words scrawled on the pock marked leather cover, but they were in a language he didn't understand.

Crowley's mouth curved into a sly smile. "It's a grimoire."

"A grim what? It's bloody grim alright."

"A grimoire, you ignoramus, is a book of black magic. It contains the names of demons. Tells you how to raise them and how to command them to do your bidding."

Jonas flicked though the ancient text, sneering at the strange words and diabolical images dotting the pages. "Oh, come on! You don't actually believe all this mumbo jumbo, Crowley? You said yourself in interviews the Satanic imagery was all for show."

"Yeah, what I said and what I believe are two different things, old son. Don't believe everything an artist tells yer."

"You expect me to believe this shit? You conjured up the fucking Devil, and what, sold your soul for fame and fortune? Come on!"

"In this very house."

Jonas waved the book. "Bullshit!"

Crowley's voice rose, his eyes sparkled. "The Prince of Darkness rose up. It was incredible."

"Oh, fuck off!" Jonas hurled the book at Crowley. It bounced off his chest and hit the floor with a dull thud.

"It's true. It's all true. The devil weaved his magic in song through me. All those tunes, all those money-making hits, he wrote through my hand. Made me his muse."

Jonas's voice rose an octave, verging on the precipice of hysteria. "What about the band? They in on this bollocks? Didn't help them. They're all fucking dead."

"Everyone has to make sacrifices. I had to make...choices. Had to fight to keep what I had."

Jonas shook his head. "You're not making a lot of sense, Reggie boy."

"Think about it, son. I had fame, I had money, but what did I not 'ave?"

"What?"

"Love, son."

Jonas saw the old rocker glance toward the fallen doll. "Oh, come on. You don't mean...?"

"Lily fuckin' died. Drug overdose." Crowley lowered his head into his hands. "I was heart-broken, desperate, wanted her back. It was complicated. There were incantations. It needed blood."

"Fuck off with this horse shit. Where's the rest of the money, you old charlatan?"

"There is none. I spent most of it on hookers and blow… The rest I just wasted." Crowley laughed bitterly at his own joke.

"So help me, old man, I'll…" Jonas rushed the metal god and slid his hands around the fallen idol's withered throat.

"Blood…" the ancient rocker spluttered.

"I'll bloody kill you…" Jonas squeezed tighter. Letting all the pent-up rage of his shitty life filter though his fingers. A steady flow of crimson from the rocker's busted nose oozed over his hands. He yanked the old man to his feet in a death grip. Crowley's eyes blazed as he looked over Jonas's shoulder and pointed, gasping, fighting to speak.

"No…don't!"

Jonas's foot slid on the cover of the grimoire at his feet. He kicked out angrily, squeezed his hands tighter round the old man's throat, watching his eyes widen and bulge in their sockets. Then he heard a loud crack and felt a sudden sharp pain, like a razor blade digging into his skull.

Jonas looked into the old man's face in confusion, to see it spattered with his blood. His grip loosened, and Crowley let out a coughing wheeze and staggered over to the bed. Behind Jonas, the life-sized doll raised the guitar and smashed it into the back of his head again.

Jonas crumpled to the floor and rolled over on his back. Above him, he saw the doll, impossibly alive, glaring down at him. Blood smeared its silicone features. Its mouth curled into a snarl. Somewhere inside him he felt a row of lights flickering out into darkness.

He opened his mouth to speak, to protest, but the doll raised the shattered guitar again and slammed it into his face. Deep in his mind, the music stopped for Colin Jonas.

Ace Crowley put a restraining hand on the doll's arm as she raised the weapon again. "Lily, Lily, Lily…that's enough, me darlin'."

When she did his bidding and retreated, Crowley bent to examine the wreckage. He picked through bits of splintered bone and gore and cradled the broken pieces in his arms. He shook his head slowly and quietly wept. Lily, standing aside, reached across and placed her cold hand on his shoulder.

Crowley heaved and sobbed. He turned to look at her, and held the shattered, blood and brain-soaked remnants up toward her pale, placid face. "Lily," he whispered, gazing into her soulless eyes. "How could you? Not the Les Paul."

STORY PUBLISHING HISTORY

All stories are copyright Anthony Ferguson. Stories are original to this collection, unless listed below (first publishing instance).

'Rest in Pieces' – original to this collection
'Brumation – *Midnight Echo* issue 15 (2020)
'Demontia' – *Underbelly* issue 2 Autumn (2018)
'Road Trip' – *In Sunshine Bright and Darkness Deep* (AHWA anthology 2015)
'With a Whimper' – *Weird Mask* Volume 1 issue 6 (2018)
'Burn for You' – original to this collection
'The Ardent Dead' – *Rom.Zom.Com.* (Knightwatch Press 2014)
'Overboard' – *Trickster's Treats 3 The Seven Deadly Sins* (Things in the Well 2019)
'A Rip in Time' – *Out of the Gutter* zine (2016)
'House of Cards' – *Ripples* issue 12 (2008)
'Blind Date' – *Breach* zine issue 10 (2019)
'Christmas Past' – *Hells Bells* (AHWA anthology 2016)
'One from the Heart' – *Burning Love and Bleeding Hearts* (Things in the Well 2020)
'Leave of Absence' – *Lost Souls* issue 12/13 (2006)
'Sins of the Father' – *Darkness Abound* (Migla Press 2016)
'Thicker than Water' - *Melbourne Zombie Convention short story competition* 2013
'Love Thy Neighbour' – *Fire and Brimstone* (Specul8 Publishing 2019)
'Protégé' – *Monsters Among Us* (Oscillate Wildly Press 2016)
'Ointment' – *Gallows Hill* Volume 2 No.1 (2019)
'Black Vine' – original to this collection
'Not Like Us '– original to this collection
'She Ain't Heavy' – *Dark Horses* No.4 (May 2022)